MERLINE
LOVELACE

"Strong and clever characters populate the Lovelace world in stories that sizzle with a passion for life and love."
—*New York Times* bestselling author Nora Roberts

"Merline Lovelace's stories are filled with unforgettable characters, scintillating romance, and steeped with emotional depth. She's the brightest new star in the romance genre. Each new book is an enjoyable adventure."
—*New York Times* bestselling author Debbie Macomber

"This absolutely wonderful story will alternately steam your glasses with sizzling romance, make you chew your nails and laugh hysterically. Wow!"
—*Romantic Times* on *Bits and Pieces*

Dear Reader,

I'm thrilled to see my first two novels packaged together in this special Signature Select Spotlight edition. Both stories take place at Eglin Air Force Base, where I was privileged to serve as Support Wing Commander.

Maggie and Her Colonel looks at the research and development phase of Eglin's incredibly vital test mission. I had such fun with that novella I jumped right in and wrote a longer story. *Bits and Pieces* explores the operational end of the test business, which occurs after a weapon system completes initial R & D. I've updated the story to reflect Eglin's current mission. I also had fun rewriting a few scenes to allow the characters in both stories to interact for this edition.

So here you have 'em—two highly educated, supremely qualified heroines matching wits with two super-sexy colonels. I hope you enjoy these glimpses of test operations at the biggest and best base in the air force!

All my best,

Merline Lovelace

SPOTLIGHT

MERLINE LOVELACE

One of the Boys

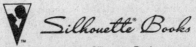

Published by Silhouette Books
America's Publisher of Contemporary Romance

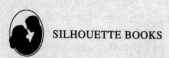

SILHOUETTE BOOKS

ISBN 0-373-28508-6

ONE OF THE BOYS
Copyright © 2005 by Harlequin Books S.A.

The publisher acknowledges the copyright holders of the individual works as follows:

BITS AND PIECES
Copyright © 1993 by Merline Lovelace.
Revised text copyright © 2005 by Merline Lovelace.

MAGGIE AND HER COLONEL
Copyright © 1994 by Harlequin Books S.A.

BITS AND PIECES was first published by Meteor Publishing Corporation in 1993.

www.eHarlequin.com

Printed in U.S.A.

Dear Reader,

The editors at Harlequin and Silhouette are thrilled to be able to bring you a brand-new featured author program beginning in 2005! Signature Select aims to single out outstanding stories, contemporary themes and oft-requested classics by some of your favorite series authors and present them to you in a variety of formats bound by truly striking covers.

You may notice a number of different colored bands on the spine of this book. Each color corresponds to a different type of reading experience in the new Signature Select program. The Spotlight books will offer a single "big read" by a talented series author, the Collections will present three novellas on a selected theme in one volume, the Sagas will contain sprawling, sometimes multi-generational family tales (often related to a favorite family first introduced in series) and the Miniseries will feature requested, previously published books, with two or, occasionally, three complete stories in one volume. The Signature Select program will offer one book in each of these categories per month, and fans of limited continuity series will also find these continuing stories under the Signature Select umbrella.

In addition, these volumes will bring you bonus features...different in every single book! You may learn more about the author in an extended interview, more about the setting or inspiration for the book, more about subjects related to the theme and, often, a bonus short read will be included.

Watch for new stories from Vicki Lewis Thompson, Lori Foster, Donna Kauffman, Marie Ferrarella, Merline Lovelace, Roberta Gellis, Suzanne Forster, Stephanie Bond and scores more of the brightest talents in romance fiction!

We have an exciting year ahead!

Warm wishes for happy reading,

Marsha Zinberg

Marsha Zinberg
Executive Editor
The Signature Select Program

BITS AND PIECES

Chapter 1

Within five minutes of opening the door, Maura Phillips knew she'd made a mistake. A *big* mistake!

She'd come flying in from the back patio and swung open the door on the third ring of the bell.

"Hello, Jake," she said breathlessly, smiling up at the tall, dark-haired man standing on the step of her rented cottage. "Sorry I didn't hear the doorbell. I was out on the patio."

Colonel Jake McAllister, deputy commander for Operations at Eglin Air Force Base, lifted a brow. "Hello, Maura. I didn't get the dates mixed up, did I?"

"No," she laughed, raking a hand through her breeze-tossed brown bob. "I'm just running a little late. I still can't get used to this gorgeous Florida sunshine after all those years of L.A. smog. Every time I go out on the patio and see sunlight sparkling on the water, I fall into a daze."

Maura stood aside as he entered the house. Her own brows arched delicately at her first full view of Jake McAllister in something other than his air force uniform.

Tonight he wore tailored dark slacks and a crisp blue cotton shirt with the sleeves folded back neatly to reveal tanned forearms. Shiny leather loafers and a chain-link ID bracelet on his right wrist gave him a casual, elegant look. With his dark hair and cool gray eyes, he exuded an aura of restrained sophistication. Very restrained. Even in civilian clothes, the colonel carried an air of authority.

The first warning bell sounded in Maura's mind.

"Why don't you wait in the living room? I'll just be a moment."

Nodding, he followed as she wove a path around the half-unpacked boxes littering the hall.

"Just moving in?"

"No. Actually, I rented this place through a real estate agent sight unseen and had my things shipped out from L.A. Bea and I have been here going on a month now."

She nodded to the massive ball of orange fur rubbing itself against a chair leg. Turning back, she just caught the expression on Jake's face as he did a quick sweep of her disordered living room.

Uh-oh, she thought, he's not into clutter. The second warning bell began to ping.

"I call it the primitive look," she told him, a deliberately bland look in her hazel eyes. Housekeeping wasn't very high on her list of priorities in life. In fact, it didn't even *make* the list. But she was darned if she was going to apologize or explain herself. She'd done enough of that before she'd left L.A.

Jake sensed he'd offended her, and his face softened. One side of his mouth drew up in a rueful smile, crinkling the skin at the corners of his eyes.

"I guess we military types are more used to packing and unpacking. Moving every few years or so, we get compulsive about putting the nest in order quickly."

Maura took the proffered olive branch with a smile only a few shades less brilliant than her normal cheerful grin. "I'll bet you're one of those disgusting types who have all the boxes unpacked, the shelves put together, and your books lined up by color and size before the moving van even leaves."

"Well, no. I line them up alphabetically by author," he confessed, his smile widening.

Fascinated by the way a simple rearrangement of a few facial muscles could transform the strong, angled planes of his face into a lopsided—and devastatingly potent—male grin, Maura almost missed his next comment.

"I'm probably a little early," he continued. "Another compulsive military trait, I suppose. Please, take whatever time you need to get dressed."

Maura blinked and caught her jaw in middrop. She was as dressed as she intended to be for a casual dinner at the home of a co-worker. All she had left to do was drag a brush through her hair and dig through the boxes in her bedroom for a light wrap.

She glanced down at her turquoise leggings and matching, thigh-length silk tunic. Okay, they might look a bit like lounging pajamas to the uninitiated. Or to conservative, polished-loafer types.

Warning bells were going off like Klaxons now. For a few moments, a desire to tell a certain colonel what he could do with his gracious offer of time warred with her ready sense of the ridiculous. Her sense of humor won. The man wanted dressed, dressed he'd get.

"Thanks." She responded to his offer with only the tiniest hint of dryness in her voice. "I shouldn't be long. The bar's over there. Help yourself to a drink if you like."

Nodding to the antique sideboard shoved up against one wall, she started down the short hall leading to her bedroom. She'd taken only a few steps when Jake's startled exclamation stopped her.

"Hey! Let go, cat."

Maura turned to see him extracting a set of claws from his pant leg. "Beatrice! For heaven's sake, behave yourself."

Hurrying back, she scooped up the lump of orange fur. The cat hung from her arms, its eyes a picture of limpid innocence.

"Sorry about that. If it's any consolation, Bea just used up her entire energy supply for the next week. You're safe now." Stroking her pet's thick fur, Maura turned a wide, guileless gaze on the man watching them both warily. "She doesn't seem to like men for some reason."

"She probably senses it's mutual."

With another stern admonition to behave, Maura put the cat down. The animal settled itself on its haunches and fixed the visitor with an unwavering stare.

As his date for the evening disappeared down the hall, Jake's glance drifted to the malevolent-looking creature hunkered at his feet. Nothing like a set of claw marks to start the evening off right. Deciding to take Maura up on her offer of a drink, he made his way through the jumble.

There was no other word to describe it. A sophisticated computer perched precariously on an impromptu desk made of heavy boards and concrete blocks. The laptop battled for space with stacks of manuals and haphazardly piled books. A miniaturized set of stereo components sat in one corner, with speaker wires strung carelessly to the four corners of the room. Bright floral rattan furniture, obviously rented with the house, sat side by side with what his assessing eye pegged as genuine antiques. That makeshift bar was a genuine Sheraton sideboard, Jake knew. His ex-wife hadn't left him with much, but she had given him an appreciation of fine old furniture.

As he poured a neat Scotch, his thoughts turned to the owner of all this clutter. From the little he'd seen of her at work, the woman had a personality as contradictory as her interior decorating scheme, or lack thereof. With her sleek brown mane, colorful attire and cheerful grin, Maura Phillips turned heads every time she breezed by. The fact that her undeniably delectable body housed a razor-sharp mind only added to the stunned amazement she left in her wake.

Jake had been in one or two meetings with her since her arrival and had to admit she knew her stuff. He just couldn't reconcile someone with a Ph.D. from Stanford with her flashy good looks and this hodgepodge house. An engineer to his bones, he liked things neat and precise on the outside as well as the inside.

As he made his way back across the room, a long, slow hiss warned him to watch where he stepped. He restrained the impulse to hiss back and wished he'd declined this dinner invitation.

Absently, Jake swirled the Scotch. What was it about his divorced state that made his friends and coworkers think they had a moral obligation to fix him up with every available female of their acquaintance? Usually Jake managed to finesse their not-very-subtle matchmaking attempts. He and his wife had split up more than three years ago, but the regret—and wariness—still lingered.

Their daughter was the one bright, shining joy to survive the bust-up. She was staying with Jake for the summer and he'd planned to take her to a movie tonight. Against his better judgment, though, he'd let himself be talked into dinner with Pete Hansen, his wife, and Maura Phillips.

Assuming they even made it to Pete's in time for dinner, Jake amended, glancing down at his watch. He tried to shrug off the delay, but lateness, like untidiness, offended his orderly soul. He downed a swallow of Scotch and wondered what the heck was taking so long.

Down the hall, Maura attacked the boxes stacked beside her bed with a determined glint in her brown eyes. Someday, she thought. Someday she'd learn to listen to her instincts. So this Jake McAllister was a world-class hunk, not classically handsome but lean and strong and all male. So he looked as good in his air-force uniform as he did in the casual clothes he wore tonight. So he had a breath-stopping smile that made her heart thump. He was all wrong for her and she knew it.

The man radiated cool authority in every inch of his body. Having worked for most of her adult life in a career field dominated by men, Maura had long ago learned to hold her own against these authoritarian types. She'd also stopped trying to curb her own ebullient personality to fit their preconceived notions of how she should look and dress.

Still, she hadn't missed the faint disapproval in Jake McAllister's gray eyes when he surveyed her home—and herself! Maura wished fervently she'd declined Pete's invitation. Or at least insisted on driving herself when he suggested Jake pick her up, since she was still learning her way around the Gulf Coast.

Oh, well. She might as well make the best of the situation and have some fun. With a grin, she pulled a wide magenta belt out of the box and fastened it low on her hips. The purply red stood out like a bold slash against her turquoise tunic. More digging produced dangly earrings composed mostly of bits of seashells and feathers on varying lengths of colored leather. On impulse, she exchanged her low-heeled sandals for strappy platforms with ties that wrapped around her ankles.

Teasing her hair unmercifully, she pulled a thick swatch to one side of her head and caught it with a sparkly gold lamé scrunchie left over from some Christmas party. A few quick strokes dramatically deepened the eye shadow and blusher she'd put on earlier.

There, she thought with a wicked smile as she surveyed herself in the mirror. That's dressed!

Stopping to pick up the bouquet of fresh flowers she was taking as a hostess gift, she sailed down the hall.

"All set."

Her transformation put a startled look in Jake's eyes, but he refrained from comment. Smart man, Maura thought as they strolled out into the Florida night.

* * *

From that inauspicious beginning, things went downhill fast. As they drove through the soft summer evening, Maura's suspicion she had little in common with this man aside from the fact they both worked at the base became absolute certainty. Politely, they agreed to disagree on music and their preference in cars, and not so politely on the St. Louis Rams' chances this season. Obviously struggling to find a safe topic, Jake finally steered the conversation to work.

"So how do you like Eglin?"

"I love it," Maura responded with a touch of her usual enthusiasm. "A friend of a friend who used to be stationed here told me about the base. When I saw an ad in a trade journal for a test manager with my specialty, I decided to send in my résumé. But I had no idea how gorgeous this area really is, or how exciting the work would be."

He shot her a quick look. "You made a major career move based on third-hand information from a friend?"

"I believe in following my instincts," she replied, a distinct challenge in her tone.

Most of the time, she amended silently. She just had to learn to follow them better when it came to uptight, controlled men.

"Haven't you ever done anything just because you knew instinctively it was right, not because it was logical or prudent or expected?"

"Not since I passed puberty," he responded dryly.

"Oh, come on, Colonel. You're a test pilot. Surely flying one of the world's most advanced high-tech aircraft is as much instinct as skill?"

An amused smile hovered at the edges of his mouth. "You've been watching too many Tom Cruise movies. What we do up there takes years of training and a precise mind, along with the ability to make split-second decisions."

Maura battled a growing irritation. The analytical side of her intellect knew he was right, but the romantic in her didn't want her illusions about dashing test pilots reduced to cool calculation and a slide rule.

"So how did you get into the business of flying?"

"It's all I've ever wanted to do," he replied with a shrug. "Even as a kid, I planned on going to the academy and then flying. Every assignment helped improve my skills."

Maura caught the unspoken message. He'd set a deliberate career path and followed it. Unlike her, whose professional goals were erratic at best. With a sigh, she gave up all attempts at conversation and turned to watch the scenery rolling past the open car windows.

They crossed the bridge linking the small town of Fort Walton Beach with Santa Rosa Island, a long, narrow strip of sand that ran for fifty miles along the Gulf of Mexico. On one side of the island Maura could see the emerald-green waters of the Gulf crashing in lacy waves against snow-white beaches. On the other side, Choctawhatchee Bay stretched to the horizon. Along a distant curve of the bay, she could barely make out the huge hangars and tall buildings of Eglin Air Force Base.

Since Eglin owned most of the eastern half of Santa Rosa Island, the land was protected in its natural state. Maura relaxed, enjoying the sharp tang of the ocean and the sight of tall, feathery sea grass swaying in the evening breeze.

After crossing a second bridge over the narrow inlet where the bay washed into the sea, they reentered civilization. High-rise condominiums crowded against neon-lit tourist shops and restaurants in what had once been the sleepy fishing village of Destin. Pete Hansen lived in the tallest of the condominiums along the shore.

When her co-worker opened the door a few moments later, he eyed her bright plumage appreciatively.

"Maura, you look so, er, vibrant. Come on in. Honey, this is Maura Phillips, the new test manager I told you about."

"I've heard a lot about you, Dr. Phillips," the cool blonde at his side responded, offering a delicate hand in greeting. "Pete's raved about the way you've brought the latest technology and a California look to our little redneck corner of the woods."

Smiling, Maura shrugged off the cattiness of the woman's remarks. "I prefer to think of it as my own look."

She doubted if her hostess even heard her. The woman had turned to greet her other guest, upping the wattage of her smile considerably.

"Hello, Jake."

"Hi, Carol."

She stretched to give him a warm kiss. The natives were friendly, Maura thought as Jake bent and took the kiss on the cheek. *Very* friendly.

"This way," Pete said, ushering his guests into his home.

Maura's smile came out in its full, natural force when she followed him into the spacious living room.

"Oh, this is fabulous!"

The room combined understated elegance with sweeping vistas. Berber carpets and walls textured in grass paper reflected the shifting sand dunes outside. The far wall was a solid sheet of glass with a spectacular view of the Gulf.

"Carol did all the decorating herself." Pete beamed at his wife as he escorted his guests out onto the balcony. "She could go into interior design professionally if she wanted to."

"And I thought I was lucky to find my little bayside cottage," Maura said with a sigh, sinking into one of the lounge chairs to absorb the full glory of a flaming-red sun hovering above the dark green waters.

"It wasn't easy to get into this condo," Pete confided. Pouring margaritas from a frosty pitcher, he passed them to his guests before settling his lanky frame onto a lounge chair. "The pittance we poor civil servants earn barely covers the maintenance fees. I thought we'd have to hock Carol's jewelry for the down payment."

"Oh, come on, Pete." His wife's voice carried a hint of annoyance. "You know it's not that bad."

"Well, I hope you saved enough for insurance," Jake put in, and deftly steered the conversation away from the apparently rocky shoals of domestic finances to the upcoming hurricane season. Maura had already participated in one hurricane watch since her arrival. Weather was a favorite topic of conversation on this part of the coast, she'd discovered, right after Miami Dolphins football.

She tried to warm up to her hostess over dinner. Carol had obviously gone to considerable effort on her guests' behalf. Heavy gleaming silver and sparkling crystal decorated the table, with an exquisite bird-of-paradise blossom in a Lalique holder at each place setting.

"Pete's right," Maura offered sincerely. "You have a wonderful flair for decorating."

"Thank you." Her long, manicured fingers stroked her crystal goblet sensuously. "I think a beautifully ordered setting helps create an inner serenity, don't you?"

Amusement flickered in the gray eyes directly across the table from Maura. She could see Jake waiting expectantly for her response.

"Yes, I do." She gave her hostess a polite smile. "Of course, we all find beauty in different ways. I, for one, like lots of splashy color."

"I know Jake appreciates clean, pure lines," Carol purred. "He's got a fabulous place across the bay." The look she sent him from under lowered lashes suggested an intimate knowledge of his home—among other things.

A tinge of red crept up Jake's cheekbones as he gave a light answer and changed the subject.

Sooo, Maura thought. Our hostess has the hots for the dashing Colonel McAllister. Repressing a twinge of something she couldn't quite analyze, she glanced at her host. Pete was energetically tossing the Caesar salad, but the faint crease between his brows told her he hadn't missed his wife's provocative remark.

Maura stepped in to cover the awkward moment. "You'll have to tell me where to shop around here. I've been so busy at work I haven't had time to hit the malls."

"Sandestin has some nice little shops," her hostess replied with a polite smile. "Although I doubt they'll have anything quite as stylish as the boutiques in L.A."

"Or as expensive," Maura agreed, laughing.

Pete gave her a grateful glance and kept the ball rolling by pumping her about L.A. Allowing her natural liveliness full rein, Maura exhausted her store of anecdotes about traffic tangles, star sightings and mail carriers on in-line skates. By the time Carol brought in the coffee, she couldn't wait for the awful evening to be over.

Riding home through the soft, starry night, she fought the beginnings of a headache. Her gushing chatter had drained both her energy and her enthusiasm. With a small sigh, she leaned her head back against the soft leather seat.

"Would you mind telling me what that was all about?"

The deep, gravelly voice coming at her out of the darkness made Maura jump. "What do you mean?"

"I mean your performance tonight. You played the breathless California girl to perfection."

Maura's eyes narrowed to dangerous slits. She forgot that she'd been late and kept this man waiting. She forgot that she'd deliberately dressed like a refugee from a floating rummage sale. She even ignored the fact that she'd prattled inanely for most of the evening, giving even herself a headache with her chatter.

"I'm not sure what qualifies you as an expert on California girls," she responded with soft, deadly sweetness, "but I'm surprised you wanted to go out with me if you have such a low opinion of the species."

He shot her a cool look. "Let's keep the record straight. This wasn't a date. When and if we do go out, we won't spend the evening dueling over everything from sports to how we should have finished the job in Iraq."

"I stand corrected," Maura said icily. "This wasn't a date. And for the record, there won't be any 'when' or 'if.'"

Her temper was still simmering when they pulled into the crushed-shell driveway beside her house. She had the passenger door open before the car rolled to a stop.

"Thanks for the ride, Colonel. I won't say it's been fun. You don't need to walk me to the door."

With another cool glance, McAllister levered himself out of the low-slung sports car. Following in her wake, he waited while she fit her key in the lock.

Determined to end this fiasco, Maura turned. Too quickly, as it turned out. The ridiculously high platforms wobbled. She teetered on the small stoop and pitched forward.

McAllister moved fast. Whipping out an arm, he snagged her against his chest. She looked up, totally embarrassed, to see a wicked glint come into his eyes.

"You're right," he drawled. "This evening hasn't been fun. Until now."

It was that damned grin that threw her. Maura was still trying to figure out how the man could go from cool and remote to rogue male in the blink of an eye when he swooped in for a kiss.

The kiss stunned her. It was the last thing she'd expected after the disaster of the evening. While her mind struggled to deal with his impulsive act, her body cataloged the sensations he was bringing to it.

The man could kiss. She'd give him that. His mouth moved over hers with a skill that sent tingles rippling down her spine. She was almost disappointed when he set her back on her feet and tipped her a casual salute.

"See you around."

"Not if I see you first," she muttered as he headed back to his car.

Confused and irritated at her body's reaction to the man, she let herself into the house, wandered into the living room and tossed her bag at the closest chair. When the chair let out a yowl, she nearly jumped out of her skin.

"Sorry, Bea!"

Scooping up the indignant cat, she dropped into the chair and leaned her head against the high cushions.

"I was right. The man is everything I don't like. Stuffy, conservative, judgmental. I should have taken my own car tonight. I should have avoided the darned dinner altogether when Pete told me he'd invited McAllister, too. And I sure as heck should have been the one to break off that kiss!"

Maura rubbed the cat's fur and tried to relax, but the night had left her with a jumble of contradictory feelings that wouldn't go away.

That's what she got for letting a long, lean body and sexy grin overcome her better judgment. She and take-charge, in-control types just didn't mix. She ought to know. She'd left one just like him behind in L.A. Shaking her head, she kneaded the cat's spine.

"When am I going to learn?"

Bea's heavy body rumbled in a purr, but otherwise she ignored the question. Scooping her up, Maura marched them both off to bed.

A frown creased Jake's forehead as he drove through the soft Florida night. He couldn't believe he'd given in to the impulse to kiss the woman who'd tumbled so conveniently into his arms. She was a mass of contradictions, as prickly as she was outspoken. He couldn't figure her out, and his neat, orderly mind hated that kind of ambiguity.

One thing was clear, though. His body wasn't experiencing the least ambiguity. Just the memory of her mouth under his put a kink in his gut that wouldn't quit.

He shifted in the bucket seat, trying to erase the discomfort with a healthy dose of common sense. The scars from his divorce had pretty much healed, but he'd learned his lesson. He intended to look long and hard before he took another leap into the pool. Particularly with a woman as confusing as Maura Phillips.

With a distinct twinge of regret, Jake decided he'd best avoid her in the future. Eglin was a big base, the largest in the world. It had more than five hundred square miles of test range and ate up half of the Florida panhandle. Surely that was enough room to keep some distance between him and this particular female.

Chapter 2

"Hi."

The tentative greeting drifted through the brim of the floppy straw hat shading Maura's brow. Angling her head, she squinted into the late-afternoon sun at the silhouette standing ankle deep in the water just a few yards away. The hazy figure gradually resolved itself into a smiling, dark-haired teen.

"Hi, yourself."

"I didn't mean to wake you," the girl offered as she waded closer to Maura's lawn chair. The chair was set in two feet of warm, shallow water with the seat just inches above the lapping wavelets.

"Don't let the closed eyes and snoring fool you," Maura responded, shifting Bea's dead weight to a more comfortable spot on her stomach. "I wasn't sleeping, just soaking up some rays."

The girl giggled. "I was just surprised to see anyone in this cove. I come here just about every afternoon, and it's always deserted. It's my special place."

Intrigued, Maura studied the gangly teen. She guessed her age at about fifteen or so and wondered why the girl would spend her summer afternoons in a deserted cove. Her own experience with half a dozen nieces and nephews made her think trips to the mall and beach parties with hordes of noisy friends were more usual pursuits.

"I just discovered the cove myself," Maura confided. "It's only a short walk from the cottage I've rented. It's so quiet and peaceful, I thought it would be a good spot to contemplate nature, even with eyes closed."

Actually, she'd thought it was a good spot to let her tired body rest in the sun. Still trying to get a handle on her new job, she'd worked late every night last week and all day Saturday. This morning she'd woken late and toyed briefly with the idea of unpacking a box or two. Instead, she'd lingered over coffee until the unnatural urge went away, then decided to go exploring. The vast Choctawhatchee Bay called to her.

Pulling on a bathing suit and a pair of sneakers that had passed their prime years ago, she dug through the boxes for the straw hat one of her nephews had won at a county fair and wouldn't be caught dead in. With a lightweight folding chair under one arm and Bea under the other, she'd set off along the narrow beach that edged the bay.

Following the shoreline from the cluster of cottages surrounding her own, she'd soon left all traces of civilization behind. Minutes later, she'd rounded a curve and found herself in this picturesque, deserted cove. Fallen tree stumps littered its bank, and shells washed up onto the ribbon of sand that constituted its tiny shore.

With a sigh of contentment, Maura had unfolded her lounger in the shallow, lapping waves, settled Bea atop her stomach, and let the sun soak into her tired bones. The sunlight dancing on the waves had soon lulled her into a light doze.

All thoughts of sleep were gone now, though. Wide-awake, she surveyed the engaging young woman facing her. Well, not really a woman, she amended. Halfway between girlhood and budding femininity, she showed promise of real beauty. Her cutoffs and tank top revealed slight breasts and long, slender legs. Short, feathery dark curls brought out the glow of her tanned skin and blue eyes. Maura felt herself drawn to the girl's smile. It was both charming and tentative, as if she wanted to talk but wasn't sure of her welcome.

"Here." Scooting up, she swung her legs off the lounge to dangle in the shallow water. "Have a seat and tell me why you think this cove is so special. My name's Maura, by the way."

The girl perched precariously on the end of the lounger and folded her legs under her with coltish grace. "I'm Lisa. I live just around the bend. Didn't you know this stretch of shore is an old Indian camping ground?"

"No, I didn't."

"It's a historic site. Registered and everything."

"So that why no one's built along here."

"They can't. It's protected by the government." The girl's blue eyes gleamed as she warmed to a topic that obviously fascinated her. "There's an Indian museum in downtown Fort Walton Beach that has artifacts found around this cove. Pots and utensils and stuff. Even bones."

"Bones?"

Nodding, Lisa grinned ghoulishly. "Real bones. Skulls and leg pieces and teeth. Some of them have been carbon-dated from prehistoric times."

"How in the world do you know so much about it?"

"My dad's best friend is married to a woman who works here on base. Maggie's an environmental engineer."

"Dr. Maggie Wescott. Yes, I know her."

Mostly by reputation, although they had attended one or two meetings together. Maura had felt an instant rapport with the leggy, green-eyed blonde, but so far she hadn't had time to follow up on her friendly offer of a personal tour of Eglin's Natural Resource Management operation.

"Maggie got me interested in archaeology," Lisa explained with engaging enthusiasm. "That's what I'm going to study in college. I got to spend a month last summer on a dig in Utah, sponsored by my school. It was really fun. I mean, we lived in tents and cooked our food over campfires and shifted about a ton and a half of dirt a day. I even found a dinosaur bone." She smiled mischievously. "Or at least I thought it was a dinosaur, until the instructor said it was actually a coyote's left foreleg."

Maura laughed at the droll recital. "Well, coyote or tyrannosaur, I'm impressed. The only remains I've ever found belonged to a bird Bea dragged in."

At the mention of her name, the cat twitched one slightly ragged ear, but otherwise declined to stir enough to be properly introduced.

Lisa reached out to stroke the mottled orange fur. "What a strange-looking cat. She reminds me of the fat Cheshire in *Alice in Wonderland,* except she's the wrong color and she's not grinning."

"No, that would take too much energy. Bea saves her strength for the important things, like sleeping."

Lisa's strokes drew rumbles of pleasure from the cat's massive chest. "How old is she?"

"I don't have any idea. I found her asleep in the front seat of my car one afternoon a few years ago, with no tag and a bleeding paw. She objected to being dislodged, so we sort of adopted each other."

For a few moments they sat contentedly, letting the sun warm them and the lapping waves tickle their ankles. Lisa glanced around her special place with a proprietary look, then pointed to a dark opening in the bank just a few yards away.

"See that small indentation in the cove? Either the tide or a storm washed out part of the bank. Lots of times buried artifacts are uncovered that way. You can find them easily in the shallow bay water."

At Maura's skeptical look, she crossed her heart.

"Honest!" Untangling her legs, she jumped off the lounger. "Come on, I'll show you."

"I believe you."

"No, seriously, come on. I bet we can find all kinds of stuff here."

Unable to resist such eager enthusiasm, Maura got to her feet. Bea observed with an inscrutable expression from the safety of the lounge as the two humans began a slow, slogging shuffle.

Following Lisa's example, Maura peered down at the water and stared intently into the muddy swirls her sneakered feet stirred up. She found a couple of pieces of dark stone, which Lisa laughingly dismissed, and was ready to call it quits when the girl called out excitedly.

"Come look!"

Lisa knelt in the shallow water to wash dirt from what looked like a small brown rock. Crouching down beside her, Maura watched as a symmetrical pattern slowly emerged from the mud.

"I've seen a design just like this on a pot in the museum," Lisa said breathlessly. "The Indians used to arrange pieces of straw around the pots before they fired them. Each tribe had its own special pattern, sort of like a designer's signature. See how this one weaves over and under."

Despite herself, Maura felt a thrill as she ran her fingers over the surface of the shard. Her mother was an amateur potter, happily shutting herself away from her noisy brood in a converted garage. Having zero artistic talent of her own, Maura was convinced that observing her parent create such beauty from natural materials had influenced her own decision to specialize in ceramics.

"Yes, I can see the design." She was almost as excited as the girl. "I can't believe we actually found this here."

Lisa clambered to her feet with an excited splash. "Let's see if we can find some more."

An hour later, a dripping but triumphant pair knelt in the shallow water and spread their cache out on the lounge.

Bea gave a disgusted twitch of her tail and moved to the end of the lounge. Eyeing the sandy bits disdainfully, she settled herself on the pillow.

Their largest find was only about six inches square, but it was definitely part of a pot. It had a round lip and curved in, then out, with a delicate line. Rows of slanted markings filled its entire surface.

"I didn't really think we'd find anything," Maura

admitted, "but I'm a believer now. This is really exciting. I can't wait to tell my mother about these. Are we supposed to turn these pieces in to the museum or something?"

"I'm not sure. I know the shore is a protected area, but we found these pieces in the water. I'll ask my dad," the girl said after a moment. "He knows everything."

"Thanks for the endorsement."

Both woman and girl jumped as the deep voice penetrated their absorption.

"Dad!"

The teenager's pretty face lit up. Splashing through water, she jumped up on the bank and laid her pieces in his hand.

"Look what we found."

Maura straightened slowly and barely suppressed a groan. Of all the people this engaging child could have picked for a parent, she had to choose Jake McAllister.

"This is Maura, Dad. She found some really super pieces, but we're not sure if we can keep them. Can we? I told her you would know."

"Maura and I have met," McAllister replied with a wry glance over his daughter's head. "And I hate to destroy my image of all-seeing, all-knowing omnipotence, but I don't know the rules about finds like this."

Momentarily deflated, the teen quickly recovered. "I know! We take the pieces down to the museum and ask the folks there. Can you come with us?" she inquired, turning to Maura. "I know the museum's open on Sunday afternoons. We can ask them about these pieces, and you can see the exhibits that they have."

"No, I can't, Lisa."

"Not today, honey."

The teen blinked at the two simultaneous responses, looking from one adult to another in confusion.

"We can't go downtown now, Lisa. We're supposed to go sailing with the Camerons this afternoon. That's why I came looking for you."

"I forgot." Not quite ready to admit defeat, she tried again. "Do you think the museum is open tomorrow evening? We could go after you get home from work."

"Why don't I do some research?" Maura suggested instead. "I'll check out the rules regarding finds like this."

There was no way she wanted to get involved with Jake McAllister again, even for a quick trip to the local cultural center.

"Okay," Lisa agreed reluctantly. "I'll meet you here tomorrow afternoon and you can tell me what you found out."

"I may have to work late," Maura warned.

"That's okay. We live just around the bend. I'll watch for you."

She hesitated, searching for another excuse. As

much as she liked this engaging young girl, she'd prefer not to tangle with her father again. Before she could come up with an out, however, Lisa scampered off.

"See you tomorrow. Come on, Dad. We're late."

"I'll be right there."

While his daughter splashed around the bend, Jake turned back to the woman almost lost under a floppy hat half the size of Texas. Despite himself, he couldn't help running appreciative eyes over the body displayed so enticingly by her bathing suit. The high-cut tank showed off her neat curves and trim, tight behind to perfection.

Appreciation surged into out-and-out lust when she scooped the cat under one arm and bent to fold up the lounger. Jake's throat went dry, but he managed to keep his expression neutral as he reached down to help her climb the bank.

He snatched his hand back again just in time to avoid a vicious swipe from a huge orange paw. "What is it with that animal?"

"I told you, she doesn't like men."

"Is that why you keep her?"

"Hey, McAllister, you have your friends and I have mine. Bea happens to be the best kind of pet. She loves junk food and doesn't care whether the bed ever gets made."

Ignoring what was obviously intended as a jab at uptight colonels with precisely arranged bookshelves, Jake reached down again. More warily this time. Maura hesitated a moment before putting her fingers in his.

"Speaking of friends," he commented when he got her on dry ground, "Lisa seems to have taken a liking to you."

The floppy hat tipped up. Hazel eyes narrowed. "And…?"

"And I've only got my daughter for a couple of months each summer. She tends to get a little lonely."

"I see." A foot clad in a wet, sandy sneaker tapped the bank. "So you're worried Lisa may get desperate and attach herself to a breathless California ditz, is that it?"

Jake had figured that would come back to haunt him. "Actually," he said with a rueful grin, "I just wanted to explain that Lisa doesn't have many acquaintances here. She might try to take advantage of you and your time."

Some of the belligerence went out of the woman facing him, but the stiffness still colored her voice.

"Lisa's a nice kid. I wouldn't mind spending some time with her. But I don't like the idea of her hanging out at this cove alone. Please tell her I'll call her as soon as I find something out."

Nodding, Jake watched her stroll away. His own reactions to the woman remained decidedly mixed, but he'd sensed the instant rapport that seemed to have sprung up between her and his daughter. Maybe a little of Maura's outgoing ebullience was what Lisa needed.

The divorce had left her too serious, too quiet. Although Jake tried to involve her in local activities when she came to visit, she tended to withdraw into a reserved, self-sufficient shell. Her favorite activities seemed to be reading and the interest in archaeology she'd developed after talking to Maggie Wescott.

Jake hadn't missed the excited sparkle in Lisa's eyes when she ran to show him the pottery shards. He'd felt a surge of love for his child so strong it almost overwhelmed him. If digging around in the mud with Maura Phillips gave Lisa that kind of pleasure, he wasn't about to deny it. He'd just make sure he kept out of their way.

"What do you think?"

Spreading the pottery shards out on her desk Monday morning, Maura summoned several of her co-workers to show them her treasures.

Pete poked a finger at the brown and red shapes. "They look like rocks to me."

"No, look at the designs," Maura insisted. Somehow, in the space of a single evening, she'd become a devotee of prehistoric pottery. She'd even called her mom, who'd added to her enthusiasm about the little pieces.

"Okay, they're rocks with designs." Pete grinned at the others peering over Maura's shoulder.

"Well, what tribe do you think made them? What do you know about the prehistoric Indians in this area?"

Laughing, Pete edged away from her desk. "Look, I'm an electrical engineer. What I know about Indian artifacts you can fit sideways in a transistor."

"You might try the base civil engineers," a short, gray-haired woman volunteered. "I think they're responsible for that sort of stuff. Why don't you start with them?"

"Thanks, I will."

A call to the Environmental Protection Branch got Dr. Maggie Wescott on the line. After a brief exchange of pleasantries, Maura described the find and asked about the rules governing their find.

"Our regulations are pretty straightforward if artifacts are found on base," Wescott advised. "Off base is a different story. We have an archaeologist on call from the University of Florida who comes in and catalogs the major finds. I can give you his number. Or the State Environmental Protection Agency in Pensacola. Also, there's a historical society in downtown Fort Walton Beach that might help."

Maura took down the numbers and tried the last first. There was no answer at the historical society, and the other two were long distance, so she decided to call them from home. She scooped the pottery shards into the little box she'd found for them last night, put them in her desk drawer and turned to her work.

Within minutes she was glued to her computer screen, running a series of simulations for the AGM-88 HARM—High Speed Anti-Radar Missile.

Charts and computer runs were scattered across her desk and littered the large worktable in the center of the room. The good part about working in a secure area was being able to leave all this stuff lying out.

The bad part was working in a windowless vault, of course. Shrugging off the closed-in feeling, Maura typed in the simulation parameters. She was soon so absorbed in her work that the shrill ring of her intercom caused her fingers to jump on the keyboard. With a muttered curse, she backspaced carefully and picked up the phone.

"Dr. Phillips, this is Janet Simpson. The boss needs to see you. Can you come down now?"

"Sure, Janet. Anything in particular I need to bring?"

"Not that he mentioned."

"Okay, I'm on my way."

Carefully saving her work on both hard disk and a floppy file, Maura gathered up her scattered charts. Vault or no vault, years of working on highly classified advanced projects had ingrained a security awareness that made her especially cautious. She gave Pete a cheerful wave as she left the common work area and went down a short flight of stairs to the director's office.

Her boss was waiting for her. She liked Ed Harrington. He was one of the original good ole boys—a local who had gone to the University of Alabama for his engineering degree, then come right back to start work at Eglin. He'd climbed his way up the bureaucratic ladder until he was promoted to this, the highest-ranking civilian position on base. He exuded a crusty, tough aura that didn't fool Maura for a minute.

"What's up?" she asked as she strolled into his office. She was halfway to the big, overstuffed chair in front of his desk before she noticed the other figure standing off to one side.

"Have you met Colonel McAllister?" Ed asked.

"Yes," Maura managed to say.

She was beginning to feel haunted.

Oblivious to the sudden electricity in the air, Ed chomped on the unlit cigar that never left his mouth and waved them both to a chair.

"Jake just got called in to see the general concerning a special project we're working on. The old man wants us to pull out all the stops. I'll let him explain."

McAllister took the seat opposite Maura's. He was in uniform—dark blue slacks, light blue short-sleeved shirt with the silver eagles glistening on his shoulder tabs—and didn't look particularly happy about this special project. Maura soon understood why.

"We've been tapped to test a new mount for the Maverick missile on the F-117."

"The Nighthawk?"

Maura's pulse kicked up. She'd cut her teeth on the swept-wing Stealth fighter.

"With all that's going on in the Middle East,"

McAllister continued, "the air staff wants to move up the test milestones. The general's put me in charge of the project."

"So how does this involve me?"

"I've told Ed I need his best test manager for this project. He tells me that's you."

The compliment should have tickled her. Coming from anyone else, it would have.

"I haven't done much work on the Maverick," she hedged. "Surely one of the other engineers who've handled the missile would be better for this project."

"We don't need missile expertise as much as we need someone who knows the F-117," Ed explained. "You worked the Nighthawk at Lockheed, Phillips. You know the plane's material structure. I want you on this one."

Maura sat back in her chair. Excitement rippled through her at the prospect of working a modification to the weapons load of the Stealth.

"Pete Hansen has been working on the project part-time," Ed advised. "I want you to take the lead from here on, full-time. Pete can help, if necessary."

In his earnestness, Ed puffed energetically on his cigar. After a few seconds of wasted effort, he remembered it wasn't lit, pulled the thing out of his mouth and stared at it in disgust.

Maura bit back a grin at her boss's disgruntled look and flashed a quick look at Jake. His gray eyes held banked laughter, but he managed to keep a straight face. The tension between them eased a bit, only to come back in full force with his next words.

"I think we can work together as professionals on something as important as this," he said quietly.

His meaning was clear to Maura even if it went right over Ed's head. Nobody, but nobody, had ever questioned her professional integrity before.

"Yes, Colonel, I'm sure I can find a way to work with you on this."

Her voice dripped ice. Even Ed now noticed the tension crackling between them. His shaggy brows rose in a question. But before he could speak, Jake got to his feet.

"I'll need a complete rundown of where the project stands by tomorrow, including a synopsis of the simulations done to date. Call my secretary and schedule a time to brief me," he ordered crisply, then left with a nod to them both.

Chapter 3

"Geez," Maura muttered as the door closed behind the man who was fast becoming her nemesis. "Who does he think he is?"

"One of the best deputy commanders for operations we've ever had at Eglin," her boss replied with an understanding smile. "Jake can come on strong at times, but since he took over as D.O., we've doubled our test-flight sorties. Even more important, the sorties have produced results. Those bunker-busters that blasted al-Quaeda out of their caves in Afghanistan were developed and tested right here."

"I know, I know. The man just rubs me the wrong way."

"Well, get over it," Ed advised. "I want you to give

this your best shot. Stop by Security on your way back and get cleared into the project."

"Aye, aye, Admiral."

Snorting, Ed shifted his cigar to the other side of his mouth. "I don't know why I let you get away with your lip, Phillips."

"Because I only give it to you in private," she tossed back, getting to her feet. "And you need someone to prick your bubble once in a while. You may have everyone else around here buffaloed with your 'senior statesman' routine, but I know you're just a frustrated engineer at heart. You'd give this fancy office up in a flash to get your hands on a slide rule again."

She opened the door to let herself out. "Too bad we don't use slide rules anymore," she tossed over her shoulder.

Ed chuckled as the door closed behind her. He'd never admit it, of course, but he thoroughly enjoyed sparring with Maura. The woman possessed a lively sense of humor that had brought a healthy dose of laughter, among other things, into his staid engineering department.

When he'd read the résumé she sent in response to their ad for an engineer, he'd almost bitten through his cigar. Ph.D. from Stanford. Elected into the prestigious International Society of Engineers within a year of graduation. Eight years in the research and development division at Lockheed, with hands-on experience in composites.

Although she couldn't detail all her experience in her résumé due to security considerations, Ed had been around long enough to read between the lines. He'd made a couple of phone calls to friends to verify her credentials and hired her, sight unseen.

He had expected a female version of the stereotypical engineer, complete with plastic pocket holder full of pens and laptop computer. He was as amazed as everyone else in the directorate when a woman in silky red walking shorts and an animal-print blouse breezed in and announced she was his new test engineer.

After the first five minutes of her incoming interview, Ed knew he had a winner. Her knowledge of the latest in materials engineering almost made him drool, but he'd restrained his enthusiasm enough to start her on a series of what he labeled category B projects until he could assess her work personally.

Within two weeks he'd moved her to category A projects. And now she would be working this mount problem. If anyone could get the test back on track, Ed was certain she could.

Maura had her doubts as she climbed the stairs after a quick detour to the security office. Although her heart thumped at the thought of working with the Nighthawk again, she worried that her knowledge was too dated, her expertise too stale. She'd have to get up to speed on this modification, and fast.

"Hey, Pete," she called as she hurried down the row of modular workstations. "I need your help."

"What's up?" he asked, sauntering over with coffee cup in hand.

"The Nighthawk, that's what," Maura answered. "Ed says all the milestones for the Maverick mounting mod have been moved up, and he's put me on it full-time."

"But that's my project."

"Ed mentioned you've been working it part-time, along with several other hot projects. I guess he figured I had more time available to work this one than you did."

Her attempt at diplomacy failed. A scowl settled over Pete's face. "I've spent almost six months on this one already. Ed should have put me on it full-time."

Maura kept silent. She could understand his disappointment, but she wasn't about to question Ed's decisions in public. He was her boss and had her loyalty.

"I need everything you've got, Pete. McAllister wants a status brief tomorrow morning."

Her co-worker made an obvious effort to shrug off his personal feelings. "I've got a couple of drawers full of data in addition to my electronic files. I'll transfer them to you."

Maura gulped when he laid a stack of fat folders on her desk. Flipping on her computer, she started taking electronic notes as she scanned the files.

Although still obviously upset, Pete's professionalism surfaced. He stayed late to help her sort through the data. It wasn't until early evening, after a break for a stale sandwich from the vending machines, that Maura found a note with a scribbled telephone number under the last file folder.

"Oh, no! I forgot to call Lisa."

"Lisa who?"

"Lisa McAllister. At least, I think that's her name."

"Jake's daughter?"

"I met her on the beach yesterday. In fact, she was the one who got me digging in the sand for those bits of pottery."

"I forgot she was down here again. I think she spends every summer with Jake."

"How long have her parents been divorced?" Maura inquired casually. Not that she was really interested, she told herself. She just didn't want to hurt Lisa by inadvertently saying the wrong thing.

"Three or four years, I think. I know Jake was divorced, or at least separated when he came here. He's been fighting off the local beauties ever since he arrived."

She looked up, startled at the touch of bitterness in his voice. She had a feeling he included his wife among those local beauties. Maura felt a little sorry for him but made herself shrug it off. Everyone had to work out their problems, as she knew all too well.

Maura and Ed Harrington arrived at the test wing's secure briefing room in the basement of the headquarters a few minutes before ten the following morning. She'd run through her briefing a couple of times, making last-minute changes with Pete's help right up until she'd left her office a few minutes ago.

"All set?" her boss asked.

"Yes."

She took a deep breath and smiled as they entered the plush conference room, where she gave her slides to a young captain. Ed introduced her to the group in the room, half of whom were military and the other half civilian. She was just getting herself a cup of coffee when everyone scrambled to their feet as Jake walked in.

"As you were. Dr. Phillips, if you're ready?"

Nodding, Maura set down her coffee and assembled her notes.

Jake hid a wry smile as she took to the podium. As many times as he'd been in this room, he'd never been briefed by a staffer wearing a blouse in a shade of yellow so vivid it could have stopped traffic on Eglin Boulevard. The chunky bracelet on her left wrist clinked as she picked up the control device and pressed it to bring up the first slide.

"Good morning, gentlemen. The purpose of this briefing is to update you on the status of the engineering efforts to modify the Maverick missile mounts on the F-117 Stealth fighter. Our goal is to design a rack-mounting assembly that will increase the loads in the Stealth's internal weapons bay.

"The fundamental issue is, of course, whether the

internal support structures will hold a bigger payload and release it cleanly without destroying the light-weight composite materials that give the Stealth its radar-evading capability."

Jake leaned forward, totally fascinated with this cool, crisp woman. She was so different from the one he'd spent that interminable evening with. And from the bay-walker with the floppy hat and breath-stealing bathing suit cut high on her thighs.

This one delivered slide after slide in precise fashion. The briefing was perfectly pitched to her audience of pilots and test engineers. She explained every detail in operational terms, illustrated every potential issue with drawings or charts. The briefing lasted nearly an hour, after which she fielded questions from the floor.

Jake sat quietly, letting his staff quiz her. She handled the questions without once resorting to her notes.

"An excellent briefing," he commented when the questions wound down. "Your estimates for completing the structural simulations are more optimistic than those my staff gave me. Do you really think we have the capability to do them in-house?"

"Yes, I do. Particularly with the new supercomputer that just came online. I'll run the simulations and have the results for you by next week, Colonel."

Jake raised his eyebrows. "Fine. I'll expect daily progress reports. Dr. Harrington, anything you'd like to add?"

Ed gave Maura a broad wink and shook his head. "I think Dr. Phillips has covered everything."

When the group broke up, Jake moved through the crowd. Her face showed a wary caution as he approached and waited for the others to depart.

"Was there something else, Colonel?"

"Look, about my remark yesterday morning in Ed's office. The one about rising above our personal differences to work together."

"Oh, yes. When you implied even a ditzy California girl had to occasionally put aside her half-baked prejudices in the interests of national defense."

Jake winced. "Well, I don't think that was quite the meaning I intended, but in any case, I apologize."

The apology surprised Maura. The wry grin that accompanied it melted some of her cool reserve.

"Apology accepted, Colonel."

Pete was waiting for her when she got back to her office. "How did it go?"

"Great! Fine! Well, okay. Tell you what, why don't I buy you lunch at the Dock and fill you in. I owe you for all your help last night."

By the time they settled down on the outside deck of a popular seafood restaurant, Maura's adrenaline had receded to normal levels and she was able to give Pete the gist of what had happened. They couldn't talk specifics in the open, of course, but each knew enough about the project now to communicate in totally unclassified code.

"Jeez, Maura, I'm amazed at how much you've learned so quickly," Pete said finally as he leaned back. "Not just about the Maverick, but about the test business as a whole."

"I may be new to Eglin," she reminded him gently, "but I'm not exactly new to the airplane business."

"Yeah, but still, working concept designs for big aircraft is a lot different from building bombs and missiles."

"Not that different. Our initial design work included the weapons that would be carried on the platform. Still, it is exciting here at Eglin to actually see the things fly and the systems work."

Their conversation turned desultory as the noon sun beat down. Maura felt the tension drain from her and a comfortable lassitude creep in. When they left the little restaurant, she was too tired to go back to work. She'd been at the office until almost 2:00 a.m. the night before.

The lack of sleep was catching up with her. She didn't want to start the computer simulation she had to do in this condition. That would require total concentration and every ounce of her energy for long hours in front of the terminal. Instead, she made a quick call to Ed's office to let him know she was taking a few hours' comp time, and grabbed the little box of pottery shards from her desk drawer.

Driving the few miles from the base to downtown Fort Walton Beach was pure pleasure. A thrill shot through her as she crossed the bridges over the little inlets that divided the town and saw how the sun sparkled on the blue-green water. When she turned into a parking spot behind the little cinder-block building of the historical society, she'd shrugged off most of the stress of preparing for the briefing.

"Good afternoon, dear. May I help you?"

Maura bit her lip as a slight, elderly woman came into the musty outer room. If she'd ever stopped to wonder who would work in a historical society, she probably would have pictured a woman like this one. But she wouldn't have pictured a museum docent in high-top sneakers and a baggy sweatshirt with Save the Turtles picked out in neon letters.

Maura tipped some of the pieces out of her little box, then held out her palm. "A friend and I found these in the bay a few yards off the shore. We think they may be Indian pieces."

"Oh, yes, I recognize some of the designs. Come on back to our Early Ancestors Room. You'll see very similar type of work."

Mrs. Bowman, or so her hand-lettered name tag proclaimed, led the way through a couple of rooms filled with early black-and-white photographs of the town to one that contained a haphazard jumble of Spanish, Indian and what looked like pirate paraphernalia.

"Our collection of Indian pottery isn't as complete as the one in the Indian Temple Mound Museum downtown," Mrs. Bowman continued, shifting a stack of pamphlets sitting atop a glass case filled with pottery and arrowheads.

"You really should visit it."

"I thought about it, but the museum was closed today. I had your address, so I thought I would try here. Oh, look, there's a design exactly like one of my pieces."

"The Cherokee didn't actually live in this area, but they did trade with our local Creek tribes, as well as with the Seminoles to the south. The pieces in this case are relatively recent. Over here are some of the older finds, from the prehistoric tribes who hunted and fished on the bay."

Maura lingered for a good half hour, examining the pieces and looking for design matches. Mrs. Bowman found an old, yellowed pamphlet written by an early scholar on southeastern Indian tribes, and offered to make a copy for her. When questioned, she didn't know the exact laws concerning retention of relics found in the bay, but suggested the state offices in Pensacola.

Maura got home late that afternoon and finally tracked down the right person to talk to in the Pensacola office. After a brief debate, she decided to call Lisa. She found Colonel Jake McAllister's number easily enough in the local directory and arranged to meet the excited teenager in fifteen minutes at the cove.

"Gosh, this is really awesome." Lisa sat on the edge of the bank beside Bea and skimmed through the photocopied pamphlet. "Look, here's a pot with a design just like one of the pieces we found."

"I know. And look here." Maura thumbed through the pamphlet. "Here's another that's estimated to be more than two thousand years old. Wouldn't it be exciting to find a piece from that era?"

"Yeah, if we could keep it."

"Well, the woman in Pensacola wasn't very specific. She said that they're only concerned if the piece has intrinsic value. She indicated the little bits we've found wouldn't have to be reported."

In fact, the woman had been downright harried and less than helpful.

"Let's play it by ear," Lisa suggested. "If we find something really neat, we can always ask about it."

"Okay, but I hadn't planned to make this a full-time occupation."

Maura smiled down at the girl to soften her words. She needn't have worried. When it came to her hobby, Lisa was as single-minded as any teenager.

"You can't quit now! Who knows what's out there waiting for us. I bet I can do a whole term paper on this when I get back to school. My teacher will be so overwhelmed, he'll recommend me for a scholarship to Harvard. You wouldn't want to deny me the chance to go to Harvard, would you?"

"Heavens, no."

Laughing, Maura clambered to her feet and joined Lisa for another wade in the bay. Bea gave them a long, steady look, as if wondering why any creatures in full possession of their senses would go splashing around when they could stretch out in the sun. Slowly, majestically, she laid her head back down, rolled on her side and shut the capricious humans out.

Woman and girl shuffled happily through the shallow water for more than an hour. They didn't find any special pieces, only a couple of small nondescript shards, but the paucity of treasures didn't dim their high spirits.

"You're a lot of fun for a grown-up," Lisa confided ingenuously when they collapsed, wet and sandy, on the bank.

Maura felt a little glow in her heart as she looked over at the smiling teenager.

"Almost as much fun as my dad."

The glow dimmed a bit.

"Would you like to come over for a sandwich or pizza or something?"

"I don't think I'd better. Your father isn't expecting guests."

"Dad's got a late flight tonight. He won't be down for hours."

The loneliness behind the appeal tugged at her. Maura herself came from a large, loud, boisterous family that augmented its natural numbers with dogs, cats, turtles and the occasional rodent brought home by her brothers. She tried to imagine being an only child, especially one whose parents had separated. Lisa obviously adored her father and seemed happy about her summers with him, but it had to be a lonely life for a child.

"Okay, but only for a quick sandwich. Come on, Bea." She scooped the boneless, lolling animal up in her arms. "We're dining out tonight."

Two hours later, Maura and Lisa sat cross-legged on the polished wood floor of Jake's living room, the remains of a large pizza and several soda cans scattered around them. Bea occupied a large leather recliner in solitary splendor, calmly licking anchovy from her mouth and paws.

"I'm stuffed," Lisa groaned, slumping back against the leather couch.

"Me, too. Whose idea was it, anyway, to order a deluxe?"

"Yours," the girl giggled.

"Yeah, well, it was a dumb idea. Next time it's a small, plain cheese."

"I love pizza," Lisa confided. "I never get to have it at home because Mom is always watching her weight, but Dad and I pig out during the summers."

Wondering idly how many deluxes it would take to fill up Jake McAllister's tall frame, Maura sipped her soda slowly and glanced around his home. Her gaze lingered on polished wood surfaces, rich leather furniture and a high-tech entertainment center set precisely in the middle of one wall. The opposite wall was filled with windows and gave a glorious view of the sun sinking into the bay in bloodred splendor.

Everything was so neat, so orderly. A direct contrast to the boxes still piled up in Maura's rented cottage. She was musing over the differences when the rumble of the garage door brought Lisa's head around.

"That's dad."

With a sense of inevitability, Maura folded the pizza carton and waited for Jake to make an appearance.

"Hi, Daddy. You're back early."

"We had to abort the flight because of a broken fuel pump," he replied, his surprised glance taking in both his daughter and her guest. "What's up?"

"Maura and I went sharding this afternoon and I invited her back for supper. She didn't want to come, but I told her you wouldn't be home until late and I couldn't eat a whole pizza by myself. You owe her seven dollars for my half."

Maura reddened slightly as she met Jake's amused gaze. Even if Lisa hadn't blurted it out, they both knew very well she wouldn't have set foot in the house if she had any idea he would be there.

"Any pizza left?" he asked, reaching down to ruffle his daughter's hair.

"Sorry, we didn't save any."

"And it was my treat," Maura put in, pushing to her feet. "I'd better be going before it gets too dark to find my way."

"I'll drive you home," Jake said. "Just give me a few minutes to change."

He crossed the room, dragging the checkered scarf from around the neck of his flight suit. Maura had to admit there wasn't anything the least bit loose or baggy about the way the fire-retardant material clung to his wide shoulders and lean torso. Sternly repressing the memory of that lean torso mashed against hers, she swiped her hands on her shorts and reached for Bea.

"It's just a short way, and I really need the exercise after all that pizza."

"It's too dark to walk back. Wait here."

The brisk tone probably had lieutenants snapping to attention but produced the opposite effect in Maura. Lips pursed, she made a face at the broad back disappearing up the wide oak staircase.

"Yes, sir! Anything you say, sir!"

Lisa's giggles brought her head around.

"Does he order you around like that, too?" she asked the girl.

"Sometimes. But I keep my Discman on and pretend not to hear him when he gets too bossy."

Jake came back downstairs just as Maura and Lisa finished cleaning up their impromptu supper. He had on a short-sleeved Air Force Academy sweatshirt and a pair of athletic shorts that made Maura's throat go dry. She couldn't remember when she'd seen quite that much male thigh before.

"I'll be right back," he told his daughter.

Guiding Maura out through the kitchen, he led her past a low, gleaming sports car to an older Jeep Cherokee.

"Smart move," she commented as she climbed into the cab. "You must have guessed what Bea's claws can do to leather seats."

"I saw what they did to my ankle."

A small silence settled between them as they drove through the winding streets of the exclusive development. Jake broke it with a glance in her direction.

"That was an excellent briefing this morning."

"Thanks. I won't tell you how nervous I was." Idly, she stroked Bea's fur. "Splashing around with Lisa in the bay this afternoon helped me recover. She's a great kid, Jake."

"I think so, too. Did the two of you find any treasures?"

"A few small pieces. By the way, I did some checking up this afternoon. I'm fairly certain we won't go to jail if we keep what we've found so far. It becomes somewhat of a moral issue, though, if we turn up anything resembling a whole pot or bowl."

"You think you'll have much time to go sharding with the Maverick project looming over you?"

Instantly, the barriers went up. "Don't worry, Colonel. I'll get your precious project done. What I do in my spare time is my business."

Jake's breath hissed out. "I wasn't challenging your right to some free time. I just don't want Lisa to become a pest."

"Sorry," she murmured. "Don't worry about it. I like her, and she seems to have hooked me on this pottery business."

He glanced over at her and hesitated. "At the risk of putting my foot in it again, I'd like to thank you for spending time with Lisa. She hasn't connected with any of her old friends down here this summer."

"She told me she met one boy," Maura ventured, thinking to help the cause of young love. "I think she said his name was Tony."

"That kid's a hood, as far as I'm concerned. He wears an earring in one ear and drives a truck with tires two stories high."

"I hate to be the one to break it to you, but an earring isn't an indelible mark of delinquency these days. Most of my nephews sport at least one stud. And I think the tires have something to do with puberty rites."

"That's exactly what I'm afraid of," Jake said dryly as he pulled into her driveway.

"Oh, come on. Lisa's pretty levelheaded. Surely you don't think she'd be overwhelmed by a set of tires?"

"I don't *think* so." His mouth curved. "But even in my day, a dude with a slick set of wheels could get lucky in the front seat occasionally."

"I'll bet! But then, they made front seats a lot larger in the old days."

"Back seats, too," he agreed, switching off the ignition.

He slewed sideways, determined to stretch out their unexpected truce a little longer. When she turned to face him, her hair brushed the hand he'd propped on her seat back. Idly, Jake burrowed his fingers in the soft, silky curtain. Not quite as idly, he stroked the soft, warm curve of her nape.

The sudden change in the atmosphere inside the Jeep caught Maura by surprise. One minute she was laughing and more relaxed with this man than she ever thought she could be. The next his fingertips were brushing the fine hairs on her nape and sending tiny shivers down her spine.

She knew she ought to pull away. Her hand groped blindly for the door handle. But she didn't pull on it, and Jake didn't stop.

"This isn't very smart, Colonel."

"Probably not, but I tried to warn you how a hot set of wheels can make a male lose his common sense. Particularly when it contains an equally hot female."

Despite the shivers racing along her spine, Maura had to grin. "Somehow I have difficulty believing the cool, composed Jake McAllister ever loses control *or* his common sense."

His brows waggled in a ferocious mock scowl. "Are you questioning my manhood?"

"No, no, honestly!"

Her laughing protests did no good as slowly, inexorably, he tugged her toward him. Her neck bowed, but she held on to the door handle and refused to give way. Even that anchor was lost when his arm slid down to wrap around her waist. An indignant Bea was dumped to the floor of the cab as he hauled Maura across the space between the seats and onto his lap.

For the second time in her tumultuous relationship with this man, Maura found herself in his arms. Half rueful, half aroused, she pushed against his ribs and managed to put some air between them. No easy feat with the steering wheel jabbing in her back.

"What is it with us, McAllister? We don't even like each other, yet we always seem to end up chest to chest."

His lips twitched. "Maybe we need to work on the liking part."

With one hand at the back of her head to hold her still, he lowered his lips until they nuzzled the edges of her mouth. He brushed them back and forth, over and over, until Maura gave a breathless murmur.

"What the hell."

Eyes closed, she put herself into the kiss. Her teeth scraped along his lower lip. Her tongue tasted his.

Sucking in a sharp breath, he moved his mouth over hers to give her full access. Maura pulled her arms free of his loosened hold and slid her palms up his arms. The muscles bunched under her fingertips, the skin warm to her touch. Tentatively at first, then more aggressively, she explored him with eager hands and tongue.

Jake held himself back, letting her play, allowing her to set the pace. But when her hands slid under the loose armholes of his sweatshirt to move across the bare skin of his back, his muscles twitched involuntarily.

All of them.

Including the one cradled against her soft, warm rear. When her eyes flew open in surprise, he grinned down at her wickedly.

"I told you, it's the hot wheels."

Maura gaped at him a moment, then laughed and pushed herself quickly, if ungracefully, off his lap.

"If a Jeep does this to you, fly-boy, I'd hate to see you when you come down out of the sky after joy-riding in one of your supersonic airplanes."

"Why do you think the fire vehicles are always standing by to hose us down?"

"God," she groaned, "you're sick."

"Nope, just your average all-American horny test pilot," he responded, opening his door to come around and help her down from the high cab.

Maura slid out of the truck, Bea held up to her chest as a shield. Despite the way her nerve endings still tingled, her rational mind questioned what her senses were feeling.

"Jake, I'm confused. I'm not real sure how this happened. I don't know if I want it to happen again."

"Don't worry about it so much," he told her gently. "Just be thankful Lisa is waiting at home or there'd be a lot more confusion to follow."

He ran his knuckle down the slope of her nose,

then jerked his hand back quickly as a warning hiss filled the darkness.

"Good night, Maura. And go take a flying leap, cat."

Chapter 4

After Jake left, Maura wandered aimlessly through her small cottage. Too restless to attack the full briefcase waiting beside her makeshift desk, she switched on the CD player. The soaring tenor of Placido Domingo performing a special collection of John Denver songs filled the night. But instead of soothing her as it usually did, the music only made her more restless.

With Bea padding at her heels, she opened the sliding glass doors to her small patio and settled on the lounger. The cat soon found her favorite spot on Maura's tummy.

Soft, starry night surrounded them. The sky was just darkening to deep blue velvet, and a glowing three-quarter moon hung low over the black waters of the bay. Crickets chirped in the bushes dotting her sloping backyard, providing a light counterpoint to the occasional deep, throaty call of a frog.

Maura stretched out on the lounger and let the night wash over her, but her body refused to surrender to the music or the magic of the breeze rustling through the palmettos. She was too restless, too wound up. Too physically aroused, she admitted with rueful honesty. Jake's kiss had stirred more than her curiosity.

Another shiver rippled through her, this one of pleasure, and her hands tightened involuntarily on Bea's coat. The cat lifted its head and opened one eye to fix her with an accusing stare.

"Sorry!"

Stroking the animal back into its normal state of boneless relaxation, Maura tried to rationalize her re-action to Colonel Jake McAllister. Despite every warning her head sent out, her body refused to lis-ten. She could still feel his lips on hers and the warmth of the arms that had circled her waist.

Okay. All right. These lingering sensations weren't that difficult to understand. She was a healthy female confronted with an attractive man. A *very* attractive man.

Maura gulped, remembering the long length of male thigh his jogging shorts had revealed. Not to mention the tight, iron-hard muscles displayed so en-ticingly by the sweatshirt. Her fingers tightened once more in Bea's rough coat.

The long-suffering animal didn't even open her eyes this time. She just used the tips of her very sharp claws.

Wincing, Maura gathered the cat on her chest. With Bea draped across her like a slightly used feather boa, she lay back on the lounger.

Her objective, analytical mind went to work dissecting the problem. She could admit now she was attracted to Jake. Had been since day one. Unfortunately, she wasn't skilled enough to separate her physical and emotional responses to a man. She'd learned that lesson the hard way in L.A.

Now this Stealth-modification project had been thrown into the mix. Maura could see only one solution. She'd have to nip physical attraction in the bud. Now, before business got all mixed up with pleasure.

She'd tell Jake that tomorrow.

Thoroughly depressed but determined, she unwrapped her fur tippet, turned her back on the low-hanging moon and went to bed.

Three weeks later, Jake McAllister sat in the Central Control Facility and watched the preparations for their first test shot. The modified missile would be launched from an F-15 Eagle first. If it separated without problem and the guidance system activated, they'd fly in a Stealth for the next test.

The three screens before Jake flickered with different views, adding to the unearthly glow permeat-

ing the room. The left screen showed the target—a
solid wall of concrete fifty feet high and ten feet thick,
with two intersecting lines painted in luminescent
black. The right screen showed a panoramic sweep
of Eglin's runway from a camera mounted in the
chase plane. When the chase plane was airborne, it
would maneuver in below the F-15 Eagle carrying the
modified missile and track the weapon during release.

The center screen showed only a hazy gray pattern. An hour from now, that small square would be
the focus of fifty anxious pairs of eyes. It would
show a view from a camera mounted in the missile's
nose cone. Everyone in the room would watch,
breath suspended, while the Maverick flew across
miles of sparsely wooded terrain toward the concrete wall.

Jake sat quietly at the console and listened while
the test engineers, range safety and telemetry people all ran through their checklists. Eglin employed
some of the finest, most experienced test personnel
in the world. The weapons they developed had
proved themselves time and again. These were the
men and women who'd fielded the systems that had
put a two-thousand-pound bomb down a factory
smokestack in Iraq while a hospital sat untouched
just a block away. These people knew their job, and
Jake let them do it.

In his normal capacity as deputy commander for
operations, he was responsible for the aircraft and

crews that flew these dangerous test missions. With more than forty of the world's finest test pilots and a fleet of thirty of the most technologically advanced test aircraft to oversee, he had plenty to keep him busy. This particular test, however, added even more responsibility. This would be the first launch of the modified missile his special team had been working on night and day for the past three weeks.

Jake rested one arm on the console and let the low, muted voices drift around him. He knew the pretest routine by heart. Having been assigned to Eglin as a test pilot some years ago, he'd flown hundreds of similar missions. Since he'd returned as D.O., he'd planned and directed many more. There really wasn't any need for him to be here this early. But an uncharacteristic restlessness had led him to cancel a scheduled staff meeting and drove him to the control facility.

He knew his still face and relaxed posture gave no clue to his inner unrest. People responded to their leader's body signals, and Jake had learned to project calm even during the worst crises. That control had seen him through more than one dangerous test, and had saved his life during a nightmarish period on the ground in northern Iraq.

Still, projecting calm and feeling it were two very different matters, Jake acknowledged ruefully. His glance strayed to the woman seated among the folks crowded in the viewing area off to the right. In her fire-hydrant-red dress, she was hard to miss.

Silently, Jake admitted Dr. Maura Phillips was the source of a good part of the tension now wrapping its insidious coils around his body. Ever since she'd taken him aside and calmly informed him it wasn't smart to mix business and personal involvement, his physical frustration had grown. He hadn't been so tied up in knots since high school.

His assessing eyes watched while she reached up one hand to push a thick swatch of honey-brown hair behind her ear. Her movement clearly outlined small, high breasts against the red material.

Damn! The woman was making him ache in parts of his body he'd forgotten he owned. Shifting uncomfortably, he cursed under his breath.

Jake knew very well she was right, that neither of them had time for distractions right now. But he was also more used to directing events than being directed. Instead of turning him off, Maura's polite dismissal had only made him more and more aware of her during their enforced intimacy the past two weeks.

"Eglin three-six-four ready for takeoff."

The scratchy voice of the pilot of the launch aircraft came over the speaker. Instantly, Jake tore his eyes and his thoughts from Maura.

"Eglin three-six-four, you're cleared for takeoff on runway one-nine."

The pilot acknowledged the tower's clearance and the right screen switched from the chase plane's camera to one mounted on the roof of Eglin's main hangar. A tense stillness descended over the control facility. Everyone watched the specially modified F-15 move into position at the end of the runway. The chase plane sat on the apron, waiting its turn.

The F-15 Eagle began its takeoff roll. Moving down the runway, it gathered speed and lifted into the air with a thrust of power and smooth grace that made Jake's hands itch to be on the throttle. The chase plane followed close behind, and both planes headed for the wide, blue waters of the bay. Their flight pattern would take them out to the Gulf, where they would turn and begin their run back over the vast test range.

"Test planes launched."

"Launch acknowledged."

The range safety officer, a senior civilian with twenty-five years' experience, took over. At this point, he was in charge. Although this missile didn't carry an explosive payload, the most detailed pre-planning and sophisticated computer systems in the world couldn't prevent a seagull from being sucked into a jet engine or a sudden updraft hitting just when a weapon was launched. If anything occurred to endanger the pilot, the mission or the surrounding communities, the safety engineer had full authority to abort the test or destroy the missile in flight.

Maura edged forward in her seat. The viewing area was separated from the main control console by a solid glass wall that gave her an unobstructed view of the action. The theater-style seats on either side of her were filled with nervous contractors, tense engineers and sharp-eyed test pilots. The test center's commander, a tall, dignified major general, sat in the front row. Another half dozen or so team members stood behind the rows of seats.

Pete had his shoulders to the wall at the rear of the small room. Although not an official member of the team, he'd provided much of the basic information and had an interest in this first test. Judging by his white face and intense, fixed stare, he was as nervous as Maura.

"Ten minutes to launch."

The camera mounted in the chase plane captured the image of the F-15 tearing through a brilliant blue sky. Maura tore her gaze from the spectacular imagery to dart a quick look at Jake. He was sitting straight and tall in his green flight suit, his eyes on the screen, showing no signs of the excitement rippling through the rest of the team members. Marveling at his control, she gripped the armrests, sure she would bounce out of her seat in her nervousness.

"Two minutes to launch."

"Launch systems on," the pilot confirmed.

The chase plane's camera zoomed in closer to show the missile mounted under the F-15's wing. It was long and sleek and white, its clean lines belying the deadly power of its normal payload. The missile fluttered on its modified mounting, buffeted by winds as the fighter streaked across the Florida sky at Mach one speed.

Two seemingly endless minutes later, the pilot's voice crackled over the loudspeakers. "Missile away."

The central screen lost its fuzzy blur. All eyes riveted on it as the camera in the missile's nose activated and began to record the short flight.

"The guidance system won't activate."

The already thick tension in the control facility kicked into overdrive. Maura watched, breath suspended, as the missile's downward trajectory sharpened. The pilot tried again, and then again, to activate the Maverick's internal guidance controls, without success.

A collective groan swept the control facility when the missile flew into a stand of trees fifteen miles short of the scheduled impact point.

The central screen went blank, and Maura's gaze whipped back to Jake. Amazingly, his lean face showed none of the raging disappointment she knew must be coursing through his veins. She shook her head at his iron control and glanced back at the blank screen. Heaven only knew how much of the missile had survived the impact.

Slowly the crowd filed out of the control facility. They'd get together tomorrow to go over the data from the pilot's debriefing and the recovered missile. Maura lingered as the room emptied, her eyes straying once again to Jake. He stood and spoke briefly with the general, who nodded once or twice, then left.

"I guess it's back to the drawing board," she said when Jake joined her.

"That's what the test business is all about," he responded with a roll of his shoulders. "Trial and error. A miss, followed by a hit. You can't expect to field a modified system without getting out all the bugs. We'll find out what went wrong and fix it."

"If there's enough left of our missile to even try again."

"If not, we'll modify another."

Maura groaned, thinking of the backbreaking hours spent over their computers to come up with the original design.

"We should get most of this one back," Jake said, obviously trying to reassure her. "The missile most likely cut through the trees and plowed into sandy earth. That's one of the reasons Eglin is such a good test bed. We recover most of what we have to drop."

He hesitated, his glance roaming over her face. "I'm going out to see what the recovery team digs up. Want to come?"

"Yes, I do! I've been out on the range a couple of times for orientation, but never to see the results of an actual shot. The remains of an actual shot," she amended with another groan.

They took the range vehicle assigned to Jake. A modified jeep, it was designed to take the narrow, unimproved dirt trails that crisscrossed Eglin's vast reservation.

Some of Maura's crushing disappointment lifted as they left the main base and headed north. Tall pine trees towered above them on either side, thrusting out of the thick scrub brush that thrived in northern Florida's sandy soil. Late afternoon sunlight flickered through pine branches and dappled the road in a shifting pattern of light and shade.

Jake kept in contact with the range patrol via his handheld radio. Following their instructions, he turned twice onto smaller, numbered side roads. Within a half hour, they picked up the flashing lights of the response team that had sealed off the impact area.

A security policewoman inspected both Jake and Maura's badges closely before passing them through the initial checkpoint. A mile or so farther down the road, they pulled up behind a cluster of official vehicles.

Even though this test involved an unarmed weapon, there was always the danger of a small explosion or fire on impact. Fire trucks, range safety vehicles, police cars and ordnance-disposal trucks cluttered the road. While Jake went to talk to the officer in charge, Maura unbuckled her seat belt and slipped out the passenger door, only to teeter precariously when her high heels sank into the soft soil.

Grimacing, she glanced down at her shoes. She'd bought these bright red strappy sandals because they matched her dress so perfectly, but they certainly weren't the right footgear for traipsing through the brush after downed missiles.

"They've found it," Jake told her when he returned a few minutes later. "It's about a half mile off the road and appears to be in pretty good shape." His glance went to her shoes, sunk to the heels. "I've got some boots in the back of the truck if you want to trek through the woods to the site."

"That's what I came for, Colonel."

Unbuckling her sandals, Maura pulled on the boots and tried a few experimental steps. The rubber slapped at her knees and sucked away from her foot every time the heel hit the soft sand. Disregarding these unpropitious signs, she clumped over to Jake.

"All set. Lead the way."

She had to stop several times to tug a boot back on, but they finally made it to the perimeter of the impact site. Yellow tape was wrapped around tree trunks, enclosing a circle approximately the size of a basketball court. Explosive-ordnance personnel in heavy safety suits maneuvered a backhoe around a blackened hole. Inside the hole was the Maverick, buried up to its tail fins.

The rest of the response team waited outside the circle. They greeted Jake respectfully, nodded to Maura and turned to watch while the crew inside the taped area worked to unearth the missile. The shadows cast by the tall pines gradually lengthened. The only sound was the steady grinding of the backhoe's gears and a dull thud as each load of earth was dumped aside. Finally, after what seemed like hours, a recovery-team member slipped into the widened pit and fixed a harness around the exposed tail.

At his signal, the crane operator slowly, inexorably, pulled the white tube from its shadowy depths. Maura breathed a relieved sigh when she saw the missile appeared pretty much intact.

"Wait here," Jake instructed. Ducking under the tape, he went to examine the missile.

Maura soon found herself engaged in friendly conversation with two of the range-patrol officers. In the ensuing twenty minutes she learned more about the strange events that could occur on Eglin's half million plus acres than she would ever have imagined possible. The range officers had wild tales of marijuana growers and poachers and more than one party of skinny-dippers caught in the buff enjoying the reservation's creeks and streams. One enthusiastic officer was just beginning a gruesome account of decomposing bodies found recently when Jake returned.

Excusing herself, Maura shuffled beside him through the tall trees. When she lost her boot for the third time, he took matters into his own hands. Literally.

"We'll never make it out of the woods at this rate."

Before she realized his intent, he'd bent, slid one arm under her knees and lifted her easily in his arms.

"Grab the boot," he instructed, dipping so she could retrieve the errant footwear.

Her twisting movement brought her breast in direct contact with Jake's palm. His body went on instant alert as the soft flesh filled his palm. He could feel the lacy pattern of her bra and the hard little bud of her nipple.

Maura's startled eyes flashed up at him. Her little speech about not mixing business and pleasure slid into Jake's mind, then slid right out again. The stress of the past weeks, the crushing disappointment of the failure, the tension of the work still ahead—everything coalesced to this one point in time. All he could think of in the endless moment when her eyes held his and the soft flesh burned against his hand was how much he wanted her.

This contradictory, tantalizing, vibrant woman had lodged like a burr under his skin. She filled his thoughts more than he'd allowed any woman to in a long, long time. And she filled his body with a surge of desire so raw it slipped past the rigid guard he kept on his emotions.

Maura saw the raw hunger that leapt into his eyes. Her breath caught in her throat as an answering flame seared through her veins. The trees, the trail, the dappled shadows, faded from her vision. Her entire world narrowed to a lean, tanned face and a pair of gleaming silver eyes.

All these weeks of sternly denying her attraction to this man slowly dissolved. Her mental barriers crumbled, and resistance flowed out of her consciousness like sand sifting gently through a sieve. What was left was a rock-hard core of absolute desire.

"Well, what do you know?" she said on a shaky breath. "We're chest to chest again."

"Yeah, we are."

A small, savage smile lifted Jake's lips. He could read the dawning desire in her expressive face as clearly as he could feel the tension quivering in her body. Slowly he let her slide down his body. He kept her pinned against his chest with one arm, feeling every inch of her long, soft form pressing into him. His other hand moved up to tangle in her silky hair.

Maura waited, breathless, her head drawn back. The pounding of her heart filled her ears. His warm breath washed across her face, and the faint scent of tangy cologne drowned out the rich, verdant odor of the pines. When he finally lowered his head and took her lips, she was aching for his taste.

Jake moved his mouth over hers needily. His hands slid down her back to shape her buttocks. Effortlessly he lifted her into the cradle of his thighs. His hips pressed against hers, grinding, rolling.

A faint sound teased at the edge of his consciousness. When it gradually resolved into a pattern of footsteps coming through the brush behind them, he gave a frustrated growl and lifted his head.

The sight of Maura's thoroughly kissed lips and heavy-lidded eyes sent another blade of desire knifing through him. He felt a primitive urge to drag her into the underbrush, cover her body with his until the intruders passed, then plunge into her right then and there.

Instead, he took a deep, unsteady breath and swung her into his arms once more. Striding down the last quarter mile of trail, he lifted Maura into the truck.

"Buckle your seat belt."

Maura fumbled with the metal clip. Her breath still came in short little gasps and she wondered wildly if her heart would slow to only double time, or even triple, during the long ride home.

It didn't. Every time she stole a glance at Jake's profile, her pulse speeded up once more. He didn't say a word during the whole drive home. He didn't have to. He radiated such a devastating aura of male potency that Maura shivered in erotic anticipation.

Her doubts about getting involved in a physical relationship with this man came back to haunt her. Some small corner of her rational mind tried to send out a warning signal, but she ignored it. This time the sensual part of her brain, the side that loved bright colors, glorious sunsets and romantic tenors drowned out the analytical side. She could handle it, she told herself. She could keep the compartments separate. Work. Sex. Jake.

Which didn't explain why her heart was hammering against her ribs when he pulled to a stop beside his own car in the lot outside his office.

He slammed out of the truck and came around to lift Maura out. Caught up in a daze of quivering, simmering expectation, she forgot her shoes and her purse. Nothing registered but the feel of his arms as he settled her in his car. They were pulling into the driveway of her cottage before she even realized she still wore one boot. She pushed it off just as Jake came around to the passenger door.

Thankfully, she kept a spare key under a flower-pot beside the door. Jake kicked the door closed be-hind them, Maura in his arms. To her surprise, instead of heading to the bedroom, he stopped in the hallway and let her slide slowly down his body. Her toes curled on the cool parquet floor. Still held in the circle of his arms, she looked up at him, a question in her eyes.

"I want you, Maura," he told her softly. "I want to make love to you until we both explode, then love you again."

Maura nodded, long past the point of being able to disguise her own need. "I want that, too."

"No worries about mixing business and plea-sure?"

"Some," she replied honestly. "But I've decided we're two mature adults. Surely we can keep a phys-ical relationship in perspective."

"A physical relationship?" Jake's eyes nar-rowed. "Are you saying all you want is sex, no strings attached?"

Some of the romantic haze surrounding Maura faded just a bit. "Isn't that what you want?"

"No. I want to make love to you."

Exasperation feathered at the edges of her sensual haze. Having been swept off her feet in the most dashing, romantic style and driven home in a fever of anticipation, the last thing she expected was to be standing in the hall, arguing semantics.

"Well, what's the difference?"

Jake stared down at her, an arrested expression in his silver eyes. A little embarrassed now, Maura fidgeted under his look. This wasn't going at all as she expected. Just when she was about to push herself out of his arms, his mouth curved.

"If you don't know the difference between having sex and making love, Maura m'girl, it will be my pleasure to teach you."

And he did.

Slowly. Deliciously. Wonderfully.

Holding her against him with one arm, Jake tipped her chin up for his kiss. Maura had a moment to wonder just what she'd got herself into before his dark head lowered and his mouth covered hers.

On a scale of one to ten, she decided, just before she lost all ability or desire for analytical thought, the kiss rated a twenty-two. It began lightly, a quick, whisper-soft brush of his mouth across hers. Then Jake caught her lower lip in a little bite, running his tongue over the sensitive inner flesh, and she felt a tiny flame flicker in parts of her body she'd never realized were connected to her lip. She reached up to steady herself with a hand on his shoulders, then slid both arms around his neck.

Widening his stance, Jake let her fit her body to his. It took every ounce of his willpower not to crush her against him, but for all his raging desire, he fully intended for Maura to experience every exquisite sensation of the act of love. He wanted to draw this out, show her every pleasure, even if it damn well killed him.

Soft little moans were coming from the back of her throat when he lifted her in his arms. He used the short walk down the hallway to her bedroom to take deep, steadying breaths. They were a serious mistake.

Every expansion of his chest muscles brought them into intimate contact with her breasts. Even through his flight suit, he could feel her tight, taut peaks. His iron control almost shattered right then and there.

In the dim bedroom, he laid Maura on the wide bed and let his eyes feast on her. The red dress rode halfway up her legs. Her breasts rose and fell rapidly in the soft light, and her arms lay above her head in an unconscious gesture of invitation. Soft brown hair spilled across the pillow, framing a face both shy and welcoming.

Jake sank to the side of the bed and reached out with hungry hands for the tiny coral buttons on the front of the dress.

"Dammit!"

He barely got his hands back unscathed as a long, hairy paw lashed out, claws extended.

Chapter 5

Biting her lip to hold back a smile, Maura scooted off the bed. A hissing Bea glared at Jake from the safety of her arms.

"Sorry 'bout that." She swallowed a smothered laugh as she took in his thoroughly disgruntled expression. "I'll put her in the guest room."

Maura muffled her laughter against Bea's coat as she hurried across the hall. Obviously Colonel Jake McAllister wasn't used to having his seduction scenes interrupted. She deposited Bea on the guest-room bed and closed the door firmly behind her. Taking a deep breath, she walked back across the hall. Any lingering inclination to laugh fled when she entered the bedroom.

Jake was sitting on the side of the bed. He'd used the last few minutes to unlace his boots. While Maura watched, fascinated, he slipped them off, then stood and unzipped the one-piece flight suit. What emerged from that green cocoon took her breath away.

He was long and lean and superbly muscled. A cotton T-shirt stretched across his shoulders, molded itself to his rib cage and trim waist. Her throat tight, Maura ran her gaze down muscled thighs covered with dark, curling hair.

"Come here."

His husky voice sent shivers dancing down her spine. Slowly, she crossed the room. Jake waited patiently beside the bed, his eyes never leaving her face. When she stopped in front of him, strong, tanned hands reached again for the buttons on her dress.

"Are you protected, Maura?"

She nodded up at him, and his fingers burned against her flesh as he worked the tiny coral buttons, one by one.

Mesmerized, Maura kept her gaze locked on his, seeing the silver flames in his eyes, feeling the backs of his fingers brush against the insides of her breasts. She felt a slow heat begin once more, low in her belly. When Jake's hands pushed the red dress off her shoulders and down her hips, she swallowed convulsively.

Standing in a pool of red, clad only in a lacy half

bra and bikini pants, she felt more exposed than she'd ever felt in her skimpiest bathing suit.

Jake stepped back and took her in. "You're so beautiful."

In a last, dying wheeze, her stubbornly analytical brain cells refuted his raspy words. They reminded her that her hips were a bit too generous and her breasts on the small side. Then the sensual side kicked into overdrive. Maura saw the naked desire in his eyes, and suddenly she *felt* beautiful. And sexy and wanton. Every spot his eyes touched seemed to heat.

When Jake reached out to brush his fingers across the swelling flesh above her bra, Maura's stomach danced. When his hands lifted first one and then the other breast out of the concealing lace, her breath stopped. And when he bent to take one aching nipple into his mouth, her legs almost collapsed from under her.

She clutched his dark head against her breast to steady herself. His teeth rasped against the tender peak, sending rivulets of fire streaking to her belly. He kneaded the other breast, shaping its soft flesh, tugging gently on the nipple with finger and thumb until Maura thought she would go mad. She must have made some sound, some indication of her need. Jake stopped his assault on her breasts to lay her back on the bed. With steady hands, he unhooked her bra. Maura barely noticed when he disposed of it and her panties. She had time for one deep gulp before he got rid of his shirt and shorts.

Her hungry eyes raked his lean length as he stretched out beside her. She felt a stab of satisfaction at the rigid hardness of the shaft against her thigh. She wasn't the only one throbbing in anticipation.

A sudden urge to shake Jake's control, to change the pace of his deliberate assault on her senses, seized her. Her eyes gleamed in the darkness as she moved one hand slowly down his chest. Her nails tugged at the springy hair, etched a line of quivering flesh. A bolt of primitive satisfaction shot through her when her hand continued its journey down across the flat plane of his stomach. The hard muscles jumped under the sharp, teasing tips of her nails.

When she slid one nail gently, erotically, along the length of his shaft, Jake's control slipped. Considerably. With a savage grunt, he rolled on top of her. His weight pressed her down into the mattress, and one thigh wedged impatiently between her legs.

His mouth over hers, his tongue plunged deep into her throat. Maura returned each thrust, incredibly aroused by the primal rhythm. His hips ground against hers, his hands roamed at will over her body.

When he bent to take an aching breast into his mouth once more, she arched under him. Alternating tiny bites with wet, sucking kisses, Jake set her flesh on fire.

She was hot and wet and all too ready when he fastened his mouth on hers again, and one hand slid between her legs. Maura moaned, far back in her throat, as his fingers found and teased her damp flesh.

She arched into his hand, using her own to return stroke for stroke, until the fire coiled low in her belly began to spread. As if sensing her gathering climax, Jake nudged her legs even farther apart.

Maura joined eagerly in the wild rhythm he set. Every thrust, every withdrawal, fired her need. Pressure built in slow, thundering waves, until it exploded in a blinding rush of pure, white-hot sensation. She cried out in the darkness, and moments later heard Jake's answering shout, muffled against her neck, as he followed her over the edge.

Later, much later, her senses stopped whirling. Raising heavy, languorous lids, she couldn't resist a teasing smile.

"So that's making love."

Jake propped himself up on one hand. "That's part of it."

"You mean there's more?"

"Oh, yes."

Long after midnight, Jake left Maura sleepy and sated, released an indignant Bea from her prison and drove home. He'd called Lisa and given her a number to reach him if necessary, but he still felt uncomfortable leaving her alone in the house all night.

Driving through the soft darkness, he smiled to himself at the vision of the woman he'd just left. Sprawled in exhausted abandon across her mismatched sheets, her hair spread in wild tangles, she looked well and thoroughly loved.

His smug satisfaction at having pleasured her to the point of exhaustion lasted all of two miles. Bit by bit, satisfaction gave way to the half exasperated, half rueful confusion Maura always engendered in him.

He shook his head in the darkness, remembering her blithe admission she was ready for sex. Well, he'd been ready, too. More than ready. He'd ached with wanting her. But when she looked up at him with her wide hazel eyes and demanded to know the difference between pure, unadulterated sex and making love, something in him had hesitated.

In that instant his desire shifted focus, changed imperceptibly in its intensity. He still wanted her, but suddenly he wanted the whole woman, not just her body. Not that he'd understand the woman who was Maura even when he had her. She was such a bundle of contradictions. Coolly professional on the job, stubbornly individualistic in her personal life, she refused to fit into any neat category. Just when Jake thought he'd pegged her and her motivations, she surprised him once more.

Driving home in the darkness, Jake accepted the truth that had been staring him in the face. He was ready to take the plunge again. Hell, he'd already dived in headfirst. And after the way Maura had blazed in his arms tonight, he was finding the water to be just fine.

* * *

For Maura, the next weeks passed in a kaleido-scope of passion, play and work. The team threw all their energies into the redesign effort, staying late every night, working weekends. They drew on the resources of the test center to analyze the data from the first shot and rework the mountings for the missile. Pete offered his services once more, insisting he could help with the complex computer work.

Although Maura had most of the analyses already programmed, she knew how much Pete resented being left out of this project. When he pleaded his case to their boss, Maura told Ed she could use the help. Once Pete joined the team, some of her pressure eased and she managed to steal a few evenings to meet Lisa at the cove.

As the days passed, Lisa acquired a healthy tint to her creamy complexion and shed some of her quiet shyness. Maura's lighthearted banter and enthusiasm for their now-shared hobby encouraged the girl's emerging liveliness. More than once Jake found the two of them up to their knees in water, T-shirts sopping wet, sneakers full of mud, exclaiming over a treasured bit of clay.

But it was the nights that seemed to color Maura's existence. Whenever they weren't working late and Lisa had some scheduled activity, Jake would proceed with another lesson in the art of making love.

One night would be wild and hard and fast, another so slow and sensual, Maura thought she'd die before he lowered his body onto hers and brought them both to a shattering climax. Then there was the night they simply held hands and went wading in the moon-washed bay behind her cottage.

At least, they started out holding hands. Once around the corner of the shoreline, out of sight of the other cottages, they held a lot more. Even now, the memory of making love with tiny waves rippling like silk along her naked body and Jake sliding in and out in an ancient, primitive water dance made her stomach clench.

Lisa's sixteenth birthday rolled around right in the middle of the hectic, busy weeks. In honor of the occasion, Maura had decided to do something she rarely did—cook. Unfortunately, she lost track of time and got home from work late.

"Hello, cat."

Ruffling Bea's fur, she dashed into the bedroom to change. She was scrambling into a tank top and shorts when the doorbell rang. Breathless, she caught it on the third ring.

"Hi, guys! Happy birthday, Lisa."

"Thanks."

Holding the door open with one hand, Maura pushed her hair behind her ears with the other. "I'm running a little behind schedule," she confessed. "You'll have to help with kitchen duty."

"No problem," Lisa replied. "Dad's a great cook, you know. He's been giving me lessons."

"No, I didn't know." She aimed a small, private smile at Jake. "But I bet he's a great instructor."

"No complaints so far," he said with a grin that was all smug male.

Once in the kitchen, Maura pushed a stack of unopened mail and magazines to one end of the counter. "Okay, here's the drill. Lisa, you do the salad, your dad can grill the amberjack and I'll fix the spaghetti."

"Fish and spaghetti?" Lisa asked with a giggle.

"Why not? You told me they were your favorite foods after pizza. This is your birthday dinner, and you ought to have exactly what you like."

"Sounds like a plan to me," Jake agreed as Maura retrieved the salad fixings from the fridge.

This was the first time he'd ever seen her in a kitchen. He figured it would be an interesting experience.

He was right. While he seasoned the white fillets, she opened an assortment of jars and dumped them into a heavy pot. If she had a recipe for her spaghetti sauce, she didn't bother to use it. She just pulled whatever took her fancy out of the cupboard and added it to the bubbling concoction.

Jake took the foil-wrapped fish out to the patio, only to discover the coals were still in their sack. He laid a neat pattern of briquettes in the rusted grill, fired the charcoal, then went back into the kitchen to warn them the fish might take a while.

"Hmm." Maura looked down at the pot of boiling

water filled with noodles. "We might have to be a little flexible on the courses tonight. You don't mind, do you, birthday girl?"

Laughing, Lisa shook her head.

Hours later, Jake polished off the last of the charbroiled amberjack. It was, he decided, a perfect ending to a perfect meal. So what if the spaghetti sauce tasted like a cross between West Texas chili and tomato stew? Who cared if the garlic bread was slightly charred around the edges? And who was he to protest when Maura brought out a five-layer cake ablaze with candles while the fish was still grilling?

They'd laughed so much and pored over the glossy book of Indian pottery Maura gave Lisa for a birthday gift for so long, that they were hungry again by the time the amberjack was finally ready.

Jake settled back in his chair and watched a light brown and a dark black head bent close together over the glossy edition. Absently his fingers stroked the fine grain on the antique dining table. Littering its polished surface was a huge pot of fresh flowers in a riot of colors, delicate Rosenthal stemware and a collection of heavy crystal candleholders, each one filled with a sputtering candle. These elegant touches accented mismatched china and placemats in varying shapes and sizes. Or maybe it was mix-matched china, Jake thought. He was getting so used to Maura's own eclectic style of decorating that the cheerful patterns and glowing colors were beginning to take on their own cachet.

Slowly his eyes roved over the small cottage. There were still a few boxes stacked in corners, but many had been cleared out. After Jake had banged his shins the second time on inconvenient obstructions during one of their more playful sessions, Maura had solemnly sworn to clear a path straight from the front door to the bedroom.

A vision of his own home superimposed itself on this tiny, cheerful cottage. Jake had had it built to his own specifications and had it professionally decorated. He'd always considered it airy and spacious. Now the glass and chrome seemed sterile and the high ceilings echoed, even with Lisa's welcome presence.

His house, he decided as he stretched his long legs out under the table, could use just a little of Maura's clutter. And he could use...

A furious snarl interrupted his musing, causing all three diners to jump. Dipping down, Maura peeked under the table.

"Oh, Jake, you must have accidentally kicked Bea." Her head popped back up. "It *was* accidental, wasn't it?"

"It was," he drawled. "When that cat and I finally have it out, rest assured you'll have a ringside seat."

Lisa giggled at his ferocious scowl. Her giggles turned to peals of laughter when she and Maura took Jake on in a three-sided game of Pictionary.

Father and daughter departed an hour later. Clutching the glossy book, Lisa snuggled down in her seat.

"This is the best birthday I've ever had."

Jake gave her a quick look in the darkness and felt his heart thump painfully in his chest. Whatever else he and Anne had done wrong, they'd somehow managed to produce a warm, bright, loving child. Reaching across the bucket seats, he gave Lisa's hand a squeeze.

"I'm glad, honey."

"Isn't Maura fun? I really like her. You do, too, don't you?"

The question held a distinctly teasing tone. At fifteen, no, sixteen, Lisa probably had a good idea about those stops Jake made at Maura's after work. She must have guessed they weren't all strictly business.

"Yes, I do. I like her a lot."

"How much? I mean, you spend a lot of time with her. Are you in love or something?"

Jake took a deep breath. Was he in love? He sure as hell was in lust.

"I don't know, honey," he answered truthfully. "I guess it's 'something' at this point."

He struggled with the answer to Lisa's question over the next week. He needed some time to sit back and assess just what he felt for the woman who filled his mind and hardened his body at the oddest moments. Unfortunately, the pace on the Stealth project picked up to such an intense, frenetic level that Jake had to settle for observing Maura across a conference table littered with drawings and computer runs and post-test analyses.

Twice he managed to get her alone for a cup of coffee, if sitting in the crowded cafeteria under the watchful eyes of half his staff could be considered alone. Each time he found himself more bemused than ever by her analytical engineer's mind and sensuous, laughing femininity.

The team racked up two spectacular successes. On the second test shot, the missile made a clean release and flew straight and sure to the target. Maura cheered with the crowd of onlookers when the concrete wall blossomed into a cloud of dust.

A third test of the modified missile, this time armed with a conventional warhead, was just as deadly. After that success, the entire team threw themselves into the next critical phase. Now that they understood the characteristics of the missile on the F-15, a known, stable platform, they planned to test it on the Stealth itself.

Sleek, black and shaped like a pointed boomerang, the Stealth flew into Eglin three days before the scheduled test. Working night and day, contractor and in-house personnel fit mounts in the fighter's internal weapons bay to hold the modified missile. To her surprise, Maura learned that Jake himself would fly the first Stealth test.

He was one of the few officers at Eglin qualified on the F-117 Nighthawk. She learned he'd commanded the first operational Stealth squadron. Jake had left that squadron to assume duties as deputy commander for operations at Eglin.

As the day of the test approached, she viewed it with a growing mixture of excited anticipation and nervousness. Somehow the knowledge that Jake was going to be in the cockpit made it seem less of an adventure. More than ever before, she began to appreciate the deadly serious aspect of the test business. A good number of the test pilots who'd pushed their machines to the edge of the performance envelope, and then beyond, had died in the attempt.

During all the years she'd spent in design, helping to produce the next generation of fighters, Maura had never felt the vulnerability of the man strapped into those supersonic designs as personally as she did now.

She was a bundle of raw nerves when she and Pete grabbed seats in the viewing area the day of the test.

"Don't worry," he told her for the third time. "Jake knows this plane. He can handle anything the Stealth has to offer."

They sat side by side in the darkened Central Control Facility, eyes glued to the screen. The chase plane's wing-mounted camera clearly displayed the F-117 to the assembled crowd. With its distinctive boomerang shape, flat undercarriage and black radar-absorbing paint, the Nighthawk sat like a small thundercloud at the end of the runway. Its coated canopy windows reflected the sun's rays, hiding any sign of the single pilot from Maura's anxious eyes.

Her nails dug into her palms as both planes taxied down the runway, then lifted off into the blazing noon-day sun. Every second seemed to last a lifetime. She followed each terse exchange between pilot and tower, between lead and chase, between test controller and drop pilot. A tense, expectant silence filled the small gallery until Jake's voice came over the speakers.

"Two minutes to launch."

Afterward, Maura would shudder every time she recalled the next terrifying sequence of events. One moment, Jake was counting off the seconds to launch. In the next, she and the entire control facility watched, horrified, as the launcher descended through the bay doors and the missile detached.

Lifting in a lethal arc, the modified Maverick slammed into the Stealth's black-painted aluminum fuselage, then somersaulted along the length of the plane toward the tail.

The watching crowd gave a collective gasp when a piece of the tail flew off into the blue sky. Maura felt her heart stop as the Stealth began to pitch and roll violently. The chase plane tried desperately to keep it in sight, but for long, terrifying seconds the TV screen showed only bright blue sky.

The speakers crackled, but Maura couldn't understand a word. Her ears filled with a jumble of

Jake's steady voice, the controller's rapid responses and the roar of her own pounding terror. She thought she heard Jake say he had the plane under control, that he was circling over the bay to empty his fuel tanks. In the background of the tower speaker, a steady Klaxon sounded.

Oh, God! The fire trucks and emergency-response vehicles were scrambling.

Maura waited, her throat closed with fear, her eyes on the screen. The center monitor switched from a view of the target to the camera mounted on Eglin's largest hangar. The camera zoomed in on a tiny black speck far off across the bay, streaking out of the clouds. The speck resolved itself into the Stealth's distinctive triangular shape.

"His wheels are down!" Pete shouted, thumping his fist on the chair arm. "He's coming in."

Maura couldn't breathe, couldn't move. She sat frozen until the plane touched down and the crowd around her broke into unrestrained cheers. Rescue vehicles converged on the plane in a whir of flashing lights before it even came to a complete stop. Two heavily suited firemen plopped a ladder against the fuselage and opened the canopy.

When Jake climbed out of the cockpit, she gulped in her first full breath and fought the tears that burned in her eyes.

Knowing it would be hours before Jake finished debriefing the safety and operations people on the accident, Maura let Pete drive her home. Her legs were still too shaky and her hands trembled too violently to manage her own car.

With a muted word of thanks, Maura let herself into the house, dropped her purse on a chair and scooped up a sleeping Bea. Holding the cat close, she wandered aimlessly through the house. Finally she went outside and settled on the lounger. Eyes closed, she relived those heart-stopping moments in the control facility.

She could hear Jake's voice, cool and steady, even a few seconds from possible death. Shuddering, she gave a silent prayer of thanks for his iron control, knowing full well only nerves of steel and flying skills honed by years of experience could have brought him down safely.

How could she have expected him, or wanted him, to be any different from the man his training and background had made him? And how could she have thought she couldn't love him just as he was?

Burying her face in Bea's fur, Maura tried to reconstruct just how and when she'd fallen for a man she cordially disliked only a few short weeks ago. She wasn't sure exactly when it happened, and at this point, she didn't really care.

"I knew it, Bea."

She hugged the protesting cat tighter.

"I knew I wasn't sophisticated enough to separate emotion from physical involvement. The man disapproves of my lifestyle, raises those sexy eyebrows at every piece of clothing I own, and he'd probably trade you in for a poodle if I let him. Am I crazy for loving him, or what?"

Bea squeezed herself out of Maura's grip and planted four heavy paws on her chest. She stared steadily at her agitated mistress, as if to indicate she couldn't care less for a mere male's opinion.

"I know, I know," Maura wailed. "But I can't help it. I've fallen for the guy."

With a disgusted flick of her tail, Bea circled once or twice, plopped back down and closed her eyes.

Chapter 6

The debriefing room emptied slowly. Foam cups and scattered manuals littered the polished surface of the large rectangular table. Jake stayed in his seat long after the last uniformed officer left. He wanted to run the videotapes again.

Although his hands were steady and his adrenaline had long since stopped surging, the near miss still occupied every corner of his mind. He was torn between exhilaration at having brought his aircraft back despite the odds, a wrenching disappointment that the test had failed and a nagging uncertainty over the cause of the failure.

He'd been in the business long enough to know the risks associated with every test of a modified system. Still, after all they'd learned from the first attempts on the F-15, he'd been confident they'd get a clean release on the Stealth.

Pressing the hand control that governed the projectors, Jake brought the room lights down and ran the tapes again. He didn't move a muscle as he watched the missile take off part of his aircraft's tail rudder, but the blood began to drum in his ears.

He rewound the tape and played it again. This time the hand holding the controls began to shake. Sitting alone in the darkness, staring down at his hand as if it belonged to someone else, Jake felt a cold sweat break out on his body. The flickering scenes of sky and swirling black plane blurred in front of his staring eyes. Abruptly he punched the controls and cut off the tape. Driven by a deep, overwhelming need, he left the operations center and headed for Maura's cottage.

A lone shrimper bobbed far out on the bay when he found her. He stood in the open patio doors for a few moments, surveying the two females sprawled in the lounge. Maura was sound asleep, her head at an awkward angle. Her miserable excuse for a pet covered most of her lap, and even from across the small patio Jake could hear Bea's contented, deep-chested purr.

He must have made some sound, some movement, because Bea jerked awake. Her sudden hiss woke Maura. Blinking the sleep out of her eyes, she took in the man standing in the doorway.

"Jake! I didn't hear you come in."

Abandoning both her pet and the lounge chair, she crossed the patio. Her anxious gaze searched his face.

"Are you all right?"

Now he was.

Almost.

"I smell like something your cat dug out of a trash can, my hands are shaking in delayed reaction, and I want you with an ache so fierce, it's doubling me over. Otherwise I'm fine."

A slow, sweet smile spread across her face. "Come with me, Colonel. I think I can fix all three of your problems."

Jake followed her through the cottage. Her tiny bathroom barely held the two of them. He stood still, absorbed by her frowning concentration as she knelt to unlace his boots, then loosened the Velcro tabs at his wrists and unzipped his flight suit.

Slowly, tenderly, she peeled back the green fabric. Her hands stroked his chest and arms, then his waist, each of his legs. Jake leaned back against the wall and savored the featherlight touch of her hands on his body. He watched as she stepped back to strip off her own clothes. The only light came from the small, translucent window set high in one wall. The soft glow outlined her body perfectly for his hungry eyes.

Jake feasted on high-tipped breasts, a narrow waist that gave way to generous, swelling hips. His hands itched to touch her, but he waited, letting her set the pace this night.

Light tendrils of steam curled out from behind the glass shower stall when Maura took his hand and coaxed him in. Jake felt the heat envelop him, the steam seep into and cleanse his lungs. Needle-sharp pellets of water drummed on his head and shoulders. Welcoming the stinging sensation, Jake lifted his face to the pulsing stream. His muscles were just beginning to relax under the pressure of the water when Maura created a wholly different tension.

She washed and soothed and stroked him. The surface of his skin tingled every place she touched. In her caressing hands, the soap and washcloth became instruments of erotic stimulation. The nerves in Jake's chest and arms and legs were on fire before she finished with them.

He sucked in a sharp breath when her fingers slid into the thatch of hair at his groin, then cupped him in her hands. All the tension of the day surged up into a driving, savage need. An urge to plunge into Maura's warmth, to bury himself in her, shook him to the depths of his being.

Jake backed her against the tile wall, his fist in the wet silk of her hair, and tipped her face up for his kiss. Driven by a primal instinct, he thrust his tongue into her welcoming mouth. His hips ground her against the tile, his chest crushed her breasts. In a fever of need, Jake reached down to find her core.

She was hot and slick and ready for him. Cupping his hands under her rear, he lifted her against the tile wall.

Maura's tight channel slid down around him, sheathing him to the root. Her legs locked around his waist, she pulled him even deeper. Jake bent one knee, pulled out a few inches, then surged back. The force of his thrust lifted her, filled her. Water drummed on his shoulders, and steam shrouded them in a gray haze of passion and heat.

Feverishly Jake used his hands and his mouth and every ounce of his strength to bring himself and his woman to a shattering, explosive, life-renewing climax. His blood drummed in his ears, blanketing their muffled groans. But just before he slipped over the edge, Jake thought he heard her moan his name.

The insistent ring of the doorbell woke Maura the next morning. She pulled a pillow over her head, willing the noise to go away. After Jake's ferocious lovemaking the night before, all she wanted to do was sleep for the rest of the day. Maybe the rest of the weekend. She was sore and aching in places she never even knew existed. Considering the small shower stall's size, they had managed to make creative use of every cubic inch.

The ringing gave way to a determined pounding. Groaning, she dragged herself out of bed, tugged down her tangled sleep shirt and opened the door to glare at two grinning McAllisters. In the bright early morning sun, they looked like two sleek, dark, very wide-awake purebreds.

Jake's clear gray eyes and tanned face didn't show any aftereffects—of either his near accident or his late night. Lisa's skin had tanned to the same deep color as her dad's, making her blue eyes stand out in sharp relief. Her short, feathery curls gleamed with the same blue-black shine. Maura felt her heart flip over in her chest just looking at the two of them.

"We've come to take you to the Mullet Festival," Lisa announced.

"Who or what is a Mullet Festival?"

"Just the biggest social event of the year in this corner of the panhandle," Jake answered with a grin. "In all the excitement yesterday, I almost forgot I promised to take Lisa there today."

His private smile told Maura exactly what excitement he was referring to. She felt a little glow at the thought that she might register higher on his internal Richter scale than a near plane crash.

"I'll go change. You guys help yourselves to some coffee or juice or something."

She took another quick glance at Jake and Lisa to make sure she knew the proper dress for this big event. Lisa wore loose, flowered shorts and a bright pink tank top that matched her sneakers. The shorts showed off her long, coltish legs, while the pink top hinted at the woman she would become.

But it was Jake who held Maura's eye and stopped her breath. Thin, faded jeans rode low on his hips and hugged his thighs. A crisp blue-and-white-striped cotton shirt opened at the neck to reveal a dark thatch of hair. Maura ran her eyes appreciatively down his long, lean body. Even in jeans, the man managed to exude an air of cool male elegance.

"Move it, woman. We want to get there in time for the hose-laying competition." His grin widened at her blank stare. "Eglin's got a good chance to win this year," he told her solemnly.

"Ooo-kay."

Shaking her head, Maura went to get dressed. The August sun would make the humidity unbearable, so she pulled on a sleeveless tank top in emerald green and paired it with a gauzy calf-length skirt in a swirling pattern of cool greens and blues. She tugged a brush through her hair, then caught it up in a wide plastic clip. Some cheerful bangle bracelets, hooped earrings and blue sandals completed her quick ensemble. A dab of lipstick, a few strokes of blusher, and she headed back down the hall.

"All set. Do I need a hat?"

"If you mean that monstrosity you wear when you and Lisa go wading, no, you don't need it. We'll get you a visor or something if the sun bothers you."

"Honestly, Lisa, I don't think your father approves of my wardrobe."

Slipping on some oversize sunglasses, she followed the two of them out into the dazzling sunshine. Lisa gave her bright, colorful plumage an admiring glance.

"I think you look great."

"So do I," Jake said to her as he backed out of the driveway. "I'm getting used to rainbow colors and feathers. I don't think I'd even recognize you if you showed up at work in a plain blue suit one day."

"I don't own one, so you don't have to worry about it," Maura told him grandly, then settled down beside Lisa to enjoy the drive.

The Boggy Bayou Mullet Festival turned out to be a combination of country fair and arts and crafts show. Held each year on a large, cleared area of the Eglin reservation just north of the main base, it attracted thousands of people from all along the coast and from Alabama and Georgia, as well. A long line of cars was backed up, waiting for parking.

Eventually Jake, Maura and Lisa joined the throng of people meandering past crafts booths and food stands. Organizations from the base and surrounding towns all hawked their wares, filling the air with sizzling scents and humorous incentives to try their products. Loudspeakers announced the ongoing entertainment at the pavilion. High school bands and glee clubs performed at intervals, adding to the cheerful din.

After a couple of hours spent admiring the local crafts, including an astonishingly professional series of seascapes and delicate gulls carved from driftwood, they'd worked up an appetite. Maura sampled the barbecued shrimp and a spicy steak on a stick.

Lisa opted for a slice of pizza and a sticky sweet German crumb cake.

"Save room for the pièce de résistance," Jake warned, herding them toward a crowded booth.

"Aha!" Maura guessed. "The ubiquitous mullet."

"Right. And if you've ever tasted anything as scrumptious as this before, I'll eat your straw hat."

When they finally worked their way to the front of the line, an aproned Pete dished up heaping platters of fish, fries and hush puppies.

"Here you go. The Shriners always serve the best mullet. We have a secret-batter recipe. It's more tightly guarded than the Stealth!"

"I didn't know you were working here today," Jake commented as he passed plates to Maura and Lisa.

"You don't think I'd miss this big event. And the chance to see all the pretty girls."

Winking at Lisa, Pete teased her unmercifully about how much she'd grown in just one summer. With the line pressing them from behind and platters of hot food in either hand, they exchanged a few more words and settled at one of the scattered picnic tables.

"The hat's safe," Maura declared a short time later, licking her fingers. Although the fish tasted a little gritty at first, its succulent, tender flesh was deep-fried in a seasoned batter and melted in her mouth. Replete, she sat back to enjoy the noisy throng and the country music from a local trio coming over the loudspeakers. Some moments later, a tall, sandy-haired youth appeared beside their table.

"Hi, Lisa."

A blush crept up Lisa's cheeks. "Hi, Tony. Um, you know my dad, don't you? And this is my friend, Maura Phillips."

"Yeah, hi, Colonel McAllister. Ms. Phillips."

The boy gave them each a polite nod, and Maura caught the flash of a small metal stud in one ear.

Uh-oh. The hood.

But despite the earring, Tony gave the appearance of a neat, gregarious young man. And he certainly had his eye on Lisa.

"Niceville High School has a booth with some of the students' artwork on display. I've got a couple of pieces there. Would you like to go see them with me?"

"Well…" She looked at Jake uncertainly.

"Didn't you mention something about a hose-laying contest?" Maura asked him casually. "I'd like to watch it, but I doubt Lisa is all that interested. Why don't she and Tony meet us later?"

Jake gave her a dry look, but acquiesced with good grace. After setting a time to join them, the teenagers disappeared into the throng.

"I wonder if any father ever thinks a boy is good enough for his daughter," Maura teased as a slight scowl settled over Jake's face.

"It's just that Tony's hormones seem to do double time whenever he gets in Lisa's vicinity. Didn't you see the look in his eye?"

"Yes, and I don't think you have anything to worry about. She's a smart girl. She can handle Tony and his hormones."

"Is that so?"

"Yes. Just stop worrying! That's an order, Colonel."

Jake gave her a mock salute and unfolded his long frame from the picnic table. "Yes, ma'am. Whatever you say! Let me help you up."

"Why? It's comfortable here in the shade."

"As I recall, you expressed an overwhelming desire to see the hose-laying. We'd better head over there or we'll miss it."

"Just what *is* this contest, anyway?"

"You'll see."

It turned out to be a friendly test of skills between the various fire departments in the local area. Eglin had two teams entered. With three active airfields and more than five hundred square miles of wooded terrain to protect, the base had one of the largest fire-protection branches in the air force. And one of the best trained.

Maura found herself caught up in the excitement and cheered as loudly as any of the onlookers when the teams raced out onto the field, laid out the heavy hoses and aimed pressurized streams at targets well down the field. Vehicle maneuvering followed the hose-laying contest, then pole climbing. Sweltering in their protective gear and laden with ropes and axes and oxygen bottles, the firefighters scrambled up poles in the ninety-degree heat. Watching them gave Maura a new appreciation of the rigorous training these men and women had to endure.

Recalling the image of two heavily suited rescue personnel climbing up to release Jake from the Stealth canopy, she shivered and hoped she never had to see these fire-protection personnel in anything other than a friendly contest again.

At midafternoon they wandered back to the center of the festival grounds. Jake stopped at a booth and insisted on making a purchase.

"Your nose is getting red."

He leaned down to give the body part under discussion a quick kiss, then settled a gray-blue visor on her forehead. The logo depicted a large, dancing fish with knife and fork in one fin and a pennant proclaiming this year's Mullet Festival the best ever in the other.

"Thank you. I'll treasure this forever." Laughing, Maura surveyed the souvenir booth. "You could use a little cover yourself. Here, try this one."

The straw Stetson fit perfectly. It also shaded Jake's eyes and cast the high angles of his cheeks into sharp relief. Maura gulped at the picture of pure masculinity he made.

She insisted on paying for the hat, informing him

that she'd decided to take his conservative wardrobe in hand, and this was the first step.

Jake linked his arm through hers and they headed for the central pavilion for the introduction of honored guests. The senior commanders from the base were onstage, as well as the local politicians and, of course, the Mullet Festival Princess and her court. Since this was an election year, the dignitaries' comments tended to take on a distinctly campaigning flavor.

After the speeches, the guests dispersed to mingle with the crowd. Some time later a surprisingly talented vocal group from the local community college summer program gave a medley of "golden oldies." Jake swept her into his arms, and as they swayed to the music, Maura marveled at her contentment.

A few short months ago, she would never have pictured herself dancing to the dreamy strains of "Deep Purple" on a swept dirt dance floor while afternoon sunlight filtered through tall, spindly pines. Closing her eyes, she let her head drift down to a warm, muscled shoulder. She felt cocooned in a web of happiness, part of, yet apart from, the cheerful, sweaty crowd that jostled around them. Tightening her arm around Jake's neck, Maura fit her body into his.

They spent the rest of the afternoon at the festival. Lisa checked in, then disappeared once more with Tony. The shy glow in his daughter's eyes had overcome Jake's reservations about her companion.

A tired, contented trio headed home after a late supper of more hush puppies and, of course, mullet. Maura had a napkin-wrapped chunk of leftovers in her purse for Bea, and the scent of fried fish filled the Jeep as they wound their way out of the traffic.

Jake headed for his bayside house to drop Lisa off first. Maura was entertaining fantasies about a late-night repeat of their spectacular performance in the cool waters of the bay when they pulled up behind a rental car parked in Jake's circular driveway.

"Who's that?" Lisa asked.

"I don't know," her father replied, then blinked in surprise as a slender, petite brunette opened the front door.

"Hello, Jake. I hope you don't mind. I let myself in."

"Mom!" Lisa jumped out of the Jeep and threw her arms around the smiling woman. "What are you doing here?"

"I was at a regional auction in Mobile, so I thought I would drive over and see how you're doing. I miss you, sweetheart."

Maura held back while Jake and Lisa greeted their unexpected visitor. Suddenly she could feel every drop of dried perspiration and every particle of dust she'd acquired during the long, hot day. Beside this exquisitely groomed woman in her white linen pant-suit and gold jewelry, she felt clumsy and definitely worse for wear. Nor did it help when the newcomer's slightly mocking gaze slid from Maura's fish-bedecked visor to Jake's straw hat.

"Going native, darling?" she asked with a bland smile.

"Yes, as a matter of fact. And enjoying it. Anne, I'd like you to meet an associate of mine, Dr. Maura Phillips."

Anne McAllister's penciled brows arched delicately at the title. Obviously Maura didn't quite fit her image of a physician, or any other kind of doctor. Resisting the urge to wipe her sweaty palm on her skirt, Maura held out her hand. She also managed not to squeeze Anne's limp fingers, although she detested weak-wristed, two-fingered handshakes.

In fact, Maura thought as she ran her eyes over the brunette's slim figure and stark, high-cheeked beauty, there wasn't a whole lot about this woman she liked at all. Recognizing pure, unadulterated jealousy for what it was, Maura gave herself a mental shake.

"How long are you staying, Mom?" Lisa asked eagerly. "I've got lots and lots to tell you."

"Just this evening. I thought we might all have dinner together." Her glance swept over the trio. "If you don't have other plans, Jake."

"We've already had dinner, but we'll go with you if you haven't eaten yet," he replied easily. "You don't mind a late dessert, do you, Maura?"

"Oh, no, Jake. You three have lots to talk about. I'll just go on home."

There was no way she intended to share a table in some restaurant with this elegant woman. Not in her dusty clothes and displaying her shiny, sunburned nose.

Both Jake and Lisa tried to convince her to join them, but she resisted. "Seriously, after all that mullet, the only activity I can handle now is lying in the lounger on my back patio."

Jake conceded with good grace. "I'll take Maura home and be back shortly," he informed mother and daughter.

The atmosphere in the Jeep was considerably different from that of a quarter hour ago. Jake was distracted, and Maura felt a curl of unaccustomed jealousy.

"She's lovely," she finally offered, as much to break the silence as to give in to that perverse need to scratch a fresh sore.

"I suppose so."

She scratched a bit more. "So how long were you married?"

"Almost twelve years."

"Does it still hurt? The divorce?"

"At times." His voice was low, reluctant. "Anne and I stopped loving each other long ago. What hurts is knowing that two reasonably intelligent adults who started out caring so much for each other could let their feelings just...drift away. We didn't even realize they were gone until it was too late."

The sore was open and running now. Maura wrapped one arm tightly around her waist.

"I was too busy to see it coming," Jake admitted. "I went from test-pilot school to flying secret missions at a classified site, and then to the Pentagon. If I had any time with Anne and Lisa on Sunday afternoons, it was a rare occasion. It took me a long time to realize I was getting more fulfillment from the air force than from my marriage."

He stared out the windshield, as if seeing the years behind instead of the road ahead.

"Anne was just as busy. She started her own antique business and built it into an exclusive consulting service. When I left the Pentagon, she decided to stay in Virginia. She'd acquired a distinguished clientele and enjoyed her work. More than she enjoyed our marriage. More than either of us enjoyed it by then."

"So you both used work as a substitute for love."

"Guess we did."

"Even then, it must have been so hard to end the marriage. There was Lisa…."

"Yes."

"And all you and Anne had invested in each other. I can't imagine how difficult it was to pull up stakes and start over."

Jake glanced sideways, a faint smile lifting one corner of his mouth. "This from the woman who changed jobs on a whim?"

"That was different. I needed a change, and I believe in following my instincts."

"Well, your instincts were certainly right in this instance." His countenance lightened as he pulled in to the narrow crushed-shell drive beside her cottage. "Just think, if you hadn't followed them, you might have gone all through life without tasting mullet."

He slewed sideways in his seat and pulled her gently into his arms.

"Jake, I'm a mess!"

The halfhearted protest didn't deter him. He folded her against his chest and brushed her lips softly, over and over, with his own.

"You taste great," he murmured. "Better than hush puppies and cold beer, even."

He nibbled at her lips, sucking the soft flesh into his mouth. "I'm glad you followed your instincts. I'm glad you're here, in my arms."

Maura lifted a trembling hand to stroke the planes of his face, hovering close above hers. Gathering her courage, she took a deep breath. She wasn't sure this was the right time. It surely wasn't the most romantic spot, nor was she quite dressed for the moment. But she knew if she didn't tell this man of the feelings constricting her heart, she'd burst.

"I love you, you know."

He brushed his lips across hers once more. "I know."

"You do?" She straightened in his arms, needing to see his face. "How could you? I didn't even know myself until yesterday."

Jake smiled down at her. "You wear your every

emotion on your face. I've watched your eyes fill with laughter and blaze with passion. And I've seen them shimmer with love. I've known for weeks you're not the kind of woman who can indulge in a lighthearted affair."

Thoroughly disgruntled that Jake knew her better than she knew herself, Maura pushed herself away.

"This is great. You read me like an open telephone book, and I'm lucky if I can coax more than a grunt out of you, and that's only when you…when we're… you know!"

"I know," Jake laughed.

"Well?"

"Well, what?"

"Okay, McAllister. Let me put it in terms even an oxygen-starved, brain-damaged jet jockey can understand. In every romantic novel I've read, when the heroine declares her love, the hero usually admits he's head over heels, too."

"I'm head over heels."

Jake tugged her back into his arms. This time he pulled her fully into his lap and wrapped a firm arm around her waist to hold her in place. His other hand reached up to lift her chin. His eyes held laughter and a raw emotion that made Maura catch her breath.

"I'm head over heels, over knees, over every other part of my anatomy."

As romantic declarations went, it wasn't the most articulate. But it would do, Maura decided. It would do nicely. For now.

* * *

By the time she disentangled her limbs and climbed out of the Jeep, she ached with desire in every part of her body. So did Jake, judging by his taut muscles and reluctance to let her go.

Maura let herself into the house, fed Bea the mullet she'd brought home and headed for the shower. Lifting her face against the water's tattoo, she leaned back against the tile and willed the tension that held her in its grip to ease.

In retrospect, she supposed she could have stage-managed things better. Maybe waited until she and Jake were having a cozy, intimate dinner or until they were caught up in a blaze of passion before she admitted how she felt about him. If she'd been thinking clearly, she certainly wouldn't have sprung it on him when his ex-wife was waiting for him at home.

Grimacing, Maura soaped her body. Her nerve ends still tingled and her nipples ached from Jake's attentions. Sexual tension still rippled low in her belly. She'd lie awake tonight, she knew, thinking of Jake and what they didn't finish out there in the Jeep.

But tomorrow night...

A slow smile curved her lips.

Tomorrow night, he'd be all hers.

Chapter 7

"Colonel McAllister?"

Jake rose from behind his wide oak desk as the gray-suited, earnest young man entered his office.

"I'm Special Agent Dennis Thompson, commander of the Office of Special Investigations here on base."

"Right. I knew the previous OSI commander, but haven't had a chance to meet you yet."

Jake shook Thompson's hand and glanced down at the shield and picture ID the young man held out. Leading him to a round table in one corner of his office, he waited patiently while the investigator took out a small black notebook and flipped through its hand-scribbled pages.

"I'm sorry we had to meet in these circumstances." Thompson raised serious brown eyes to meet Jake's squarely. "The accident investigation board is still reviewing the data from your in-flight incident. Although they're far from finished, preliminary results show a faulty stress analysis on the modified mounts that held the missile."

"I'm aware of that."

"The accident-board president called me this morning. He told me that you suspect the faulty analysis may be deliberate." Thompson looked at him soberly. "He said you believe we're dealing with a case of sabotage."

The single word hung over them like a thick, noxious miasma. Jake had forced himself to articulate it yesterday, when he spent the day alone, agonizing over the evidence. Yet spoken by someone else, it had an ominous ring.

For days the pattern of the near crash had tugged at Jake. He'd buried his doubts in Maura's welcoming warmth the night of the accident and forced them to the back of his mind on Saturday, when he'd taken her and Lisa to the Mullet Festival. But even as he'd relaxed in the sun and pigged out on fried fish, the questions had simmered in his head.

Despite an almost overwhelming desire to spend Sunday with Maura and follow up on her surprising declaration of love, Jake had found himself back at the secure conference room in the Operations Building. As he played and replayed the videotapes and spent hour after hour reviewing the team's work, his nagging uncertainty changed to reluctant suspicion, then to gut-clenching surety. It was late afternoon when he made the call, and late Sunday night before he made it home. Now Special Agent Thompson was here to follow up on that call.

"Can you tell me what you base your suspicions on?"

Jake took a deep breath, strangely reluctant to take the next, irrevocable step. He'd been involved in enough investigations during his years in uniform to know the devastating impact even a hint of wrong-doing could have on a unit.

Taking a firm grip on himself, be leaned forward and voiced the ugly suspicion. "I think someone deliberately altered the code in the release sequence of the missile."

Thompson listened intently as Jake went into detail about the modification project. Capturing what he could of the technical issues, the special agent finally turned to the question of the personalities involved.

"You realize that this puts the members of your own team under suspicion?"

Jake's eyes narrowed to slits. "Yes, I know that. They're not the only ones who had access to the analyses, however. The contractors, our in-house engineering branch, even the load crews worked with the designs."

Thompson nodded. "I'll need a list of all your

contacts, everyone who's been cleared into the project." He paused a moment, thinking rapidly. "I worked the counterespionage branch at headquarters before I assumed command of this detachment. The standard procedure, if there is such a thing in cases like this, is to assemble a special team of agents and dedicate them full-time. Given the fact that the Stealth is involved, my bet is they'll be here tomorrow, at the latest."

Jake spent the rest of Monday morning and most of the afternoon working with Thompson and his deputy. Both had to be granted special clearances, but once that was accomplished, they dug in like bull terriers, shaking apart and worrying over every bit of information Jake could supply.

They also assembled the background dossiers and security clearances of all the Eglin personnel. Thompson had already combed through the dossiers in preparation of the interviews he'd conduct with each team member, but wanted Jake's assessment of their qualifications.

Jake shrugged off a feeling of betrayal as he provided objective, incisive comments on the various members of his team. He'd worked with these men and women for more than a month now. He knew their strengths, their few weaknesses. They were the best and brightest Eglin had to offer, and he couldn't accept the idea any one of them was responsible for sabotaging their own project.

Dennis Thompson understood and respected Jake's feelings. Not being as close to the team, however, the younger man was more willing to look for evil, to find holes in their backgrounds. Rubbing his forehead, Thompson sifted through the folders once more. His suit coat hung on the back of his chair, coffee cups left rings on the once-polished tabletop and the stack of notes had grown considerably.

"I'm sorry, Colonel McAllister, but I'll have to ask you to explain this personal relationship you say you have with Dr. Phillips."

Jake nodded. He'd known before this started, Maura would be one of the suspects. And he also knew, with every fiber of his being, she couldn't have produced the faulty analysis. He'd trust her with his soul. He'd already trusted her with his heart.

Late that afternoon, Maura sat at her workstation, her hands clenched tightly in her lap to still their trembling. A deadly, freezing fear filled her veins, racking her body with tiny shivers.

The office was deserted, most of her co-workers having left for the day. Maura's gaze was glued to the blank computer screen, as if the words echoing in her mind would appear on its opaque screen. She kept hearing them, over and over, like the low, deadly hiss of a cobra.

You have the right to remain silent.

You have the right to consult with an attorney. Your attorney may be present during this interview.

Should you decide to answer our questions, your statements may be used against you in a court of law.

Wrapping both arms around her middle, she rocked back and forth in her chair. The dull green screen blurred before her eyes.

You have the right to remain silent.

You have the right to consult with...

"Maura, are you all right?"

Blinking, she looked up to see Pete's white face hovering above her.

"Did you get called in?" he asked her.

Swallowing, she nodded slowly.

"Me, too." He moved a hand through his hair. "Man, I couldn't believe it when they suggested sabotage. How in the hell could they suspect one of us?"

"I don't know."

Her voice sounded as frozen as she felt. Still fuming, Pete collapsed in the chair beside her wide worktable.

"After all we've done for McAllister, working night and day on his damned project, how could that bastard sic the OSI on us like that?"

"What do you mean?"

"Didn't they tell you?" His lip curled in an angry sneer. "Your lover boy is the one who thinks the accident was no accident. I guess he couldn't stand the thought that he just might have screwed up, that maybe he's not such a hotshot pilot after all. He's the one who told them to open this investigation. He's probably trying to salvage his career by blaming this whole incident on one of us."

Maura recoiled at the venom in his voice. "I don't believe that."

"Oh, no? Ask the boss. Ask McAllister himself, if you don't believe me."

"I will."

Grabbing her purse, Maura stormed out of the building. Once in the parking lot, she made her way to her car. She felt dazed, as if she were walking through some unknown terrain with shifting, unfamiliar landmarks.

Late-afternoon sun beat down unmercifully, filling her small vehicle with muggy heat. Maura slid inside and opened the driver's-side window, but she couldn't bring herself to turn the key in the ignition. Her hands shook too badly to trust them with driving. Instead she sat in the hot car, shivering.

You have the right to remain silent.

She hadn't remained silent, of course. After the first few moments of stunned surprise, she'd answered all their questions. Even the embarrassingly personal ones about her relationship with Jake.

Maura shook her head in dazed confusion. She'd worked in the defense business since the day she finished graduate school. Before, actually, since some of her doctoral research involved the composite materials now used in advanced aircraft. In all those years, she'd held the highest security clearances. Her background investigation was updated every five years, and she was convinced there wasn't anything about her public or private life the Defense Investigative Agency didn't know.

But as she answered Special Agent Thompson's skilled questions, she gradually realized he was working from a shattering hypothesis—that she had seduced Jake McAllister to earn a place on his Stealth team.

Maura finally took a firm grip on the steering wheel and forced herself to start the car. Tiny rivulets of sweat ran down her neck, beaded between her breasts, yet still she shivered. Grimly determined, she drove home.

"Hello, Maura."

Jake's deep, steady voice penetrated the stillness of the night. It was late, almost ten. Maura had been waiting for him since early evening. She looked up from the lounger to see his long, lean form framed in her patio doors. Moonlight gleamed on the aviator's wings on his chest and shone dully on his polished silver belt buckle. Except for those pinpoints of light, he was a still, shadowy figure.

When Maura didn't speak, Jake moved out of the shadows, into the full light of the moon. His features slowly resolved into a face that until this afternoon, she thought she knew. His crisp blue air force uniform suddenly looked official and threatening. Moving with the controlled grace so natural to him, he slid a folding lawn chair across the small concrete slab and sat down next to her.

Still Maura couldn't force a sound through her constricted throat. Nor, now that he was here, did she know exactly how to open this painful conversation.

Jake took the initiative, watching her closely. "I understand the OSI spoke to you this afternoon."

His blue eyes glittered in the dim light. She managed a small nod.

"I know how intimidating those kinds of interviews can be. Did it upset you?"

Anger began to replace some of the ice that had been clogging her veins all evening.

"Upset me? Why should it upset me?" She formed each word slowly, deliberately. "Just because they suggested I'm having an affair with you as a means of getting on the Stealth team? Because they seem to think I'm some kind of a modern day Mata Hari, using my body to keep you in thrall?"

To her stunned amazement, a smile flitted across Jake's face. Her anger blossomed into fury.

"I'm glad you find this amusing, Colonel. I found it debasing, humiliating and incomprehensible." Swinging her legs off the lounger, she faced him directly. Searing rage washed through her. "I've all but been accused of being a traitor to my country, of sabotaging our defense efforts!"

"No one's accused you of anything."

"How the hell do you know? You weren't there."

Quivering with fury, she jumped up and planted herself in front of him.

"You didn't hear them questioning me about my motives for coming to Eglin! You didn't hear the insinuations that I had some ulterior reason for wanting to get back into Stealth work! You didn't have to try to answer their sly questions and ugly suppositions."

"Yes, I did." Jake stood slowly. "They asked me about our relationship, too."

"And what did you tell them?" she sneered. "That I moved here on a whim? That I wormed my way into your confidence through Lisa? That I'm such a good lay that you couldn't help pouring out everything you knew about the Stealth every time you came?"

"Stop it, Maura."

Jake took her arms in a hard grip, but she jerked out of his hold.

"You should let me rant and rave. Maybe you'll learn something your damned investigators missed this afternoon."

"I know everything about you I need to know." His voice was low and taut, a sharp contrast to her shrill anger.

"Oh, is that so? What did they tell you? How many men I've slept with? How I like doing it in the water? The bay or the shower, it doesn't matter which. Oh, wait a minute. You already knew that."

She flung the accusations wildly, searching for something to hurt him like she'd been hurt.

"They didn't tell me a damn thing." The rasp in

Jake's voice suggested her rage was testing even his iron control. "I told *them* all they needed to know."

Her lip curled. "Like what?"

"Like, I love you."

She waited, anger still swirling hot and furious. "That's it?"

"That's it."

"And that's supposed to make up for siccing the dogs on me?"

She knew she was being irrational. Knew Jake was obligated to take any suspicions about sabotage to the authorities. Still, the fact that he hadn't trusted her enough to share those suspicions ate at her insides like a vicious, gnawing beast.

"Just calm down, Maura. I know damn well you didn't have anything to do with any faulty analysis. You're too open, too vulnerable, too passionate, too... Oh, hell!"

Jake could see his arguments weren't getting past her hurt and anger. His own feelings were still raw enough that he acted without thinking. Whipping out an arm, he yanked her forward and bent her backward with the force of his kiss. She clutched at his shoulders to keep from toppling over. For a long, heart-stopping moment she clung to him, then reached back a sandaled foot to whack him in the shins.

Jake took the hit with a grunt. Tilting her farther off balance over his arm, he slid his other arm under her knees and gathered her high against his chest. Over her squirming, indignant objections, he carried her in through the patio doors and down the short hallway to her bedroom.

Bedsprings bounced in noisy protest when he unceremoniously dropped her, then followed her down. Maura's breath left with a whoosh as Jake sprawled on top of her, making no effort to cushion his weight. She wedged her hands between their bodies to push at his unyielding mass, but he wrapped one arm tightly around her waist, leaving her no room to maneuver.

Jake stared down at her wide, luminous eyes and for the first time in their acquaintance, he couldn't read her expression. He sensed it was a combination of anger, hurt and something else, something he couldn't define. He held her, waiting. She said nothing for long, tense moments.

"Do you really love me?" she ground out at last.

"I love everything about you."

"All I can say, McAllister, is that you've got a hell of a way of showing it."

Her tone still carried a distinct note of belligerence, but some of the stiffness went out of the body under his. Relieved and determined, Jake gathered her even closer.

"Listen to me, Maura. You fill my heart with laughter and my life with color. I didn't know how to tell you before. Hell, I didn't even know myself how much you've become part of me."

He punctuated his words with tiny, sucking kisses that covered her eyelids, her nose, her lower lip. With a long, shuddering sigh, Maura let go of the fury that had gripped her since he'd arrived.

"Oh, Jake, are you sure? We're so different. How can you love me?"

"Yes, I'm sure. And we're not that different. We both like mullet," he reminded her, his mouth kicking up. "And we have a lifetime to discover what else we both enjoy."

A slow, tremulous smile spread across Maura's face and erased the lingering doubt in her eyes.

"Well, I know of at least one other small pleasure we both enjoy."

Jake met her grin with a relieved one of his own. The stress of the last traumatic days receded, replaced by a different tension. Blood surged into his lower body, hardening him against Maura's pelvis. Groaning, he buried his face in the dark warmth of her neck.

She had a taste uniquely her own, a combination of tangy femininity and sweetness. His nostrils caught the faint, lingering scent of her perfume, something fresh and flowery. Jake covered her breast with his hand and kneaded the soft flesh hungrily. When the nipple peaked under his palm, he slid down her body until he could take her breast in his mouth. Through her T-shirt, he teased and suckled and nipped.

Maura writhed in his arms, glorying in his seductive hands and mouth. Tendrils of her hair caught on the sharp metal wings pinned to his chest. When she tried to lift her head for his kiss, her hair tugged painfully.

Surveying the way she was tethered, Jake grinned. "I'm sure Freud would have something very profound to say about this."

"I'm not sure about Freud, but I can tell you what it means to me." Maura gave him a slow, languorous look that made his heart thud painfully. "It means you'd better get undressed. Fast."

Much later, they lay wrapped in each other's arms and watched the moonlight spill through the low windows to dance along the cardboard boxes stacked along the far wall. Replete, relaxed, content to simply stroke the damp stretch of back and derriere curled at his side, Jake listened sympathetically to her whispered recount of the day's events. Their loving had taken the hostility, but not all of the hurt, from her voice.

"It was awful, Jake. By the time they finished with their questions, even I thought my answers were suspicious."

She propped herself up on one hand and stared down at him. Her hair formed a soft, silky curtain around them. "They implied I left my last job under a cloud and was out to get even or something."

"Well, not everyone would voluntarily chuck a six-figure income to become a civil servant," he commented.

"I wasn't happy there."

"You don't have to explain anything to me. Whatever you did, for whatever reasons, they were right—for you."

"Thank you…I think. I want to explain. It's not that mysterious, just private."

Tracing the line of his jaw with one finger, she searched for the right place to begin.

"I went to work for Lockheed right out of graduate school. Those years working in advance concepts were more exciting than I could have imagined. I was right in the middle of all the action and loved every minute of it."

She paused, staring down at his mouth as if mesmerized.

"A couple of years ago I started dating a brilliant financial wizard. Brian did the cost estimates on one of our proposals. I thought we were in love, and Brian thought we made the ultimate, up-and-coming professional couple. He had ambitious plans for our future. When he got promoted to corporate level, he convinced me to accept a management job, and we celebrated by getting engaged. I knew I wasn't right for that position, but to please Brian, I gave it my best. I even got another promotion. Can you imagine me as a corporate VP?"

Jake gave her hair a tug. "Well…"

"I hated it. I hated the political infighting and one-upmanship. I itched to get back to hands-on engineering the whole time. That's what I was trained for, that's what I love."

She folded her hands on his chest and propped her chin on them. Her hazel eyes held a remembered pain and self-disgust that made Jake itch to take a fist to the bastard who'd put it there.

"I don't know how I ever fooled myself into thinking Brian and I could make a go of it. He was fun and full of energy, but so focused, so ambitious. He found us a condo in just the right neighborhood and filled it with lots of neon sculpture and stainless steel. He began suggesting what clothes I should wear to work. He even wanted to get rid of Bea, for heaven's sake."

Jake silently revised his opinion of her discarded fiancé. The guy had at least one redeeming quality. Maura's next words, however, wiped all thoughts of the man out of his mind.

"That's why I resisted you for so long. You're a lot like Brian. The air force is your life. You're on your way up, and I don't see someone like me fitting into the pattern all laid out for you."

Abruptly Jake shifted, reversing their positions, pressing her down into the rumpled bedcovers. He leaned over her and measured each word clearly, carefully.

"I love you, Maura. I don't want you to 'fit in' anywhere. You're too unique, too precious, to just fit in. We'll create our own patterns."

Smiling, Jake made the ultimate sacrifice.

"I'll even learn to tolerate that misbegotten hunk of fur you call a cat."

Maura's mouth opened with an indignant defense of her faithful companion. Before she could speak a word, Jake covered her lips with a kiss that demanded as much as it promised.

Three days later, Jake sat in the office of the center's commander. Big, tough, with shuttered eyes that gave away nothing of his thoughts, Major General Palladino listened impassively while Special Agent Thompson finished briefing the assembled group.

"So there's no doubt the faulty code came from this end?"

"No, sir. Headquarters had a team of five of the air force's top engineers review the complete series of designs, from the project's inception."

General Palladino's bushy black brows drew together. Jake sat in stony silence, as coldly furious as the general that one of their own could be responsible. Palladino swiveled in his massive leather chair to pin Jake with a hard look.

"And you believe the intent was not to damage the Stealth, but to cause the missile to drop outside the target zone?"

"Yes, sir."

"Why?"

Jake leaned forward, meeting the general's gaze with a steady one of his own. He'd done a lot of thinking, a lot of agonizing, over the motivation behind the suspected sabotage.

"After one failure early in the project, we had several spectacular successes. We know this modification will double the internal payload of the Stealth, with minimum cost. Add to that the improved maneuverability of the missile, and you have a lethal combination."

Palladino nodded. A fighter pilot himself, he knew the importance of improving the payload and capability of existing systems.

Jake took a deep breath and continued. "What we've done is make the best weapons system in the world even better. You know as well as I do our allies will be badgering the State Department to make the new design available through Foreign Military Sales immediately. Similarly, every tin-pot dictator with a few oil wells and his own private fleet of fighters will want it. Any arms merchant in the business would give major bucks to get their hands on an early prototype. The black market's potential desire for this modification could be unlimited."

Special Agent Thompson added his assessment. "We agree with Colonel McAllister, sir. The faulty release code on the wing strut precluded a clean separation and caused the missile to deviate from its projected flight pattern. With five hundred square miles of test range, we were lucky to have found it. As you're well aware, we don't always recover every test projectile."

"Tell me about it!" The general harrumphed. "My first week here, I went to a cocktail party at the home of one of the local dignitaries. Damned if he didn't have a sleek little bomblet sitting on his coffee table as a conversation piece. This distinguished citizen, who sure as hell should have known better, found the thing while out hunting, poked it to see if it would detonate, then decided it was safe enough to take home as a souvenir."

"Well," Jake said, smiling, "our missile is a little large to sit on a coffee table, but it would fit easily in an average-size van or camper. If it had fallen outside the projected test area, we might have spent days looking for it. Someone else could have found it. Some innocent hunting party who just happened to wander into the area, with metal detectors and heat-seeking scanning devices."

Agent Thompson nodded vigorously. "The demand for U.S. systems has skyrocketed since their performance in Iraq. We've opened several cases of suspected illegal arms-dealing in the past six months. Any black market arms dealer would love to get his hands on this baby. He could sell the prototype to one of a number of the less-reputable arms manufacturers. Copies of the systems would be in the inventories of the nations we refuse to sell to within a year."

The general eyed the young agent. "If, as you suspect, the saboteur is one of our own, why wouldn't he or she just steal the plans? Why take the risk of going after a whole blasted missile?"

Thompson knew he was being tested. He sat up straighter and spoke with crisp precision. "Sir, the plans would be a poor substitute for the actual system. With today's reverse-engineering techniques, a manufacturer could duplicate materials more precisely and more quickly from a sample than starting from scratch with the plans."

At the general's hard look, Thompson took a deep breath and began to lay out the plan he and Jake had developed.

"You're suggesting we rig a dummy test with a fake missile?" Palladino interrupted, his thick, bushy brows drawing together once more. "At night?"

"Yes, sir. We'll make sure it 'accidentally' falls outside the drop area. Using airborne infrared scanners, we can track any unauthorized vehicles on the range. If anyone or anything heads for the downed missile, we'll get them."

"Do you know how much one of these tests costs in terms of manpower and resources? Even with a dummy missile, you're talking hundreds of thousands of dollars in people and aircraft costs. You better be damn sure you know what you're doing before you ask me to spend that kind of money."

Jake knew well the general's fierce growl belied his interest. The gruff, forceful man would have thrown them out of his office unceremoniously if he didn't think the proposal had merit.

After a half hour of the toughest grilling Jake suspected Agent Thompson had ever endured, the general agreed.

"I'll let HQ know what we're doing. Get back to

me with the final details when you have the date and flight pattern worked out."

The small group rose at his brusque dismissal.

"Colonel McAllister, I want to talk to you for a moment."

Jake stood at ease before the general until the others had filed out. At Palladino's nod, he resumed his seat in the leather armchair to one side of the massive oak desk.

"I understand Maura Phillips is one of the suspects in this case."

"She was interviewed by the investigators, like everyone else on the team," Jake replied evenly. He knew that the general was aware of the fact that he'd been seeing Maura. Hell, they'd shared more than one drink with Palladino and his wife at the Officers Club.

"I like that woman, Jake. She's bright and energetic, and Ed Harrington says she's the best damn engineer on his staff."

Palladino got up and moved out from behind his desk. He began to pace back and forth across the wide expanse of sunlit office.

"The Office of Special Investigations seems to have questions about her, though. The interim report suggests there are some unexplained holes in her background. They're digging into it."

"They can dig all they want," Jake said firmly. "There's nothing there."

"How do you know?"

"I know."

"I'm not sure how involved you are with her, McAllister, but maybe you better throttle back a bit. Until this is all cleared up."

Jake stood and faced the general squarely. "Sorry, sir, I can't do that."

"Look, man, use some common sense. I gave you this project not only because of your background but because I knew you'd do it right. Headquarters has you lined up for a wing commander's job as soon as it's over. That means promotion to brigadier general. Are you willing to risk that by getting involved with a suspect in an espionage case?"

"General Palladino, you're one hell of a pilot and a fine commander. I'd fly as your wingman anytime. But when it comes to my personal life, you're way off base. I'm telling you up front I intend to keep seeing Maura Phillips. If that makes my professional or personal judgment questionable in your eyes, then pull me off this project."

After a tense moment, a wry grin spread across Palladino's face. "I guess I'd be disappointed if you responded any differently. Get the hell out of my office, McAllister."

Chapter 8

Jake cursed under his breath as he struggled to slip tiny silver studs into the minuscule openings of a white dress shirt. There were five of the blasted things, each one about the size of a small thumbtack. When the last stud stubbornly refused to fit into the hole right under his chin, Jake's oath was more vocal and more audible. A giggle from the bedroom door brought his head whipping around.

"You didn't hear that, Lisa."

"No, sir!"

She gave a very creditable rendition of a military salute and wandered into the bedroom.

"Here, let me do it."

Relieved, Jake leaned back against a long, brass-

trimmed Korean chest and let his daughter's nimble
fingers slip the recalcitrant stud into place. When she
smoothed down the crisp, pleated front of his shift
and grinned up at him in triumph, Jake felt his heart
turn over. God, she was beautiful. So fresh and open
and loving.

"Thanks, honey."

Lisa plunked herself down in the middle of Jake's
bed. "I'd better stay, in case you need me again. I remember how Mom used to have to help you into
your monkey suit."

Jake grinned at his daughter's reflection in the
wide mirror above the chest. "As many times as I've
worn this dress uniform over the years, you'd think
I'd have learned how to manage it by now."

His fingers fumbled with a length of dark blue
satin, trying to achieve a roughly symmetrical bow
tie. Lisa giggled again when he tugged his first and
second attempts loose and tried a third time.

"Maura says she always wears comfortable
clothes that express her personality. I bet she won't
be buttoned up to the neck and choking in a tight tie
tonight."

"No, I bet she won't."

Jake felt the first flicker of anticipation for this
evening's formal function lick at his veins. Up to this
point, he sure as hell hadn't been looking forward to
getting all gussied up and spending the evening so-
cializing. In fact, he'd considered canceling out completely. The investigation had all but demoralized his

team, and he'd had to exert every leadership skill he possessed to recharge them. His interview with General Palladino a few days ago hadn't exactly contributed to his own festive spirit, either. But his sense of duty wouldn't let him cancel. A dining-out was one of the air force's few formal traditions. It was a time when officers and senior civilians suited up in fancy dress and gathered to celebrate their common fellowship.

Most of his subordinates and their spouses would be there tonight. So would Maura, although she'd been less than enthusiastic about going to a party in the midst of their frantic preparations for the next test shot. Until Lisa's casual reference to her dress, though, Jake had considered the function more a duty to perform than an adventure. Now delicious visions of what his free-spirited Maura might consider appropriate formal attire danced through his mind.

His mood considerably lighter, Jake began to look forward to the evening. He pulled up decidedly unregulation red suspenders and handed Lisa a dark blue satin cummerbund to hook for him.

"Are you sure you don't want to go over to the Camerons' tonight? I don't like you staying here by yourself. We'll probably be pretty late."

"No kidding!" Lisa teased. "Every time you're with Maura, you get home pretty late."

"Is that so?"

"Yes, and you know it."

Jake paused with one arm in his tailored mess

jacket. Although he would never consider discussing his relationship with Maura with anyone, let alone his teenage daughter, it suddenly struck him he didn't have to. Obviously, she had a pretty good idea how things stood between them.

Sometime during this long summer, his daughter had slipped past that invisible demarcation between child and woman. She still had qualities of both, but now the scale seemed to tip, ever so slightly, toward womanhood instead of childhood.

Jake felt a sharp, fleeting pain at losing the little girl who was Lisa, even as he forced himself to recognize the beauty of the emerging woman. Taking a deep breath, he sat on the edge of the bed.

"I haven't been here much for you this summer. I guess Maura and this special project both overwhelmed me about the same time. I'm sorry, honey."

"It's okay, Dad. Really." She scooted forward to give him a quick hug. "I'm glad you've found Maura. I didn't like you being alone. Everyone needs to have someone to do things with and laugh with."

Thunderstruck, Jake took her hand in his. "You're amazing. You've been growing up right before my eyes and I never really noticed it."

"Well, I'm glad you've finally acknowledged it." Lisa gave him a speculative look, then grinned mischievously. "Now that you've noticed my maturity, I can go out with Tony, right? This weekend, right?"

Jake gave her a dry look. "I trust you. Tony's another story."

"Daaaad!"

Swallowing a sigh, he gave his little girl a last, silent farewell. "Okay, okay, I cave. Against my better judgment, but I cave. Now help me get these medals straight on this jacket. If I don't kick it into afterburner, I'm going to be late."

To Jake's surprise, Maura was almost ready when he arrived at her cottage. She was missing only her shoes when she opened the door. Of course, he reminded himself as he stepped inside, there was no guarantee she intended to wear shoes. She could be planning on going barefoot or maybe donning sequined sneakers.

Whatever footwear she picked, Jake decided, it could only enhance the most seductively simple, elegantly contrived scraps of material he'd ever seen on any female. A halter of shimmering green sequins draped around her neck and fell in simple folds over her breasts. Below the halter was what Rodeo Drive probably labeled a skirt. If there was a yard of dark green satin wrapped around Maura's luscious hips and thighs, Jake would eat his best flight cap.

She'd piled her hair in a cluster of curls high on her head, leaving the long, pure line of her throat bare. Huge, star-shaped earrings trimmed with green sequins danced in each ear and deepened her hazel eyes to shimmering gold.

Or maybe it was the welcome Jake saw shining in her eyes that riveted him in the open doorway.

Whatever it was, she presented a picture of such vibrant color and femininity that he felt a slow heat begin to simmer in his veins. Reaching out with both hands, he drew her gently into his embrace.

"You look wonderful."

Maura smiled up at him. "You do, too. Now I know why so many women are suckers for a man in uniform."

He was a symphony in shadow and silver, she thought, as her gaze roamed from his eyes to the embroidered eagles on his shoulder boards.

She noted appreciatively how his massive shoulders tapered to a narrow waist and displayed to perfection the dark blue jacket with its shining buttons. Long, lean legs were encased in knife-creased trousers with a satin stripe down the side.

Almost shyly, she ran her fingers over the polished wings on his chest, then touched the double row of bright-colored medals hanging below the wings. She'd never seen so many medals and had no idea what they represented, but she suspected each one had a story.

"Are you ready?" he asked. "We'd better hustle or we'll be late. It wouldn't do for senior officers to set a bad example for the troops by sneaking in after the mess is called to order."

With a quick shake of her head, Maura broke her dreamy contemplation and dashed back to her bedroom. A shivery anticipation for the evening ahead filled her. The sight of Jake in his stark magnificence wiped away the last of her doubts about joining the festivities.

Even the dark, hovering shadow of the investigation faded from her consciousness. Tonight, she decided, they'd laugh and dance and forget the damn project for a while.

She strapped on a pair of high-heeled sandals dyed to match her green satin skirt, then rummaged through a box to find her evening bag. With a little cry of triumph, she pulled out the cat-shaped gold metallic bag and stuffed a lipstick, compact and a couple of tissues inside.

"All set," she called, dashing down the hall.

A smile tugged at Jake's lips when he saw the bag, but he refrained from comment as he ushered her out the door and into the car.

He used the short drive to the Officers Club to brief her on some of the traditions of the mess. Maura listened with mounting skepticism.

"Let me be sure I understand this. One, don't ever clap, just bang your spoon on the table, or you get sent to the grog bowl. Two, don't leave the mess to go to the potty, no matter how long-winded the speaker is, or you get sent to the grog bowl. Three, give the correct responses to the toasts, or you get sent to the grog bowl. And if, heaven forbid, you get sent to the grog bowl, down the whole glassful of the noxious brew in one swig, then tilt the glass upside down on top of your head to show it's empty."

"Or you get sent to the grog bowl," Jake finished

with a laugh. "Are you sure you wouldn't rather just grab a hamburger at the Sonic instead?"

"And miss all that grog? No way!"

The Officers Club was mobbed when she and Jake arrived and threaded their way through the crowd. Maura waved to several members of the test-program office, including her boss, Ed Harrington and his wife. Jake's buddy, Colonel Mac MacRae was accompanied by his bride, Maggie Wescott. The leggy environmental engineer greeted Maura warmly.

"I'm so glad we finally get to meet on something other than official business. How are your sharding expeditions with Lisa going?"

"I haven't had as much time for them as I'd like in the past few weeks, but we've had fun."

"Why don't you call me? We'll do lunch and you can tell me about your finds."

"I'd like that."

With Jake guiding her, they found their assigned table. Maura smiled at Pete and Carol Hansen, seated at the far end of the table. She got a wave from Pete and a distinctly cool nod from Carol in return. Refusing to let Carol's habitual cattiness spoil the fun, she filled her eyes and her mind with the rich pageantry all around her.

The military men and women looked incredibly elegant in their dark mess dress and crisp white shirts. The civilian men were in tuxes, but the nonmilitary women wore a rainbow of color. In the flickering light of hurricane lamps spaced along the long tables, the women's dresses glittered like jewels. Maura feasted on the bright gowns the way a starving man would on an unexpected banquet.

The room itself provided a colorful setting for the evening's events. A massive white parachute hung suspended from the ceiling and formed an exotic tent that billowed and swayed over the main dining area. Squadron flags on tall stanchions identified the occupants of the tables that radiated from the dais, where the VIPs and their spouses were seated.

Prominently displayed on a small table in front of the dais was the grog bowl—a bomb casing sawed in half and standing upright on its sleek, deadly fins. It was filled with a bubbling liquid that had caused more than one hearty soul to grimace in disgust when sent to sample it. Luckily, Maura wasn't among them.

The noisy after-dinner din and hilarity died down when the general rose to introduce the guest speaker. Somewhat surprised that the guest of honor at such an august gathering was a young captain, Maura leaned forward to listen intently. In short, precise sentences, the young officer began to relate the story of his last mission in Iraq. Quietly, with understated drama, he told of the ground crews working twenty hours a day in simmering desert heat to turn hot jets. Intelligence briefings by haggard, bleary-eyed officers. Last-minute target changes to coordinate with another attack force. He spoke of seeing his wing-man hit by a surface-to-air missile and explode in midair. And of feeling his own aircraft disintegrate around him when another SAM slammed through the tail.

Maura felt her heart catch when the young captain described parachuting through the dark night to an uncertain fate, then burying himself in scorching sand for two days until a rescue crew fought its way through to pick him up. Over and over, he praised the teamwork and the dedication of the men and women who fought and struggled with him during those turbulent days.

Maura glanced around the ballroom as the young man spoke. An intense stillness hung over the vast room as more than four hundred people focused on the speaker. With a shock, she realized that his story wasn't just the tale of one man's adventures. It affected every man and woman in the room. Many of these officers had served in both Gulf Wars. The fighter wing at Eglin had deployed, as well as hundreds of the base support forces. And those who didn't deploy worked long, tense months to provide special armaments needed for that conflict.

Never had Maura felt the impact of her chosen line of work as dramatically as she did at that moment. Her expertise, her small contribution to advancing weapons technology, could mean the difference between life or death to some other young captain in some other conflict.

She slanted a quiet glance at Jake. His face showed no emotion, but she could see a glittering intensity in the gray eyes focused on the speaker. The young captain concluded his speech with a round of thanks to the team he served with in Saudi, the crew who pulled him out, and the SOB who taught him to eat sand in desert-survival school. Maura joined in the burst of laughter that rocked the room, but didn't understand its significance until a grinning Jake stood to take the young man's salute.

"What was all that about?" she asked him as the crowd moved onto the dance floor and he gathered her close against his chest. "That stuff about eating sand?"

"I helped restructure the air force's survival-training program a few years ago. Captain Anderson was one of the lieutenants we tested the new curriculum on. Believe me, his comments then weren't nearly as restrained as they were tonight."

Before Maura could ask any more questions, the slow, dreamy song they were dancing to ended and a faster, much louder beat began. The lively tune made further conversation impossible, but Jake continued to hold her tight in his arms and move to his own sensuous rhythm while younger couples gyrated all around them.

Maura didn't object. With Jake's strong thighs moving against hers and his hand making lazy circles on the bare skin of her back, all she wanted to do was close her eyes and savor the feel of him. And when he lowered his head to nuzzle her cheek with his chin, the rasp of his bristly skin against hers sent tiny shivers of sensation along her cheek, down her neck, across her shoulders, through her arms. Tingling from her ears to her toes, she wondered just how long these fancy shindigs lasted.

They lasted a long time, she discovered. When one of the single officers at their table respectfully asked her to dance, then shed his dignified facade in wildly energetic movements that took her all around the floor, Maura found herself the center of attention. The other dancers fell back to form a loose circle around her and her partner, clapping and cheering and whistling encouragement. Taking care that her halter top stayed in place, she nevertheless managed to shimmy and shake and thoroughly enjoy herself.

After that, one or another of the young officers would ask her to dance whenever she wasn't in Jake's arms. He filled the time when she was otherwise occupied with what he termed his "duty" dances. She noted that the general's wife did a mean cha-cha, but she didn't care at all for the way Carol Hansen plastered herself against Jake during one number.

When he winked at her over Carol's head, Maura swallowed her fierce surge of jealousy and managed to wink back. After that, she saved all her dances for Jake.

Except one. Around midnight, the guest speaker caught her while Jake was at the bar refreshing their drinks. Luckily, it was a slow number, since Maura wasn't sure either her shoes or her breath would hold out much longer.

"I enjoyed your talk tonight," she told Captain Anderson. Out from behind the microphone, he had a devilish grin and a gleam in his eye she was coming to recognize as endemic to Eglin's test pilots.

"It's a lot more fun to talk about it than it was to do it," he joked.

"Did you really eat sand?"

"Ma'am, I was so scared, you wouldn't believe the things I stuck in my mouth to keep my teeth from chattering. Colonel McAllister... Well, he was Major McAllister then. He taught us tricks to stay alive that would shock your socks off."

"He was your instructor at survival school, wasn't he?"

"No, ma'am," Captain Anderson responded, shocked. "He wasn't an instructor. He built the current course, from the ground up."

At Maura's inquiring look, the young man shook his head. "Didn't you know?"

"Know what?"

"Colonel McAllister spent nearly a week on the ground behind enemy lines as a lieutenant. He busted a leg and an arm when he ejected but managed to crawl miles every day. The man lived off things that wiggle in daylight and glow in the dark. To escape detection, he buried himself in mud and rotting leaves, and once even in a pile of cow dung to throw some dogs off the scent. What that man doesn't know about survival probably hasn't been learned yet."

"Good heavens."

Maura gulped and glanced over to the tall, elegant man chatting easily with a group of lieutenants at the bar. She tried to envision him buried in cow dung.

"He's my hero," Anderson said softly, following her glance. "Colonel McAllister is just the kind of officer we need to lead us into the future."

Maura nodded, too overwhelmed to say anything coherent. When Jake reclaimed her, she melted against him. Wrapping her arm around the strong column of his neck, she molded her body against his solid warmth. And she didn't let go until nature and the wine she'd had at dinner forced her to the ladies' room.

Thankfully, the line wasn't too long. She'd washed her hands and was reapplying her lipstick when Maggie Wescott materialized in the mirror.

"Hello, again," Maggie said brightly.

"Hi back at you. How are you enjoying the festivities?"

"I always enjoy these bashes. As Mac would say, they're—" She broke off, covering her mouth over a fierce hiccup. "'Scuze me! I rarely drink, and all these toasts go to my head every time I attend a dining-out."

"Well, this is my very first dining-out," Maura confessed. "Wine or no wine, it's quite an experience."

"Isn't it? I'm glad you're having fun. I noticed you and Jake seemed to be going great guns. You two are obviously meant for each other. I'm glad he didn't take the general's advice."

"I beg your pardon?"

A startled expression came into the woman's green eyes. "Oops. I thought you knew."

"Knew what?"

Biting her lip, Maggie glanced around the powder room. The two women temporarily had it to themselves.

"Mac said… Well, he heard the general advised Jake to cool things with you until after the investigation."

"What?"

Obviously wishing she hadn't let the matter slip out, Maggie grimaced. "I guess I can understand where the general's coming from. Jake's a fine officer. He'll be up for a star on the next go-around. It would be a shame for anything to ruin his career."

Like a bucket of cold water, the comment doused the hot anger that had begun to build in Maura.

She remembered the young captain's voice tonight as he spoke of Jake. His reverence for the senior colonel was quiet, but absolute. Maura herself had admired Jake's skilled leadership of their little team, but until that moment, she'd never realized how many lives Jake touched in his career.

Maggie Wescott was right, she thought. It would be a shame for anything to ruin Jake's career.

Aching inside, she glanced at the clutch of women who emptied out of the washroom into the powder room. Maggie frowned and murmured under the cover of their chatter.

"God, I'm sorry I brought this matter up here."

"I'm glad you did. I needed to know."

"Are you all right?"

"Yes," Maura lied. "I'm fine."

Hands shaking, she tucked the lipstick in her bag. A crowded, noisy party was no place to sort out her chaotic thoughts. Not with Jake waiting for her and the raucous beat of *Proud Mary* shaking the rafters. Plastering a determined smile on her face, she left the small powder room.

Jake was waiting with his shoulders propped against the wall. "I thought you fell in or something," he teased. "One of your young conquests tonight volunteered to lead a search-and-rescue party, but I convinced him you could handle whatever disaster might occur."

She managed a smile, but a headache had started to pound just above her eyes. Thankfully, Jake suggested they leave shortly afterward.

Maura said nothing as they drove away from the club. The miles slid by until Jake broke the stillness of the car's dark interior.

"Are you all right?"

"I'm not sure."

"What do you mean?"

Dragging in a deep breath, Maura swiveled in the

bucket seat. "Did the general advise you to stop seeing me? Because of the investigation?"

"How in the hell did you…? Oh, never mind. This base is worse than any small town."

"Did he, Jake?"

"Yes, he did."

Maura blinked at the short, clipped response. And then again when he took his eyes off the road to offer her a taunting question.

"So?"

"So maybe you should take his advice. Maybe your career is too important to risk for a few nights in bed."

"I'll tell you the same thing I told him. My private life is just that, private. No one's going to tell me who I can and can't love."

A thousand hot words trembled on Maura's lips. Words of hurt and denial and love. But she didn't utter any of them. This was too important for an impulsive, emotional response. She had to use the objective, analytical side of her brain to think this through. Jake's career was at stake.

He shot her another hard look, but refrained from further comment until he pulled into her drive. Coming around to help her out, he would have followed her into the cottage, but Maura stopped him with a hand on his chest.

"Please, Jake, I'm too tired and too confused right now to talk, or even think. Let's let it go tonight."

In the bright porch light, she saw his face settle

into harsh, sharp angles. Impatience and restrained anger flared in his silver eyes. She waited while he fought down his emotions with his characteristic iron control.

"All right," he ground out. "No talk. No thinking. Not tonight, anyway. But I want you to keep two things in mind as you lie in bed tonight, Ms. Phillips. The first is that I know damn well you didn't have anything to do with sabotaging our project, and so does the general."

"All right. What's two?"

"This."

His kiss was unrelenting, and Maura poured every ounce of her love into her response. When his lips slanted over hers, she wrapped both arms around his neck, reveling in his strength, his primitive possession. When his tongue slid in to dance with hers, she met the thrusts with urgent ones of her own. And when he pushed her out of his arms, she had no doubt about his commitment or his love.

Only later, as she curled her legs up under the light sheet and stared into the darkness, did she question her own love.

Bea gave a low, rumbling growl from her side of the bed as her mistress shifted restlessly under the covers. Maura patted the cat absently and struggled with the thoughts tumbling through her troubled mind.

Could she let Jake sacrifice his career for her? He'd told her the air force was his life. It was in his

blood, in his heritage. He was one of the finest officers she'd ever met. Would he come to resent her if
she cost him the profession he loved?

She drew a painful parallel to her own career situation. She remembered how miserable she was during those months she'd struggled in a management
position. For more than a year, she'd juggled people
and schedules when all she wanted was to bury herself in new designs and engineering projects. She'd
done it for her fiancé, and Maura knew now that
compared to what she felt for Jake, her passion for
Brian was a pale, insubstantial thing.

Still, she had almost married the man. Yet her un-
happiness on the job ultimately overrode her feelings
for Brian. Or maybe it was resentment because he
couldn't appreciate her career aspirations. In any
case, Maura had firsthand experience with the impact
of professional decisions on her personal life. In the
deepest recesses of her heart, she knew Jake would
be miserable out of the air force. It was his element,
his natural milieu. Could she ask him to make a
wrenching career change for her?

The alternative, of course, was to give him up.
Maura shied away from the thought. Surely there had
to be another way, some middle ground. She tossed
in frustration, trying to find an out. Try as she might,
she couldn't think of a way through the maze. The
investigation could take months. By then Jake would
have lost his chance at promotion.

It wasn't fair, Maura thought mutinously. Of all

the colonels she knew, Jake was the best. He deserved to be promoted. Heck, even the young captain tonight recognized his leadership skills. In frustration, she gave the bed an angry thump with one clenched fist.

"Umph!"

Her breath left in a whoosh as a heavy, furry body landed on her stomach. Bea growled a warning that she was at the end of her patience, then kneaded soft stomach flesh with heavy paws. Circling twice, she settled her bulk squarely on Maura's middle.

With a half laugh, half sob, she soothed the disgruntled cat. Gradually her soft strokes and Bea's low purr had a calming effect. Willing herself to sleep, Maura closed her eyes. She needed rest, and time, and a fresh perspective to think this thing through.

Chapter 9

The next morning, Maura felt like something Bea might have tried to bury under the oleander bushes. Despite her stern injunction to herself the night before, she hadn't been able to sleep. In desperation she'd wandered out to the patio to watch the night sky slowly turn purple, then pink.

The sun rose in a blaze of color, shimmering bright red against the horizon. Maura sipped coffee from a battered mug, her knees tucked up under her sleep shirt. She murmured the old nursery rhyme about red skies in the morning, sailors take warning.

No kidding! As if she needed the sun to tell her this would be a horrible day. Her butt dragging, she abandoned the lounger and went to dress for work.

When the team filed in for their morning meeting, she met Jake's hard look over the conference table, but knew her wan smile didn't come close to answering the question in his eyes. Deliberately she opened her briefcase and fiddled with some papers. Knowing Jake, she only had a brief reprieve. He'd want some answer to his unspoken question before he let her out of the room.

Jake stood and faced the team. "We're going to fly our next test shot tonight."

His quiet announcement startled the weary team. A chorus of excited voices filled the small room.

"Tonight!"

"You're kidding!"

"We can't be ready by then!" Pete exclaimed with a fierce frown.

"We can, and we will."

One of the test engineers leaned forward, his face furrowed with concern. "We just got the modified missile supports certified by maintenance yesterday. The crews will have to load the weapon using new technical data."

"They're loading now."

"We'll never get range time," Pete insisted.

"We've got it. Range Seventy is ours from seventeen hundred hours on."

Maura's quiet voice cut through the excited chatter. "Will we be able to get the shot in before dark? Five in the afternoon is late to launch a mission like this. It doesn't give us much margin for error or time for recovery."

"We should have plenty of time if the daylight holds. There's a storm out in the Gulf we're watching that could impact the launch. But as of a few minutes ago, the weather detachment is predicting it to remain outside of Range Seventy's safety envelope."

Maura nodded and settled in as Jake ran the team through the final test parameters again. Then again. They all knew them by heart, but he was relentless.

He had all team members present, their analyses of the best- and worst-case probabilities for the shot, and drilled them all to see if there was anything they might have missed to minimize the risks. When he finally released the team to their last-minute tasks, Maura's palms were damp from a mixture of excitement and nervous tension. Pete was in even worse shape. His white face and worried frown reflected the strain they all felt.

"Dr. Phillips, would you mind waiting just a moment?"

Maura glanced at Jake, knowing he wasn't about to let her plead the need to get back to the office and scurry out with the rest of the team. She leaned back in her chair and waited.

Jake rounded the width of the conference table and approached her slowly. Sliding one hip onto the table edge, he studied her face.

"You look like hell."

"Thank you very much, Colonel McAllister. Nothing like cheering up the troops before the big battle."

"I take it from the dark circles under your eyes you didn't work through your problem."

"*My* problem! I'm not the one whose career is going down the tubes."

"My career isn't going down the tubes because of our relationship. And if it were, I'd say to hell with it."

Her hand reached out involuntarily to grasp his knee. "That's just it, Jake. You can't say to hell with it. You've put your life into the air force. You're a natural leader, you belong in uniform. You can't just toss all those years away!"

"Listen to me, Maura. I lost a wife because I thought my blasted career was so all-fired important. Through some incredible quirk of fate, I'm getting a second chance. I'm not about to lose you to the air force, too."

Maura felt her heart begin to pound. With every ounce of her being, she wanted to slide out of her chair and into his arms. But she forced herself to sit rigid and unmoving.

"This is too important to decide so quickly. We need to think it through, weigh the pros and cons."

One dark eyebrow hooked. "Is this the same woman who relocated from California to Florida on a whim?"

"Oh, for pity's sake, will you let go of that! This is different. You're different. I won't let you just shrug off your whole career."

"If it comes to a choice between you and the air force," he said simply, "there is no choice."

"Jake…"

"We'd better get to work." He bent down and kissed the tip of her nose. "And don't worry."

As if there were any way not to worry, Maura fumed hours later. She couldn't remember ever feeling so tense and racked by doubts. Jake's stubborn insistence that his career didn't matter warmed her romantic heart, but chilled her professional mind. In a crazy role reversal, she'd have to be the one to approach this problem with cool, detached logic.

Adding to her personal worries were her concerns over the test. In the deepest recesses of her mind she was convinced the accident had to have been the result of carelessness, not deliberate sabotage. The thought haunted her that something she did, or didn't do, might have caused it. Some calculation she failed to interpret correctly, some clue she missed about the properties of the materials used to construct the missile racks. Some error she made could have caused Jake's death.

Her fingers flew over the keyboard as she ran every analysis twice, then ran it again. She hunched over the computer all morning long, all through lunch, and then throughout the afternoon. Jake would fly this mission, as well. It had to be perfect.

By four o'clock, she'd reviewed her input into the test parameters a half dozen times. With a small sigh, she switched off her computer. Stretching her aching shoulder muscles, she strolled over to Pete's desk. To her surprise, he was in the process of stuffing his briefcase.

"Are you leaving?"

"Yeah. I have to pick up Carol's folks at the airport."

"Aren't you going to watch the shot?" Incredulity laced Maura's voice. "After the stress and strain we've been through these last weeks, how can you stand to miss it?"

"I guess the investigation took some of the thrill off it all for me." Bitterness tinged Pete's reply. "Believe it or not, I'd rather spend the evening with my in-laws than sit through another session in the control facility."

Maura watched him gather his things and leave a short time later. Too keyed up to go out for supper, she dug through her oversize straw carryall for a little plastic bag full of pottery pieces. She hadn't been able to go sharding with Lisa in more than a week, much to the girl's disappointment. Still, their find for the summer included some incredibly beautiful bits. If you could call dull gray-and-red-tinted chunks of clay with barely discernible squiggles on one side beautiful.

Fingering the indented patterns in a determined effort not to dwell on the evening to come, Maura let her mind rove back over these summer months. A smile tugged at her strained features as she thought about how rich and full the weeks were before the investigation had put everyone on edge. She'd never dreamed when she left California that she'd find so much enjoyment splashing around in the shallow blue waters of the bay with a precocious teenager— and thrashing around in bed with the girl's father. She loved Lisa's company and looked forward to a string of golden summers with the girl.

And Jake. God, how she loved him.

She wanted him in the summer, in the winter and every day in between. She wanted him in bed and out, naked and clothed, laughing and panting with his own particular, all-consuming desire.

Maura's hand closed around the pottery piece, jabbing the sharp edge into her palm. Did she want Jake so much she was willing to risk his future happiness?

She still hadn't found the answer to that question when she left the engineering facility and crossed the grassy lot to the control facility. Eyeing the dark thunderclouds piled up over the Gulf, she felt her adrenaline begin to pump. Not only would they have all the inherent dangers in the test to contend with, as well as the ominous threat of sabotage, but now they'd have Mother Nature to worry about.

As long as the storm remained out in the Gulf, they should be okay.

"Oh, come on, Lisa. Don't be such a prude."

"I don't want to do this."

Lisa's soft voice barely carried over the boisterous shouts and laughter of the crowd of teenagers.

She glanced toward the group congregating at the water's edge. As the more daring of the group began to strip off their shorts and T-shirts, she looked away again quickly. A tinge of red crept up her cheeks and she faced Tony squarely.

"I want to go home."

"For Pete's sake, haven't you ever gone skinny-dipping before?" Tony made no effort to hide his exasperation.

"No, and I don't plan to tonight. You should have told me that was the game plan before we left the pizza parlor. I wouldn't have come."

Lisa tried to keep the disappointment out of her voice as she stared up at the sandy-haired youth next to her. After she'd worked on her dad until he relented and allowed her this date, Tony was turning out to be a real jerk.

Lisa had looked forward to this evening with tremulous anticipation. She'd hoped Maura would help her with her makeup, but she was working late tonight. Still, Lisa thought her own efforts weren't too shabby. When she'd dressed in a new pair of cream shorts and a hot pink silk top very similar to one Maura wore, she'd felt deliciously adult and sophisticated.

The first part of the evening had been fun. Tony had taken her to meet some of his friends from school at a local pizza joint, and Lisa listened shyly while the gregarious group shared horror stories of vacation trips with parents and summer jobs. She'd even overcome her initial reserve enough to contribute some of her own experiences. But her enjoyment slowly turned to dismay as the group discussed and discarded possible alternatives for the rest of the evening.

The movies were out—too tame. A suggestion from one of the girls to head out to the island for miniature golf met with hoots of derision. The beach was a possibility, but with thunderclouds threatening over the Gulf, they knew the lifeguards would be overly cautious and clear the public areas at the first sign of rain or lightning within ten miles. Finally the boys hit on the idea of driving out to one of the natural ponds on the base for a private picnic.

Lisa had started to get nervous when a bold, red-headed teen with a forged ID volunteered to get the picnic "supplies" and meet them at the site. Her uneasiness increased tenfold when their little convoy turned off a main highway onto an unpaved road, which in turn led through a wide clearing and onto a barely discernible dirt track through the woods. She sat beside Tony in the back seat of one of the cars and watched with worried eyes as they drove past prominently posted signs reading Government Property, Restricted Area, No Trespassing.

The track twisted and turned through the tall pines and heavy scrub until Lisa had lost both her sense of direction and the last of her confidence. With each jouncing mile, the pines cut off more of the summer twilight and enveloped them in whispering darkness.

The breeze had sharpened with the storm far out on the Gulf, causing branches to rustle and twist high above them. When they pulled up at the wide pond that was their destination, its waters were black and uninviting.

The other kids didn't seem to mind. They spread blankets at the edge of the water and began passing six-packs. Lisa sat beside Tony with her knees drawn up and arms locked around them. Unobtrusively she refused the beer, feeling more uncomfortable by the minute. But when one of the giggling girls coyly suggested they cool off in the water, she flatly refused to participate.

"I want to go home, Tony," she repeated firmly.

"Look, we just got here. If you don't want to swim, fine. But I'm going in with the others."

He shrugged himself out of his jeans and bent over the blanket to pull off his ragged, sleeveless sweatshirt. Lisa turned away when he reached for the waistband of his shorts.

Not knowing what else to do, she stayed still on the blanket and hugged her knees once more, wishing fervently she'd heeded her dad's warning regarding Tony. The dark night had surrounded her when the laughing teenagers finally splashed out of the pond.

"Hey, let's light a fire," one of the girls suggested. "That water was freezing."

"Good idea," someone else echoed.

"No!" Tony's voice cut through the darkness. "My

dad mentioned there was a test tonight. The range patrol will be scouting the area and would sure as heck notice a fire."

"Yeah," one of the other boys concurred. "All we need is to get hauled in for trespassing. Come here, Joyce, I'll get you warm."

Shocked, Lisa tried not to watch as a beefy, still-naked boy wrestled the girl to the ground and rolled across the blankets with her. She scrambled to her feet as another couple followed the first's example.

"Lisa, wait a minute."

Ignoring Tony's impatient call, she headed for the car with the intention of sitting in the back seat until the incipient orgy was over. Thick darkness and her own welling tears blinded her. Her foot caught on a tree root and she went down on one knee. When Tony's hands closed around her arm to pull her up, she whirled on him.

"Let me go."

"For crying out loud! Don't be such a baby."

Tony held her by both arms. Even in the dark shadows, she could see his slick, bare chest. An odor of beer assailed her nostrils as he tried to gather her close against him.

"Let me go!"

Lisa twisted frantically to avoid his kiss. His lips left a wet trail across her cheek. Furious now, she forced herself to remember her father's repeated instructions on the various ways to extricate herself from just such a situation. When Tony grabbed her hair and held her head still for another kiss, she bit him on the lip. Before his yell had even finished echoing among the pines, Lisa was off and running.

She dashed around the cars, praying she could follow the faint dirt track in the darkness. Her long legs carried her swiftly down the trail, until Tony's shouts receded in the distance. Panting, she stopped at an intersection in the track. A narrow trail led straight ahead, while another bent to the left.

Her eyes swept the darkness for some familiar landmark, some sign of the way they'd come. To her dismay, both tracks seemed to carry recent tire marks. She knelt in the dirt, swallowing tiny sobs of fear. Suddenly the thought of being lost in the dark on Eglin's vast range loomed larger and more frightening than Tony and his friends. She'd just turned to head back when twin slashes of light cut the darkness. Straightening slowly, she waited as the car pulled up.

"I'm sorry, Lisa. Honest to God."

Tony left the lights on and the engine running to come stand before her. He'd pulled on his shirt, but had no shoes. A faint trickle of blood dribbled down his chin from his cut lip.

"Please, don't be scared. I'll take you home. I borrowed one of the guys' cars and told him we were leaving."

Lisa swallowed her fright and stood her ground as he advanced. Imitating her father, she met Tony's anxious, pleading look with a deliberate lift of her chin.

"I'm sorry," he said again. "Really."

After a long moment, she nodded curtly. "All right."

Without another word, she walked around him and slid into the passenger seat. The atmosphere in the car was blacker than the wind-whipped night as they drove slowly through the towering trees. Dark clouds hid the moon, and the first fat drops of rain on the windshield obscured their vision even more.

Tony kept the pace to a slow crawl as he leaned over the steering wheel, trying to see ahead. He gave a low grunt of relief when the car finally swung sharply to the left and their headlights arced across the wide clearing they'd crossed through on the way in.

"Oh, no!"

Lisa jumped at Tony's frightened exclamation. "It must be the Range Patrol."

He pointed a shaking hand toward a frozen tableau just within the arc of the lights. A minivan with its rear doors open was parked at one side of the clearing. Three figures in dark clothes bent over some equipment just outside the van. For a long, timeless minute the trio stood frozen in the glare of the headlights. Lisa had a glimpse of a vaguely familiar white face before a blinding spotlight cut across the clearing and illuminated their car. She turned her head, trying to blunt the force of the glare, and brought her hand up to shield her vision.

"We're outta here," Tony muttered, gunning the engine.

Lisa kept her hand up as the spotlight flooded in the passenger window and followed her across the clearing and onto the main road. Above the crash of the wind, she heard the welcome whine of rubber on asphalt. Tony glanced fearfully in the rearview mirror as they tore down the road, but the van didn't follow them. The subdued and shaken twosome finally pulled into Maura's driveway.

Chapter 10

Maura frowned at the pounding on her front door. She'd just poured herself a glass of wine. After this awful week and even worse day, she needed it.

What she *didn't* need this late at night was company. Unless it was Jake, of course, and she knew it couldn't be him. He wouldn't be finished with the debrief for another hour, at least. Even a mission canceled because of weather had to be picked apart.

As she headed for the door, Maura rubbed her temples to ease the headache simmering there since they'd begun setting up for tonight's test. Almost everyone had stayed late, huddled in the Central Control Facility, eyes glued to the screens and the increasingly ominous weather forecasts. When the range safety officer scrubbed the mission just an hour before the planned launch, disappointment swept through the CCF in palpable waves.

Maura combated her own crushing chagrin by promising herself wine, comfortable sweats and an evening stretched out on the couch in total, mind-numbing inactivity. Until Jake arrived, anyway.

Grumbling under her breath at this disruption to her plans, she padded through the house in her bare feet and opened the door on the chain guard just enough to recognize a wet, dripping teenager standing on her doorstep.

"Lisa! What in the world happened?"

She threw the door wide open and stared at the girl in astonishment. Her surprised glance encompassed an equally wet and bedraggled Tony waiting beside his car, seemingly oblivious of the rain now pelting down around them.

"Oh, Maura, I had to come here."

Lisa pushed past her into the cottage. Still holding her wine in one hand and the door in the other, Maura glanced in confusion from the girl to her soggy date.

"Is Tony coming in?"

"No! And I don't want to see him again, ever."

A fresh gust of wind almost whipped the door out of Maura's hand. She grabbed it again and tugged it shut. Through the narrow windows on the side of the door, she caught a last glimpse of Tony as he got into his car and began backing down the drive.

"Lisa, are you okay?"

Setting down her glass, she wrapped an arm around the shivering girl to lead her into the living room.

"Yes. I guess." Lisa lifted a shaky hand to push back the dark curls plastered to her forehead. "I'm so glad you're home. Dad's flying tonight, and I just had to talk to someone. I knew you would help me get myself back together."

"Together from what?"

Alarmed, Maura ran her eyes quickly over Lisa's dripping form, but other than one scraped knee, she couldn't see any physical signs of distress. Grabbing a sweater from the hall closet, she wrapped it around the shivering girl.

"Tony's a jerk. A first-class jerk." Lisa's hands clutched the fleece material into tight, wrinkled folds.

"Uh-oh. I gather the first date wasn't quite a roaring success."

"It was a disaster!"

A fleeting memory of her own first date with Lisa's dad flashed through Maura's mind. Too bad there wasn't some way to skip the initial courting scene and get right to the real people underneath, she thought wryly. It sure would save everyone a lot of time and misunderstandings.

"Let's get you into some dry clothes," she said. "Then you can tell me what happened."

With the teenager in comfortable sweats and munching her way through a bowl of hot, buttered popcorn, Maura left a message on Jake's recorder that Lisa was with her and snuggled down on the rattan sofa to hear all the details. Outside, the night whipped into a howling frenzy of rain and wind, but inside the small, cheerful cottage, they felt safe and cozy. Lisa quickly recovered her poise and was able to relate the night's events with a blend of rueful humor and heartbreaking disillusionment.

"Oh, Lisa, I'm sorry Tony was such a creep." Maura scrunched an indignant Bea up higher in her lap and folded her legs under her on the couch.

"Me, too," the girl sighed.

With her feet tucked up under her and Maura's Stanford sweatshirt enveloping her slight body, she looked young and vulnerable. After a moment, however, a mischievous smile lit her blue eyes.

"He really was kind of pathetic. He shook all the way home. I don't know whether he was more worried about the Range Patrol following us or having to face Dad. You should have seen the relief on his face when I told him to bring me here."

"He'd better not feel too relieved," Maura commented dryly. "I imagine your father will want to have a little man-to-man discussion with him. Or rather, man-to-jerk."

Lisa's delicate black brows drew together. "I…I don't think I'll tell him about tonight."

"Oh, honey, do you think that's wise? He'll be proud of the way you handled yourself, but he should know what you've been through."

"I'm all right. Nothing really happened. I just hate to bother Dad any more right now. He's been so busy with this project you guys have been working on. And lately he's been, um, sort of distracted. I can tell he's worried. Even though he can't talk about it to me, I know something's wrong."

They'd all been worried, Maura admitted silently. Absently she toyed with Bea's front paws, extended straight into the air as the animal lolled on her back in Maura's lap. Her loving cat lifted one eyelid, showed a quarter inch of claws in a sign of displeasure at having her rest interrupted, then settled back into slumber.

"Did you and Dad have a fight?"

The soft question brought Maura's head up. "No, we didn't. Why would you think so?"

"I don't know. It just seems like both you and Dad have been so tense lately. Last night, when you went to the dining-out, was the first time you two went anywhere together in a while."

"We've just been so busy. All of us. Everyone's worked late, just about every night."

Lisa teased some popcorn kernels with one finger, plainly unconvinced. "Are you sure that's all?"

When Maura nodded, the girl added hesitantly, "Dad likes you. A lot."

"I like him, too. A lot."

Two huge blue eyes fixed Maura with an unwavering stare. "Are you two going to get married?"

"I don't know. We, ah, haven't exactly gotten that

far yet." Maura drew a knuckle down Bea's tummy. "Would you mind if we did? Get married, I mean."

"Shoot, no! I think it would be great. Dad's been alone too much and—"

A steady knocking on the front door interrupted her.

"Maybe that's Dad now."

"Could be, although I'm surprised he's done so soon."

Maura hurried to open the door. To her amazement, Pete stood on the front stoop. Using two hands to hold the door against the force of the wind, she gestured him into the hall. He slid past in a flurry of rain, leaving Maura to drag the door shut behind him.

"What are you doing here, Pete? I thought you were with your in-laws."

His windbreaker and dark slacks were as wet as the hair plastered to his skull. He looked very much like she had the one and only time she'd tried to give Bea a bath.

"I decided to watch the test after all."

"You did? I didn't see you at the control facility."

"It was crowded, and I got there late. Just about when they canceled the mission."

Still confused about why he'd shown up on her doorstep, she refrained from any more questions until her unexpected guest sponged off the worst of his dampness.

"Come on in and I'll get something to dry you

off. You know Lisa, don't you? Jake McAllister's daughter?"

Maura nodded to Lisa, who gave him a shy smile. "Hi, Mr. Hansen."

Pete turned slowly to Lisa. His face lost all expression as he stared at her for a moment, then he managed a slight smile and a "Hello."

Maura hurried to gather the towels. Rushing back, she sensed imminent disaster. Pete had moved to stand just beside the couch where Lisa sat. Water ran off his navy windbreaker and dark slacks to pool in spreading puddles on the hardwood floor. With her ingrained good manners, Lisa was trying to carry on a polite, one-sided conversation.

Bea, however, made no bones about her feelings toward the uninvited guest. Her back was arched, and every orange hair stood on end. A low, deadly hiss vibrated in the air.

Maura rushed into the room and thrust one of the towels at her guest. He blinked at the towel as if it were a foreign object. His strange behavior only added to Maura's worry.

"Pete, what's wrong? Did some word come from Operations after I left?"

She sucked in her breath as a shaft of pure, unadulterated terror lanced through her. Something must have happened to Jake. That was the only reason she could think of for Pete's strange visit.

Trying desperately to control her fear, Maura shot Lisa a quick look. She couldn't ask Pete to blurt out bad news in front of the girl. She was just about to grab his arm and yank him into the kitchen when he shook his head.

"No, nothing happened at work."

His voice sounded so strained that Maura's heart sped up once more. He still hadn't taken his eyes off Lisa, who was surveying him with a puzzled look. Suddenly, the teenager's brow cleared and she gave a merry laugh.

"I saw you tonight, didn't I? Out on the range." She turned toward Maura with a gamine grin. "This is great. Wait until I tell Tony he shook in his shoes all the way home because he thought the Range Patrol was after us, and it was just Mr. Hansen and his friends."

Pete took a quick, jerky step toward the sofa. Bea rose up on her toes. In an effort to subdue the hissing animal, Lisa gathered her against her chest.

A look Maura could have sworn was regret passed across Pete's face. His shoulders slumping, he put one hand in the pocket of his dark, wet windbreaker. Totally bewildered, Maura turned back to Lisa.

"You must be mistaken, honey. Mr. Hansen wasn't on the range. He was with his in-laws, then at the control facility."

"No, I'm sure it was Mr. Hansen I saw. I only caught a glimpse, but I knew the face was familiar."

She turned to Pete for confirmation. After a long, tense moment, he nodded slowly.

"I thought you'd seen me. I recognized you as soon as the spotlight hit the window."

"Why were you out on the range? I thought you said you were at the control…"

Maura's voice trailed off as an insidious, dangerous thought flashed into her mind. The test. Good God, the test.

No, her brain screamed. No! Surely Pete wouldn't be involved in the suspected sabotage. He couldn't!

Her growing dismay and suspicion must have shown in her face. Pete's mouth curved in a tight, strained smile that never made it to his eyes.

"Have you figured it out, Maura?"

"The test?"

He nodded slowly. "I hoped Lisa hadn't recognized me."

"Why?" she whispered. "Why did you do it?"

"Do what?" Lisa asked.

"I needed the money."

"Do what?" Lisa interjected again.

Shaken, Maura tore her eyes from Pete to stare down at the girl. "Mr. Hansen…" She had to force the words through a throat gone tight and dry. "Mr. Hansen is sabotaging the special project your dad and I are working on."

She stumbled over the words, not believing them even as she said them. Her gaze flew back to Pete. "My God, if you needed money, I would have helped. So would Jake. You didn't need to do this."

He swept her small cottage with a look of derision. "You couldn't have made a dent in what I owe. I was so far over my head with the condo and the boat and trips to Acapulco, I was going under for the last time. Besides, it started long before you got here."

Maura gaped at him, aghast. "Are you saying you've been selling secrets for a long time? Before this project? How could you?"

"When you're desperate enough, you discover you can do just about anything. Carol was going to leave me. I was frantic. I couldn't go to my father-in-law for help. The son of a bitch never wanted Carol to marry me in the first place. I had so many loans out at the bank and with less-reputable lenders, I was about to go under."

"But the security screens… The safeguards…"

"Easy enough to get around when you're on the inside."

Numb with shock, Maura tried to absorb his bitter yet strangely gloating words. Pete sounded as if he derived some twisted pleasure from what he was doing, aside from just the money. Eerily, his next words validated her guess.

"Once I sold the first set of plans, I was trapped, of course. My contacts kept demanding more goods, more deliveries. After a while, when Ed Harrington passed me over for promotion, my little side deals gave me a chance to get even with the system."

Maura stared at him, not seeing his rain-plastered hair or taut body. It was the defiant look in his eyes that held her mesmerized. She couldn't believe she'd worked next to this man for months and not seen the evil in him. She'd sensed his weakness and some of his frustration, but not this implacable hostility.

"Don't look so damn horrified," he admonished. "I'm not doing anything half the defense-industry corporate-marketing departments aren't doing. They all try to beat the competition by selling a new prototype to foreign markets on the side. The only difference is, they get their buddies in the State Department and Congress to ratify the sales after the fact."

"Don't you dare try to excuse what you're doing with that political bull," Maura spat out. "Aside from the fact that you betrayed your country, you could have hurt someone with those rigged tests. You could have killed Jake!"

Her voice gathered both intensity and volume. She wanted to scream at the man standing so arrogantly before her. She clenched her hands into claws, ready to rake down his face.

Pete took an involuntary step back. "The missile wasn't supposed to arc back like that! It should have fallen straight."

"Well, it didn't. Jake's lucky he survived."

"It wouldn't have broken my heart if the bastard went down in flames. He couldn't keep his hands off Carol from the first day he got here."

"That's not true!" Lisa cried.

Springing off the sofa, she stood beside Maura, every slender inch quivering with anger. Her silent fury communicated itself to the animal still held tight in her arms. Bea's gums pulled back over a set of sharp-toothed fangs.

Maura's throat closed with suffocating fear. If Pete could so casually condone Jake's death in a plane crash, he was in deeper than she realized. With blinding fear, she realized he didn't intend for her and Lisa to survive his admission of guilt, either.

As if reading her mind, Pete pulled his hand out of his jacket pocket. Maura swallowed convulsively and looked down the barrel of a pistol.

A deadly silence filled the cottage, broken only by the rain pounding on the roof and the low, growling rattle Bea expelled with every breath. Whimpering in fear, Lisa pressed close against Maura's side.

She wrapped a protective arm around both girl and cat, her gaze locked on the gun. She'd never seen one before, much less had a barrel aimed straight at her. The small piece of steel looked obscene in Pete's tanned hand.

Tearing her eyes from the pistol, she lifted them to his face. "You can't do this."

"I don't have any choice."

The utter lack of emotion in his reply frightened her more than anything else. Terror, hot and metallic-tasting, choked through her.

"It's you or me," Pete said grimly. "The boys I deal with aren't exactly small-town shopkeepers. They don't tolerate mistakes or informants."

"But you can be protected from them." Maura forced the words through numb lips. Her heart hammered painfully with every breath. "I don't know what kind of sentence you'd get or where you would go to, but surely you'd be protected."

"Not hardly. My associates would see I was put away permanently before I could damage their network."

"My God, Pete, you can't do this. You can't step over the line between selling a few pieces of hardware and murder."

Maura knew her plea was futile. Pete had passed the line months, if not years, ago. He couldn't stand there so coolly, holding a gun on his partner and his friend's daughter, if he had any conscience left. She took deep, gulping breaths, trying to swallow the bile threatening to choke her.

"I told you," Pete said with a show of regret, "I have no choice."

Tightening her arm around a shaking Lisa, Maura took a backward step. A stack of boxes piled haphazardly against the wall blocked any further movement. Her frantic eyes flicked over the tiny living room in search of a weapon, any weapon. The only thing with even remote possibilities was a heavy crystal decanter on the sideboard, but Pete stood between her and the bar.

"Outside," he ordered.

"What?"

"Outside." He gestured toward the kitchen with the gun. "I'll shoot you right here if I have to, but I'd rather arrange a little accident."

He eyed them with deadly speculation. "I think you and Lisa will have to drown. Everyone will wonder what the two of you were doing out on a night like this, but they'll never know, will they?"

Lisa's terrified sob unlocked the paralysis gripping Maura's mind. She was damned if she'd let Pete harm the girl, no matter what the cost. Taking a deep breath, she gauged the distance between her and the gun. If she turned at an angle and lunged, maybe she could take the bullet in her arm or some other nonvital part. She had to hold Pete long enough for Lisa to get away.

"I said outside."

Snarling now, Pete raised the gun as if to strike her. Maura coiled her muscles to leap. Lisa screamed. And Bea, jostled roughly in the girl's arms, sprang directly at Pete's face with claws extended.

"Aaah!"

Pete twisted wildly, swiping at the animal with one hand. His gun went off, and a bullet shattered a lamp across the room. Acrid smoke filled Maura's lungs, stinging her eyes as she dived for the gun. Dragging on it with both hands, she forced the barrel toward the floor.

"Run, Lisa!"

She threw a desperate look at the girl, only to see her frozen in fear.

"Get out of here!"

"Let go!" Pete snarled.

He fought desperately to dislodge both Maura and the animal, which now had its claws dug into his shoulder. Blood ran down his face and splattered on Maura's outstretched arms. His left hand came up in a vicious blow that knocked Bea to the floor. She yowled in fury, then streaked through his legs to make her escape.

The combination of Maura's weight pulling on his arm and Bea between his feet threw Pete off balance. He staggered and fell forward into the stack of boxes. Maura almost went with him. At the last second, she jerked on the gun with all her might. It twisted out of Pete's hand and fell with him in a shower of crashing cardboard, unpacked books, assorted dishes and a long-lost steam iron.

The rubble half covered Pete, but he scrambled quickly to his hands and knees. His hands dug frantically through the jumble for his weapon.

Maura didn't wait around for him to find it. Whirling, she grabbed Lisa's wrist and yanked her out the back door into the pelting rain. She knew the cottage to her right was vacant. The one on the left housed an elderly couple. Fifty yards separated the two buildings, but the emptiness seemed to stretch for a mile.

As she and Lisa raced through the thundering night, Maura searched frantically for a light in the bungalow ahead. There was nothing, not even a glow.

Praying her neighbors were asleep and not gone, she hauled Lisa behind her. They were almost to the cottage when she heard the screen door slam behind them. She didn't have time to pound on her neighbors' door and wait for the elderly couple to answer it.

"Head for the beach," she panted to Lisa.

Altering the angle of her run, she herded the girl toward the narrow shoreline barely visible in the distance. Thank God they both wore old sweats, already darkened by the soaking rain. They should be nearly invisible in the darkness.

Crouched low, they raced for the beach. At any moment, Maura expected to hear the sharp crack of gunfire. She strained every sense to catch signs of pursuit. Listening intensely, she cataloged every sound and sensation.

Lisa's sobbing breath rasped in her ears. Stinging pellets hit her face and eyes. They blurred her vision and obscured the night as much as the suffocating darkness. With one hand locked around Lisa's wrist, Maura used the other to push her wet, heavy hair out of her eyes.

She almost sobbed with relief when her feet sank into squishy mud at the water's edge. Hanging on to Lisa, she slithered down the shallow bank. The girl tumbled down beside her. Panting, they crouched against the mud and risked a quick look back. Darkness lay like a thick blanket.

A tiny spark of hope shot through Maura. If they couldn't see Pete, he couldn't see them, either. They could slip away in the blackness.

"Maura!"

The reedy shout sliced through the wind and the rain. Their stalker was between them and the house, heading their way.

"I'll find you," he yelled. "You can't get away. There's nowhere to run."

A bright beam suddenly cut the darkness, and Maura cursed viciously. Pete must have found the little cache of hurricane supplies she'd stashed beside the back door. After the last hurricane exercise, she'd invested in a waterproof flashlight, among other survival items.

Putting her mouth against Lisa's ear, she whispered quick instructions. "We've got to get around the curve of the bay, out of Pete's range. As soon as we're clear, I want you to run for home. I'll stay behind and hide. If he picks up our trail, I'll delay him somehow while you call for help. Ready?"

"Yes."

The whisper was thin and high with fear, but Lisa grabbed the hand Maura held out. Backs bent low, they ran along the narrow beach. The bank offered little protection, but at least the soft sand muffled their footsteps.

Normally a good three feet of packed-sand beach edged the water, but tonight the wind and rain whipped the waves right up against the bank. At places, water covered the beach completely.

Rolling troughs of murky water slapped against Maura's calves and knees, slowing her pace and threatening her balance. They'd almost made the far edge of the cove when another yellow beam sliced through the darkness.

"Down!"

She dropped like a stone, dragging Lisa down beside her. The beam stabbed over their heads and aimed off to the right. Spitting out sand and saltwater, Maura struggled to her feet and tugged Lisa into another run.

Long, agonizing moments later, they rounded the curve and splashed into their own private cove. For a few moments at least, they were out of Pete's sight. Maura grabbed a tree trunk to steady herself and helped Lisa climb the chest-high bank.

"Run for home. Or for any house where you see a light. The path goes straight through from here."

"I don't want to leave you!"

"You've got to. You've got to bring help."

"Come with me," Lisa pleaded.

"I can't. Pete might come around the curve any moment. He knows where you live. He knows your dad isn't home and will try to follow us there. I've got to stop him, somehow. Now, get going, kiddo. I'm counting on you to send help."

She managed a shaky grin at the pale face hovering above hers. Lisa bent down to give her a quick, desperate hug, then scrambled to her feet and took off.

Maura waited until the driving rain had swallowed the phantom figure before she began to feel her way along the bank. Unlike the cleared shoreline around the cottages, this one was wild and undeveloped. And the storm had added even more natural obstacles. Broken branches and debris littered the narrow beach. Whole sections of the bank had given way under the force of pounding rain and relentless waves.

Mud sucked at her shoes. A twisted, half-submerged tree stump caught her foot in a hungry grasp. Swearing under her breath, Maura threw out a hand to steady herself and fought her foot free.

Halfway along the cove she found the indentation she'd been searching for. It was wider and deeper than she remembered, probably due to the storm's erosion. A tall, thin pine towered at the edge of the bank right above the opening, its roots exposed and reaching down toward the sea to form a natural curtain over the shallow cave.

Maura groped in the darkness for a branch to use as a club, then slipped behind the slime-covered tree roots. Wedging herself as far back into the dark earth as possible, she tried to slow her pumping heart and still her rattling breath. Seconds crawled by with agonizing slowness. Minutes. Hours, or so it seemed.

Sheltered in her earthen cocoon, she couldn't hear anything except the splat of rain hitting the waves outside. Her universe consisted of shades of darkness, the water distinguishable from the earth and air only by its faint, pearly sheen. Maura ran a hand along the branch she'd dragged inside, needing the reassurance of its weight and feel. To her dismay, the water-rotted wood crumbled under her shaking fingers. She wanted to scream in frustration. As weapons went, it wasn't much, but just the thought of a stick of wood in her hands had given her courage. False courage, she now knew.

Dragging in a shuddering breath, she edged toward the slimy roots. She'd have to slip out and find another branch. Just as she started to slither through the slimy curtain, a yellow shaft of light appeared.

Maura slammed back against the earth wall, her hands spread out on either side. Her fingers clawed the dirt in fear. Breathless, she saw the narrow beam of light sweep the cove. It sliced past her hiding place, swung back again. She bit down hard on her lower lip to still her rasping breath. Her frantic hands dug deeper into the wall, as if she could tunnel through the bank behind her to safety. Earth crumbled beneath her fingers.

Suddenly, she touched something smooth and cold and round. Maura snatched her hand away with a terrified gasp. Lisa's stories about Indian burial grounds flashed into her mind. She could almost hear the girl's light, high voice recounting with ghoulish delight stories of bones and remains found in this area. The thought that she may have closed herself in the darkness with a skull almost sent her plunging out into the rainswept night. Only the slow, deadly sweep of that damned flashlight kept her still.

Almost paralyzed with fear, Maura watched the

beam grow stronger. Pete was coming her way! The light stabbed the darkness in short, staccato bursts as it swept back and forth across the cove.

Knowing she had to have some weapon, Maura forced her trembling hand back to the earth wall beside her. Her fingers touched the round smoothness, jerked away and fumbled for it again. Twisting to the side, she scrabbled in the dirt holding the object. To her intense relief, it wasn't bone, but clay. Round and smooth and still half buried.

A pot wasn't much of a weapon, but maybe it had a ragged edge she could use to cut and slash with. Her fingers dug deeper around the piece, trying to pull it loose. After a few frantic seconds, she cleared enough of the dirt to get a grip on the rounded portion.

To her utter amazement, a heavy clay jug came loose and tumbled out. She ran her hands over its smooth shape, testing its solid heaviness. Around the rim the pads of her fingers could detect an intricate pattern of indentations. The handle was still whole and attached.

Her fingers closed over the handle. Heart pounding, she watched as the light stabbed closer and closer.

Okay. This was it. Edging her way to the far side of the opening, Maura filled her free hand with muddy earth. She knew she'd only have one chance.

When that chance came, she was ready. Pete was only a few feet from her hiding place when Maura slid out from behind the root curtain and let fly with the mud.

"What the…?"

He staggered back, giving her the few seconds she needed to lunge forward and swing the clay pot with all the force she could muster.

Jake pulled into his driveway and waited for the automatic garage opener to lift the heavy doors. Rain drummed on the Jeep's roof with a steady, pounding beat. The stormy weather exactly matched his mood.

They'd been so close to launch, so close to springing the trap. Even when the storm over the Gulf changed course and headed inland, they'd almost pulled it off. Delaying cancellation of the mission until the last minute, they gave the saboteurs as much lead as possible.

Sure enough, a suspicious van had entered the range and parked just outside the expected drop zone. Agent Thompson told him they'd tracked the van with infrared scopes from the first moment it crossed the sensors.

They'd tracked a few other vehicles, as well, Jake found out during the debrief. Some poachers had wandered through the area with spotlights and gun racks mounted on their truck. Then a bunch of kids had driven through, heading for the small pond and an illicit swimming party. Thompson had an agent watching them the entire time.

The kids blew the whole scheme. Just after the

van arrived, a couple of the teenagers had left the pond. They'd headed toward the van and screeched to a halt before taking off like a NASCAR challenger. Unfortunately, the kids had spooked the suspects. The van left the area just a few moments later.

Special agents trailed the van, but they didn't have much to pin on the occupants. Trespassing, for sure. If they could convince a judge to issue a search warrant on such flimsy evidence they might get lucky and find some contraband or illegal tracking equipment in the vehicle.

After weighing the risks of alerting the suspects against the slim chances of finding anything incriminating in the van, Jake made the decision to let them go and try to rebait the trap with another test. Thompson radioed his people to continue following the van in hopes of identifying the occupants. Chances were they wouldn't report anything for hours, if even then, so Jake decided to make a quick run home to change. He'd been in his bag since early morning and felt hot, sweaty and frustrated. His body ached for a cool shower and a few hours of rest.

Wearily he slid out of the Jeep and let himself into the house. His footsteps echoed in the dark stillness. Knowing Lisa was out with Tony, he decided to change and drive over to Maura's. Maybe they could relax for a few hours and talk through this overwhelming concern she'd developed for his career.

He shook his head, remembering how serious she'd tried to be, how intent. She followed her heart when it came to her personal affairs, but couldn't quite bring herself to believe Jake would do the same. He'd try to convince her tonight. On his way to the stairs, he stopped at the desk and punched the Play button on the phone recorder.

"Jake, this is Maura."

As if he wouldn't recognize her voice, or any other part of her person, he thought with amusement.

"It's 9:00 p.m. Lisa's here with me. She, ah, got back from her date with Tony a little early. Come over if you get home before too late. If not, she'll stay with me tonight and we'll see you tomorrow."

After a slight pause, she added softly, "I love you."

Jake hit the Play button and listened to the message again, feeling his heart lighten. So the damn project had cost him two months of sleep. So they blew their chance to trap suspected saboteurs. So Jake wasn't sure if he'd have a job, much less a career, by the time this whole thing was over.

Maura loved him, and he loved her with an intensity that filled his entire being. He knew with absolute certainty that's all he needed in this world. The message just finished for the second time when the back door crashed open.

"Dad! Dad!"

The panic in Lisa's voice sent Jake sprinting into the kitchen. Drenched, panting and sobbing, his daughter fell into his arms.

"Dad, Maura's in the cove! Mr. Hansen's after her with a gun. I saw him on the range and he tried to kill us."

Jake absorbed the implications of her stuttering, frantic cries in a split second. It took him another second or two to assure himself Lisa wasn't hurt. She was wet and covered with mud, but otherwise okay.

"Come on."

There was no way he was going to leave her alone until Hansen and his cohorts were accounted for. Together they ran to the nearest house with a light showing. Jake pounded on the door, thrust Lisa into his startled neighbor's arms, rapped out a brusque order to call the police, then turned and raced toward the shore.

His booted feet crashed through the litter tossed down by the storm as he left cultivated lawn area and charged along the narrow path leading to Lisa's favorite cove. Rain pelted him in the face and obscured his vision, but didn't slow him down. His mind told him he should proceed cautiously, find a weapon, approach the situation only after careful recon. Years of experience and hard-learned survival instincts screamed caution, control, care.

His heart overrode every rational thought. Maura was in danger. Jake refused to even consider that he might be too late, that Pete might have found her.

He reached the small cove in less than a minute. Heart pounding, he stopped beside a scrubby pine seedling to get his bearings in the thick murkiness.

His breath caught when he saw a faint yellow glow in the distance, close to the bank.

The light beam moved toward him in short, jerky paces. It had to be Pete, looking for Maura. Trying to harm Maura.

Driven by a cold, lethal rage, Jake crashed out of the tree line and launched for the shore. At the same instant, the light speared straight upward. A shout rang out, then a crash, followed by a dull, thudding splash. The light sank into the water to glow eerily through a dark, wavy screen.

His heart in his throat, Jake leaped down the bank. He saw a dark shadow bent over, as if fishing for something in the shallow water. The shadow turned with a startled movement toward his noisy approach. Just as his muscles gathered for a flying leap, Jake recognized the white, staring face.

"Maura! Thank God!"

With a glad cry, she splashed across the few feet of shallow water separating them and fell into his arms. Jake hauled her up against his chest. She was sobbing something, but he couldn't hear her over the hiss of rain on the water and the roar of his own blood in his ears.

His arms crushed her against his heart, his face buried in her wet hair. He could feel her shivers and convulsive sobs through the slick material plastered against her body. Ankle-deep in water, rain pounding down on his head, rivulets of cold streaming down his collar, he rocked back and forth, Maura in his arms.

"Jake, it's Pete."

"I know, darling."

"No, it's Pete. Over there, in the water." She pushed herself out of his arms enough to point to a dark lump lying half submerged a few feet away.

"I knocked him out. He may drown."

"Let him."

"Jake!"

Giving in to her urgent plea, he waded over to the fallen man. Pete lay on his back, his face half covered by the washing waves. Grabbing the front of his windbreaker, Jake hauled him bodily out of the sucking sand and water. He had him halfway to shore when a ring of lights blazed out on the bank above them.

"Freeze!"

For one heart-stopping moment, he thought Pete's accomplices had found them. Jake prepared to drop the dead weight in his hands and throw himself across the few feet to Maura, protecting her with his body.

"Colonel McAllister! Is that you?"

Dennis Thompson's incredulous voice speared through the blinding light. Jake's eyes narrowed against the glare as a figure detached itself from the ring of lights and jumped down the bank. Another figure followed and, within seconds, relieved Jake of his burden.

"'Bout time you got here, Thompson. I think we've found our saboteur. Pete Hansen will have a lot of explaining to do when he wakes up."

Jake held Maura close as the small group headed for the bank. Hands reached out to pull them up to relatively dry land. Pete lay on the ground a short distance away, two brawny men standing over him.

"Nice work, sir." The special agent's voice held awed admiration. "My men were tracking him since he left the range, but lost him in the rain and darkness. They found his car at Dr. Phillips's cottage just a few moments ago. With an empty gun holster inside it. How'd you get him?"

Jake squeezed the soggy bundle in his arms. "I can't claim any credit. Dr. Phillips took him down single-handedly."

In the glare of the spotlights, Jake could see amazement and admiration ripple through the men clustered around them. They looked like something right out of a James Bond movie. Several had blackened faces, obviously from their earlier stakeouts on the range. Most wore dark pants and sweatshirts and knit caps over their hair. And all carried either handguns or semiautomatic weapons.

Thompson slipped his pistol into a shoulder holster and turned to Maura. "Good work, Dr. Phillips. How did you disarm him?"

She gave a little hiccup, half laughter, half sob. "I hit him with a pot."

Chapter 11

Bright September sunlight warmed the afternoon and bounced off the waters of the bay in thousands of sparkling white points of light. A slight breeze stirred among the waxy gardenia blossoms woven into the gazebo's framework. Heavy, sweet scent drifted from the flower-bedecked structure to the crowd seated in rows of chairs set in the shade of majestic oaks. A long, flagged walk led from the back patio of the Officers Club to the little white wrought-iron summerhouse.

Jake stood at rigid attention, shoulders squared in his mess-dress uniform, medals glinting in the sunlight. Beside him stood his best friend, Mac MacRae.

As the music began to swell, he turned to face the

club. Its back doors opened and Lisa appeared, a vision in deep, glowing rose. The color formed a warm contrast with her creamy complexion and dark, feathery curls. She looked breathtakingly beautiful to her father's totally impartial, coolly objective eyes.

Jake bit back a smile, remembering Lisa's indignant reply when her mother had suggested via long distance that pale pink was more her shade. His daughter explained very carefully and at great length how much healthier it was to surround oneself with brightness and glowing color. How the subconscious mind absorbed and responded to the stimuli around it.

He watched Lisa advance step by careful step, her bouquet held high and her smile wide. The crowd rose as the wedding march surged into full volume and Maura came out of the club and into the sunshine. Jake's eyes fastened on her face with a hungry, aching intensity.

She wore a white hat with a wide, translucent brim and yards of netting wrapped around it that trailed behind her in a long, floating stream. The floppy brim shaded her eyes, but even in the shadows Jake could see them shimmering with love. To his surprise, she wore a creamy white dress. He'd half expected orange or maybe even neon green.

But if the color was traditional, the design was certainly all Maura. Off the shoulder, about a foot shorter on one side than the other, and adorned with layer upon layer of lacy flounces, the dress reflected her unique style and cheerful individuality.

Throughout the short ceremony that followed, Jake's hand gripped hers, and his eyes never left her face. He held her fingers gripped in his as they walked back down the aisle under the gleaming arched swords of the honor guard, and throughout the reception. He'd nearly lost her once. He wasn't about to let her go again.

Not until the long reception was over and they'd retreated to a private family dinner at his house did he relax his grip or his stance. Surrounded by Maura's lively family, with his daughter's ready laughter adding to the chaos all around him, Jake felt a sense of rightness he'd never expected to experience again.

They'd moved Maura's things out of the cottage the day before, in the midst of arriving relatives and the wedding rehearsal, just before Jake's crew hauled him off for a bachelor party he was still trying to recover from. Now his home reflected Maura's indelible presence.

Boxes leaned haphazardly in various corners of the huge, sunlit living room, books and magazines littered the tables, and cushions in deep, glowing jewel tones added bright splashes of color to the austere leather-and-wood furnishings. The antique sideboard and beautifully crafted dining table graced the dining room.

"Well, I never thought to see the day that misbegotten, hunk of fur would have a place of honor in any man's house."

Maura's father shook his head at Beatrice, regally presiding over the festivities from a velvet pillow set squarely in Jake's leather chair.

"That damn beast left furrows in the back of my hand the first time Maura brought her home for a visit."

Jake grinned at the tall, silver-haired man. For a philosophy professor, Howard Phillips was surprisingly down-to-earth and easy to talk to. In the few days Jake had known him and the rest of Maura's boisterous family, he'd come to understand where her unique blend of brilliance and decided individuality sprang from.

"Bea and I have reached a state of mutual toleration," he told his new father-in-law. "She allows me to feed her and see to her comfort, and I let her do precisely as she pleases."

Despite his sardonic drawl, his glance held a trace of affection as it lingered on the cat.

"After the way she clawed up the bastard who was after Maura and Lisa, I'd give her my bed if she wanted it."

"She probably will," Howard said dryly.

"Daddy!" Lisa called from across the room. "We need you over here."

With a nod to the professor, Jake edged his way through Maura's sisters and brothers and their numerous progeny. Joining his wife, he slipped his hand in hers.

He still couldn't quite believe the jolt that shot through him at the thought of being married to this vibrant creature. Of seeing her eyes light up with pleasure, her face crinkle in laughter, each day of his life. They shared a secret smile before turning to face Lisa and Maura's mother, both holding identically wrapped packages.

"Quiet, everyone," Irene Phillips called in a low, musical voice so like her daughter's that Jake started every time he heard it. "Settle down on any available seat. We want to give the newlyweds their wedding gifts from the family."

Jake lifted an inquiring brow at Maura, who shook her head. She was obviously as surprised as he.

"Here, Maura, Daddy. This is from me."

Lisa's bright face reflected a simmering excitement as she handed them her box. Jake held it while his bride attacked the bows and paper. Lifting the lid, she pushed aside layers of tissue paper.

"Lisa, I don't believe this!"

Her voice held breathless laughter as she slipped both hands into the box. With utmost care, she lifted out a heavy, rounded clay jug.

"I sifted through the water for days," Lisa told them excitedly. "I found almost every piece, then took them down to the museum. The people there helped me glue the bits together and even fabricated some parts I couldn't find. See, the handle doesn't quite match."

Maura turned the clay pot over and over in her hands, rubbing her fingers lightly across its red surface and tracing the patterns around its lip. She turned brimming eyes up to Jake as she handed him the jug.

"I think your daughter has found her chosen profession. We'd better plan on converting a room in the house to a museum for her finds."

Jake took the pot gingerly. "It's beautiful, honey."

Lisa's face glowed at his simple, heartfelt words. She basked in their pleasure for a few moments, then heaved a huge sigh.

"I'm afraid we can't keep it. The museum says it's from the oldest known civilization in this region. It's going to the University of West Florida, to be displayed in their antiquities collection. I just worked a deal with them to let me use it for today since I, or rather Maura, found it."

"Oh, Lisa, thank you." Maura leaned down to hug the girl with both arms. "It was a wonderful idea. We'll go over and see it as often as we can."

"They're going to put a placard on the display with your name on it and everything."

"With both our names," she told the girl firmly.

"Here, darling." Her mother stepped forward with the second box. "Just so you both have something to remind you of your memorable night."

Maura looked at her mother's twinkling eyes and

knew before she opened the box what it contained. Sure enough, an identical pot lay in a nest of tissue. Crafted by her mother's hands, the new jug flowed in the same graceful lines as the original.

"Thank you, Irene." Jake's deep voice rumbled with pleasure. "This is a work of art. It'll have a place of honor in our home. Right beside the bed."

"Where we can use it if anyone ever tries to break in," Maura finished for him.

Much later, Maura lay beside Jake in his king-size bed. The house whispered around them, filled with the soft noises of various family members settling in for the night. Moonlight filtered in through high, arched windows that faced the bay and illuminated the clay pot sitting in isolated splendor on a pedestal of boxes between the tall windows.

Despite Maura's best intentions, they hadn't unpacked or sorted out any of her belongings. They wouldn't be there long enough to bother, Jake told her. Two days before the wedding, he'd gotten word of his promotion and pending reassignment to Hanscom Air Force Base, just outside Boston.

Sighing, Maura nestled her head on his shoulder. "I really hate to leave Florida, but one of the engineers at work has a brother who used to be stationed at Hanscom. After hearing him describe the high-tech research and development going on up there, not to mention all the great places to eat and sights to see,

I'm looking forward to it. I have a feeling we're going to really enjoy this new assignment."

A rumble sounded in the chest just under her ear. She glanced up into Jake's moon-shadowed face to see him grinning down at her.

"I know we'll enjoy it. I trust your instincts implicitly."

Maura snuggled contentedly against her husband's broad chest. Tomorrow they would take Lisa to the airport to return to Virginia, and then leave for a honeymoon. They were both looking forward to those few precious days together. Jake had suggested sailing around the Virgin Islands, but Maura convinced him they should try Cancún. She'd developed a burning desire to visit the ancient Mayan ruins. Who knew what bits and pieces they might uncover there?

* * * * *

*Everything you love about romance...**and more!***

Please turn the page for Signature Select™
Bonus Features.

Bonus Features:

BONUS FEATURES

One of the Boys

MAGGIE AND
HER COLONEL
by Merline Lovelace

CHAPTER 1

"Just who the hell is this Dr. Wescott, and where does he get off disapproving my test?"

Seated in the outer reception area, Maggie heard every angry word. She shook her head and shared a wry grin with the secretary perched behind a large modular desk unit. The older woman winked, then turned to listen with unabashed interest to the exchange taking place in the commander's office.

"Dr. Wescott is our new chief of Environmental Engineering and is waiting outside to discuss the issue with you when you calm down, Mac."

Her boss's measured tones provided a sharp contrast to the visitor's deep angry growl.

"I'm as calm as I'm likely to get over this. Bring him in."

The secretary answered the intercom on its first short ring. Gray curls bouncing, she nodded toward the open door.

Here we go, Maggie thought. She squared her shoulders to take full advantage of her considerable height and entered the inner office. She could tell from the glint in her boss's eyes that he was thoroughly enjoying the situation, the old reprobate.

"Colonel MacRae, this is Dr. Wescott. She joined our staff a week ago. One of her first projects was your proposed test."

Maggie had to admire the visitor's composure, even if she *had* decided to dislike him on principle. MacRae's blue eyes narrowed dangerously for a moment when she entered, and he slanted a sharp glance at Maggie's grinning supervisor. He showed no other signs of surprise that Dr. Wescott was not the man he expected, however, and took her hand in a firm grip.

Maggie felt a strange sensation as she looked up, and up, into the man's eyes. He was a linebacker in a blue air force uniform, for heaven's sake. She couldn't remember the last time she felt dwarfed by any man. At five foot eight in her stockinged feet, she was usually at least eye level with her co-workers and acquaintances.

"Dr. Wescott, Colonel MacRae is commander of the armament division of Wright Laboratory here on base. He's concerned that you disapproved the propulsion test his lab wants to conduct and would like to discuss the project with you personally."

With that bland introduction, Ed Stockton sat back to enjoy the fireworks. He'd only worked with the young woman who now headed his Environmental Engineering department for a week, but he'd put his money on her, hands down. She'd made mincemeat of one of the other department heads who'd mistaken her blond good looks and laughing green eyes for those of a professional lightweight. The lady knew her stuff and didn't take any nonsense from anyone.

MacRae started his attack even as they moved to the conference table.

"Since you're new here, Dr. Wescott, you may not fully understand the implications of this test for Eglin Air Force Base and for the lab. It involves over a million dollars in reimbursable costs and is vital to the space program."

The hairs on Maggie's neck bristled. She could almost forgive this man for the unconscious chauvinism she'd overheard while she sat in the reception room. Most men, and women, of her acquaintance assumed engineers were of the male persuasion. But no one questioned her professional competence and lived to tell about it. Inwardly seething, she kept her voice level.

"Colonel, I fully appreciate the implications of this test for Eglin. The chemical you want to use as a propellant is highly volatile and has never been tested anywhere in the quantity you propose. Your people have done a poor job in addressing potential impacts in their environmental assessment."

Maggie seated herself at the conference table and laid the folder with her notes aside. She'd done some quick reading since the call had come to report to her boss's office. She had her facts down cold.

"The U.S. Fish and Wildlife Service has already issued a statement of concern over your test's threat to endangered species. Even if I wanted to override their objections, which I don't, Eglin would be slapped with a notice of violation. Not only would the Wildlife folks have scrubbed this test, but they might hold all our other tests hostage while we negotiated with them. This base is too important a test facility to the Department of Defense to allow a poorly planned, inadequately researched project like this to close it down, even temporarily."

Mac MacRae leveled a hard stare at the young woman across the conference table. She must have ordered her Ph.D. through the mail, he thought. With her mass of golden curls that tumbled wildly over her shoulders, she looked about eighteen. Only when he noticed the fine lines fanning out from the corners of her eyes did he revise his estimate of her age, if not her capabilities. Maybe she was old enough, but surely not experienced enough to make the kind of judgment she had.

His lips settled into a grim line, and he gave her his full attention. By the time she was halfway through her succinct review of the situation, he'd stopped seeing her curly hair and sensuous lips. Instead, he focused on clear green eyes that looked at him with distinct challenge and more than a hint of disapproval. He listened in silence, then sat back in his chair to consider the facts she'd laid before him.

Maggie refused to let MacRae's silence disconcert her. She held his gaze steadily and used the pause to take a mental inventory of the man facing her. Those penetrating blue eyes seemed out of place in a tanned face with a nose that looked like someone had taken a fist to it more than once. Or a shoulder, Maggie thought, in keeping with his linebacker appearance. She noted with some satisfaction the silver that liberally laced his dark hair. He wasn't as young as he looked at first glance, she thought, unknowingly mirroring MacRae's assessment of her. Although why that thought should give her satisfaction, she had no idea. She was so absorbed in her private review that she jumped at the deep gravelly voice.

"I apologize, Dr. Wescott. You've obviously put more effort into studying this project than I realized. I'll have my people redefine the test parameters. I'd appreciate it if you'd work with us closely so we can modify the test to satisfy all environmental concerns."

His response surprised Maggie. She'd had her hackles up and was ready for a long argument. Hard experience had taught her that some men were congenitally unable to give in gracefully to a woman. She would've bet her last dollar this hulking male was one of them. His reasonableness left her feeling slightly deflated.

Before she could frame a coherent reply, MacRae got to his feet and shook Ed Stockton's hand. He turned to take Maggie's hand again, and her pulse seemed to jump at the hard warmth that enveloped her palm. She was sure she only imagined that he held her hand longer than he had the first time. Tugging her fingers loose as nonchalantly as possible, Maggie used the excuse of gathering up her papers to put some distance between them. For some reason, this man disturbed her. Maybe it was his size. He was a veritable mountain, for heaven's sake.

By the time she'd stuffed the report haphazardly into a file, he was gone.

"Just who was that masked man?" she asked her boss.

Ed Stockton laughed at her rueful grimace. "I've known MacRae a long time, Maggie. There isn't a more brilliant physicist or better commander in the air force."

"He looks more like a football player than a scientist," Maggie commented.

"You aren't exactly the stereotypical Ph.D., either," Ed responded blandly. "Actually I think Mac did play football at the Air Force Academy. Now he's a test pilot, but one of the weird ones. He actually finds the science of what makes those tubes of steel fly more fascinating than the flying itself. He's brilliant, but when he has a hot project in the works, he's like a bulldog. The man's made my life miserable more times than I can count with his demands for range support for his propulsion tests. It did the old heart good to see him put in his place for once."

Maggie knew her boss well enough by now not to take him seriously. A senior colonel, Ed Stockton could give as good as he got and then some. His gruff voice hid a sharp precise mind and a total dedication to the air force. He needed both to command the nine-hundred-plus civil engineers, military and civilian, who were responsible for maintaining Eglin Air Force Base. The largest air base in the world, Eglin covered a land area of more than half a million acres and ate up most of the western half of Florida's panhandle. It boasted thousands of miles of roads and hundreds of buildings and test facilities.

Maggie was just beginning to appreciate the vast size of the base, as well as the scope of her job. As chief of Environmental Engineering, her responsibilities included anything and everything that might have an impact on the environment on that half-million acres. When she'd first arrived, she'd outlined a schedule to visit every hazardous-material site, fuel-storage area and restricted-test area on base. It would take her six months to cover them all.

Maggie had responded on impulse to the ad for an environmental engineer at Eglin. She'd worked for the government before on some classified projects in Washington and knew enough about the test business to win an immediate job interview. Unlikely as it seemed at first to either of them, she and Ed Stockton had hit it off from the first few minutes of the interview.

Maggie knew that her extensive credentials and her high-powered industry job she gave up to come to Florida had impressed Stockton. He'd asked her why she wanted to come to "redneck country," as he put, after working at corporate level for a major oil conglomerate in Houston. She'd responded that she needed a change and wanted to get back to field-level work. At Stockton's quizzical look, she added gently that she had personal reasons, as well, which were none of his business.

Maggie considered her private life her own affair. If the crusty colonel interviewing her wasn't satisfied with her professional credentials, she knew there were plenty of others who would be. Stockton was more than happy—with both her credentials and her feisty spirit, so like his own. He'd hired her on the spot and had enjoyed the reactions of the conservative local populace ever since she'd arrived. Just as he'd enjoyed MacRae's narrow-eyed appraisal of her. Ed leaned back in his swivel chair and regarded his newest employee.

"Work with MacRae on this test, Maggie. He's right about its importance. If there's a way to do it safely, let's find it."

"I'll give it my best, Ed, although I doubt I'll have much to do with the big man himself. He'll probably assign the task of convincing me to some lowly engineer."

"Possibly," Ed agreed. "Just don't be surprised if you find him taking a personal interest in this project. It's a big one."

12

CHAPTER 2

Maggie's next encounter with "the mountain," as she'd privately dubbed him, came sooner than either she or Ed Stockton had imagined. She ran into him, literally, the next evening.

She'd been invited by the chief of Natural Resources to join a nighttime expedition to one of the base's protected beaches. Natural Resources was responsible for wildlife and timber management on the sprawling Eglin complex. The chief of that division went about his work with a contagious enthusiasm. With Ed Stockton's support, he'd enlisted a local school to help with the annual turtle-hatching. Maggie listened with smiling skepticism as he explained how she could help.

"Really, Maggie, half the squadron turns out, as much to help supervise the kids as work the turtles. Most of the fun is watching the youngsters see nature at work."

"Come on, Pete, don't the folks in this corner of Florida have anything better to do on Friday night? Do you really expect me to believe you've got several hun-

dred adults and as many kids coming out to watch turtles hatch?"

Pete smiled through his bushy beard. Now here was
a man who fit his biologist image, Maggie thought. Unlike a certain hulking scientist.

"Not just watch," Pete protested. "We have to work
them. The loggerhead sea turtles are one of the endangered species that are protected by law. But mama loggerhead isn't a very responsible parent, and that makes
our job difficult. She deposits her eggs on Eglin's
beaches, then swims off into the gulf. My people have
spent the past few months building wire cages to protect the nests from predators."

Pete's earnestness won Maggie's interest, and she
leaned forward to peer over his shoulder at the map
showing the various nesting sites.

"The eggs are just now starting to hatch. Unfortunately, on cloudy nights like tonight, the baby turtles
can't see the moon's reflection on water to guide them
to the sea. They get disoriented, lose their way and die."

"I would think a couple of hundred inquisitive
schoolkids would only add to the poor baby turtles'
confusion," Maggie joked.

"Come out to Site 15 tonight with me and see. Trust
me," Pete said, placing a hairy paw on his plaid-covered
chest. "It'll be one of the adventures of your life."

Later that night, as the moon darted in and out of
dark clouds, Maggie stood a short distance apart from
a milling group of adults and preteens that Pete was or-
ganizing. She'd driven out with him and listened to his

detailed explanation of the night's activities, but still felt a bit foolish among a bunch of strangers baby-sitting turtles of all things. She shivered slightly in her lightweight jacket. So much for balmy Florida nights and swaying palm trees, she thought.

Even the cool May night air, however, couldn't dampen her natural ebullience for long. She stood on a slight rise and caught her breath as the moon peeked around the edge of a cloud, bathing the beach with soft light. White sand, undulating dunes and the iridescent ripple of the waves washing in combined to make a magical seascape. Maggie drank in the serene beauty of the night, disturbed only by the excited noise of a dozen children trying to be quiet.

She turned toward the nest area, noticing that the kids had formed a line from the dunes to the shore. When they switched on their flashlights, a wave of high-pitched giggles and muted adult exclamations drifted across the night air. Despite herself, Maggie felt a thrill as she saw hundreds of tiny dark forms begin to make their squiggly way to the sea. She started to run down to join the line, but crashed headlong into a very large dark form coming from the side.

Hard hands gripped one arm and one breast, trying to keep her from falling. The hand on her breast shifted almost immediately to her other arm, but not before Maggie's startled glance had looked up, way up, into equally startled eyes.

Maggie's ready sense of humor overcame her momentary embarrassment. "I know you wanted us to work closely, Colonel, but isn't this above and beyond the call of duty?"

"Dr. Wescott, I'd have recognized you anywhere."

At Maggie's indignant gasp, MacRae added, "From the moonlight glinting on that wild head of hair."

His wicked smile told Maggie that he knew very well she'd thought he was referring to his quick but very thorough exploration of her breast. The thought of his hand on it brought an unexpected tingle to the very area he had pressed so briefly. She stepped back quickly out of his hold.

"What are you doing here, Colonel? Scouting out the next site to blow up with one of your super ray guns?"

Mac smiled down at her. "You've been listening to that old goat Stockton too much. I don't blow up every part of his precious range. Only the selected portions he grudgingly allows the rest of us to use. Actually I'm here in my other official capacity tonight. Those are my two boys over there, trying not to stomp too many turtles to death as they help 'save' them."

He waved in the general direction of the line of children. Maggie saw a couple of flashlights dance wildly in response. Even in the darkness, she guessed, his kids could pick out their giant of a father. She firmly suppressed a surprising twinge of disappointment at the thought of his having children. Of course he had kids, and he probably had a dainty demure little wife, as well. Maggie took a step away from him.

"I better get over there and help, too, or I'll lose my environmentalist badge."

16

Mac fell in beside her as she headed toward the line. Inexplicably, some of the adventure of the night had dimmed for Maggie.

"Dad, Dad, can me and Danny spend the night at Joey's?"

A sand-covered shadow ran full tilt toward them out of the darkness. Maggie barely avoided her second collision of the night, but Mac wasn't as lucky. He caught the youngster, who appeared to be about nine, under his arms and swirled him around in a shower of sand, wet jeans and giggles.

"Mind your manners, Davey. Say hello to Dr. Wescott. She works at the base, too."

Davey extended a damp sandy hand to Maggie. His grin, as he introduced himself, was a miniature duplicate of one she had seen smiling down at her just a few moments ago. Heavens, there were three of these males loose on society!

"Please, Dad. Joey's mom promised to make fudge tonight. Can we go?"

"Let me talk to her first, son, and make sure it's all right."

As the child dashed back to his place in line, Mac excused himself. "I need to catch Joey's mom before they overwhelm her. I'm not sure she knows what she's getting into with those twins of mine. They've been through half a dozen full-time housekeepers in the past few years. The latest has worked out only because she used to be a warden in a woman's prison."

He started to walk away, then turned back. "What the

heck's your first name, anyway? I feel like we've passed the Dr. Wescott stage."

"I'll tell you, if you'll tell me what goes in front of the 'Mac' in MacRae."

For the first time, Maggie saw the big man slightly discomposed.

"It's Alastair, after my Scottish grandfather. Most of the folks who know me have managed to forget that. Mac'll do just fine. Your turn."

"Maggie, short for Marguerite. After my French grandmother."

He left Maggie with a smile. She wandered toward the line, thinking of their brief conversation. After their initial meeting, Maggie never would have imagined enjoying herself with the incredible hunk so much. She had just reached the point of wondering about the string of housekeepers when he was back.

"All clear. The boys are set, and I have an unexpected free evening. Do you want to go hatch turtles with me?"

The moon came out from behind a scudding cloud, lighting the beach and Maggie's night. She resisted an almost overwhelming urge to put her hand in the one he was holding out to her.

"Wouldn't Mrs. Colonel MacRae mind you going off to hatch turtles with another woman?"

Maggie was nothing if not direct. She had learned to succeed in a field still dominated by men.

Mac was equally direct. "My wife died in a car crash six years ago. It's just the boys and me." He looked out at the sea briefly, then deliberately lightened the somber mood. "Danny and Davey have been trying to marry me off for years to any woman who can cook. You don't have a diploma from a gourmet-cooking school tucked away with all your other degrees, do you?"

"Nope, you're safe."

"Good, come on, then. There's another nest a little way down the beach, minus kids. Pete told me about it. Incidentally he mentioned that he'd be here late. I told him I'd take you home if you want to leave before he does."

Maggie stared at him in wry amusement. The man sure moved fast for someone his size.

They spent the next hour alternately escorting hatchlings to the sea and sitting next to a small fire set in the protection of the dunes. Mac provided a thermos of hot coffee laced with rum. Obviously he'd done turtle duty before.

She found the man beside her fascinating. He laughed and joked easily with the other members of the small group. In between dashes to the sea, he kept Maggie amused with a light running commentary on the joys of parenting twin boys.

For his part, Mac couldn't keep his eyes off her mobile expressive face with those green eyes gleaming in the moonlight. Nor off her long legs and the firm tush outlined to perfection by her tight jeans. She had a light and laughing personality that attracted Mac even more than her trim figure. When the last hatchlings finally made their way to the surf, he took Maggie's arm and led her away from the small fire toward a Jeep parked at the edge of the dunes.

"Mac, I'm cold," Maggie protested, looking back longingly at the fire and the thermos of doctored coffee Mac had left with the remaining group.

"Me, too. We'll get warm in the car. My jeans are wet clear up to my thighs."

"That's a lot of wet," Maggie said, her voice solemn.

He grinned and helped her into the Jeep. Joining her, he turned on the ignition and the heater. Welcome warmth began to fill the cab, along with the soft strains of a country-and-western ballad from the radio.

"Better?" he asked.

"Mmm, much."

20   Maggie propped her knees up against the dash and leaned back in the seat, drinking in the sight of shadowed moonlight dancing on the sea and her tingling awareness of the man beside her. Idly she wondered if she'd have a chance to see Mac again once she started working with his people on the test project. She certainly hoped so.

Mac's low voice cut through the stillness. "I was impressed with your grasp of the issues on our propulsion test. For someone so new to the base, you've certainly picked up on our business quickly."

"I may be new to Eglin, but I'm not new to testing," she told him. "I worked in Research and Development on the Air Staff for a while before I moved to private industry."

"What made you come back to defense work?"

Maggie found that Mac's presence was proving to be a major distraction. That, and the way his arm stretched across the back of the seat. She had to think a couple of moments before she could come up with a response.

"It was time for a change," she finally managed.

"I'm glad," he said, and smiled.

At her inquiring look, his hand slid off the seat back and burrowed under the weight of her hair. It settled on her nape, and Maggie felt the tender rasp of his callused fingertips all the way down to her toes.

"I'm glad you needed a change, Maggie. I'm glad you're here."

Maggie swallowed and looked up to see his eyes glinting silvery blue in the moonlight.

"Me, too, Mac," she whispered.

With a lopsided grin, he moved his arm down to wrap it around her waist. His muscles barely shifted as he lifted her easily across the gearshift and into his lap. She half-sat, half-lay across his iron-hard thighs.

"I've been wanting to do this since turtle number twenty-seven," he murmured.

His dark head bent toward her, and Maggie felt his lips close over hers. He tasted of coffee and rum and delicious male. Letting her eyes drift closed, she savored the slow languorous way his lips moved over hers.

She smiled up at him when he pulled back moments later. "Why did you wait so long?"

Mac gave a little groan. The hand around her waist tightened as he fit her more fully against his chest, and her head angled back for his kiss. When she moaned softly in an unconscious echo, his tongue delved in to explore her mouth. Maggie's last rational thought was that she hadn't necked in a parked car since junior high. She hadn't realized what she was missing.

A long time later they surfaced. Mac tilted her chin up so he could see her face in the moonlight. With a grunt of pure male satisfaction he took in her half-closed dreamy eyes and swollen lips.

"Lord, you look great in the moonlight, woman. Especially with that hair of yours glinting that way."

When she only smiled in response, Mac ran his finger gently back and forth across her lower lip. Maggie had thought the feel of his lips on hers erotic. This finger business was about to drive her crazy. Instinctively she opened her mouth and captured his finger in a teasing nip.

"You little cat."

Mac bent her back over his arm as far as the truck door would allow and kissed her again. His hand started to move toward the zipper on her jacket, then stopped a tantalizing few inches away from her breast.

Dragging in a harsh breath, he lifted his head and dropped his hand to rest on the curve of her hip. "Lord, I'm sorry, Maggie."

She blinked. "Sorry?"

"I'm acting like some pimply teenager on his first date. I must be crazy, trying to grope you in the front seat of a car."

Flustered, Maggie stared up at him. She wasn't about to admit that she wanted to be groped, front seat or back. That she hadn't been kissed like that by anyone, pimply or otherwise, in this lifetime. That her nipples had tingled in anticipation as his hand started to open her jacket. She swallowed and tried to take in his next words.

"I can't believe I lost control to the point where I was ready to do something I'd wallop the boys for in a few years. Would it help any if I said you and the moonlight are a fatal combination and I couldn't help myself?"

A slow wave of embarrassment washed over Maggie as she listened to his apology. Here she was, a grown woman with a string of degrees, trading kisses with a man she hardly knew. In a Jeep, no less. Obviously, Mac hadn't expected her uninhibited response—any more than she had herself.

She shifted off his lap and scrambled awkwardly to her seat.

"I'd like to go home now."

"Maggie—"

"Now, please." Thoroughly mortified, and a little hurt by his rejection, Maggie stared straight ahead.

Mac studied her stony profile and cursed himself for being such a clumsy idiot. It wasn't as if he was totally out of practice. He hadn't been celibate all these years since Anne's death, but normally he managed a bit more finesse. He didn't know what it was about this woman now staring at the sea that started his hormones raging. Since his first meeting with her, he'd felt far more than a professional interest. That interest had ripened to a deep attraction as he'd watched her sparkle in the firelight and shimmer in the moonlight.

He'd responded to her looks as any healthy male would, but it was more than that. She'd put him calmly and efficiently in his place in Stockton's office. Instead of turning him off, he found himself intrigued by the brain behind the face. By the whole woman. When she careened into him tonight and he felt her firm breast in his hand, Mac had decided instantly to follow up on that promising lead. He just hadn't planned to let it go quite so far, so soon.

"Look at me, Maggie. Please."

He waited until she speared him with a cold challenging look. "I'm sorry. I didn't mean to come on to you like some sex-starved jerk. We're going to be working together closely for the next few weeks. I don't want you to be…uncomfortable around me."

Mac could have kicked himself as soon as the words were out. They sounded pompous and all wrong, and he could see that was just the way Maggie heard them. Anger quickly replaced the stony stillness on her face.

"Look, Colonel, I've never yet let private feelings interfere with my professional dealings, and you aren't the man to change that. If you're through beating your breast over this evening's fiasco, would you please take me home? Or shall I find another ride?"

Mac muttered a curse under his breath. Obviously he couldn't recover tonight. However, he hadn't risen to the top of his profession without learning his trade. Any good military man knew when to beat a strategic retreat and marshal his forces for another day. Without another word he drove the Jeep out of the tall dunes and onto the highway.

During the ride home Maggie stoked her simmering anger at the man seated next to her. So he was a world-class hunk who looked as good in his uniform as in the worn jeans he was wearing tonight. So he had a slow easy smile that crinkled his eyes. So some people thought he was brilliant. She knew better. The man was a jerk, just as he himself said, and the less she dealt with him the better. The fact that he'd stopped kissing her when she was warm and willing had nothing at all to do with the matter. At least that's what she finally managed to convince herself of by the time she'd soaked in a hot tub and buried her head under a mound of covers.

CHAPTER 3

Maggie wasn't sure whether it was the insistent ringing of the doorbell or the loud barking that woke her the next morning. She poked her head out from under the tangled covers, pushed a pile of hair out of her eyes and squinted at the clock.

26   It was only seven thirty, for heaven's sake! And a Saturday morning, as best she could recall. What idiot was making such a racket so early? It took another few moments for the fact to penetrate that the ringing doorbell was hers and the barking didn't seem to be going away.

Muttering something that wouldn't have done much for her professional image, Maggie climbed out of bed. She searched among the jumble in her closet for a robe. She hadn't had time in the week she'd been here to unpack, but household chores were pretty low in her list of priorities. By the time she'd found a short beach robe to cover her nightshirt, the doorbell had begun to grate on her nerves, and she was seriously considering changing her opinion on animal euthanasia.

Her sleepy irritation changed to surprise when she

opened the door of her rented condo. Three pairs of male eyes surveyed her. Four, if the huge creature who treated her to one more ear-splitting bark before plopping down on her doorstep happened to be a him.

"Mornin', ma'am." Mac's blue eyes twinkled down at her confusion. "I just collected the boys from Joey's house, and they swear three pounds of fudge barely kept them from starving to death last night. We're on our way to our favorite restaurant for breakfast. Since you're new in town, we thought you might like to join us for some local down-home cooking."

In answer to her skeptical look, one of the boys chimed in, "Honest, ma'am. Felix makes the best grits in town. Probably in all of Florida. Maybe in the world." Another enthusiastic bark seconded the boy's earnest opinion.

Maggie smiled down at him, then gave Mac an inquiring glance.

"This is Daniel." Mac ruffled one dark head affectionately. "You met David last night. They're otherwise known as the Terrible Twosome or, more politely, the Scourges of Northwest Florida."

"Aw, come on, Dad." Davey grinned up at him. "We're not that bad, at least not all the time."

Maggie suddenly realized that her front doorstep was not exactly the proper place to be standing in a short robe and carrying on an extended conversation. Not that she should be carrying on a conversation with these three males in a short robe at all. Correction, make that four males, Maggie amended as the big hairy beast sniffed a ceramic pot gracing her doorstep, then lifted his leg to drown her poor potted mums. Thank goodness they were artificial, Maggie thought. Gardening was another domestic task she had little interest in or talent for.

"Woof—bad boy!" three male voices chastised the dog in unison. The dog drooped his head in a semblance of repentance for a few seconds. Then a squirrel in the yard caught his attention and he bounded off.

"Woof, come back!" Davey yelled.

"Interesting name," Maggie said as the dog returned, tail wagging. She stood aside. "Why don't the bunch of you come in for a moment while I put on something more presentable?"

Mac's eyes told her that he found her eminently presentable, but he prudently kept silent as she led them into a light airy living room.

Maggie had fallen in love with this condo the first moment she'd seen it. Since it fronted the emerald-green waters of the Gulf of Mexico, the rent was high. She considered the spacious rooms well worth the price, though. At least they had seemed spacious until her three—four—unexpected guests filled them.

Mac caught her arm as she turned for the hallway. "Please come, Maggie," he said softly. "I at least owe you breakfast for last night."

"You don't owe me anything at all," she began, only

to stop abruptly as she noted two pairs of very interested blue eyes fixed on her and Mac.

"What happened last night, Dad? Did you put the make on Dr. Westly?"

Out of the mouths of babes, Maggie thought. She folded her arms and turned to watch how Mac handled this one. He got himself in. Let him get himself out.

"It's Dr. Wescott, Davey. And I guess I did come on a bit strong with her. Breakfast is my way of apology."

Maggie had to admire MacRae's honesty with his sons, even if she didn't particularly like being the subject of it. She gave a silent groan as the boys turned their bright inquisitive eyes back to her. She forestalled the highly personal questions hovering on their lips.

"Apology accepted. And it's Maggie, guys. Give me a few minutes to get dressed, and I'll take you up on your offer of grits."

"That's great, Maggie. But don't take too long, okay? You won't mess with all that female stuff, will you?" Davey, or maybe it was Danny, managed to project a superb impression of imminent starvation.

"I wonder where they picked up that little bit of sexism," Maggie tossed at Mac as she moved past him.

Five minutes later she was back, dressed in snug jeans and a soft red sweater. Her only concession to "female" stuff was a red band that caught her long curls up in a wispy concoction Mac found utterly enticing.

He forced himself to repress the mental urge to pull that band slowly back out of her hair and watch the tawny mass spill across his arm. *Come on, man,* he told himself, *you're here to make amends, not make matters worse.* With that admonishment, he shepherded Maggie and his tribe out of the apartment and into his Jeep.

Maggie found herself amazed at the variety and scope of interest displayed by the two lively nine-year-olds. During the short ride their conversation ranged from the fate of the turtles hatched last night to hockey strategy to some strange rock group whose name seemed to be composed mostly of dead things. She sat back, content to enjoy their company and let the crisp Florida air fan her hunger.

An hour later the boys watched with open admiration as she pushed back her second empty grits bowl. It joined the litter of empty biscuit platters and gravy boats on the table.

30

"Gimme a break, guys," Maggie said, noting their expressions. "I'm a big girl. I need a lot of sustenance."

The boys and their father flashed identical grins. Maggie felt her heart thump against her full stomach. It must be heartburn from all this food, she thought. She couldn't be falling for three bothersome males who wouldn't even let a gal sleep late on Saturday mornings.

She sipped her coffee, feeling full and strangely happy in the midst of the noisy clatter of the restaurant. When she met Mac's look, he let loose with one of those slow easy smiles that started at the corners of his mouth and ended up lightening his blue eyes to silvery gray. It almost made Maggie forget where she was.

"Forgiven?" he mouthed at her over the boys' heads. She smiled back and gave a slow nod.

"At the risk of overwhelming you with MacRaes, would you like to fill the next couple of hours with fresh air, terrifying suspense and unmitigated violence? The boys have soccer practice in half an hour. They always perform better before admiring females."

"Daaad," the twins chorused, but they turned identical hopeful looks on Maggie.

Maggie rubbed her full tummy as if in deep thought. "I guess I need to do something to repay the guys for the best grits I've ever had. Sure, I can cheer them on for an hour or so."

Mac's thigh rubbed against Maggie's jean-clad leg as they sat on the hard bleachers. She found his taut muscles much more fascinating than the controlled mayhem that passed for kids' soccer. She retained barely enough consciousness of the game to return the twins' waves after each spectacular play, which, given the wild charges up and down the field, didn't happen too often. The bleachers were crowded with noisy parents, all no doubt hoping their offspring would work off some energy. Maggie noticed the speculative glances other parents had given Mac when he arrived with boys, dog and herself in tow.

Mac had returned several friendly greetings, but didn't linger beyond brief introductions. He wanted some time alone with the tawny-haired creature next to him—if you could consider being surrounded by yelling soccer parents on a crowded bleacher alone, he thought with a wry grimace. Actually the strategy worked better than he'd anticipated. From long years of practice he caught all the boys' more energetic moves while he kept his attention and gaze mostly on the woman beside him. She fascinated him more by the minute.

"We all appreciated not being kept waiting for 'female stuff' this morning," he told her, gazing down at her fresh glowing complexion. "The boys, because they were about to expire with hunger on the spot. Me, because I find you look even better in the light of day than in the moonlight."

"I'm not sure you ought to bring up the subject of moonlight. I'm still trying to sort last night out."

Mac winced at her directness. She leaned her elbows back against the seat behind them and studied him from under thick gold-tipped lashes. "You confused me," she added. "My own response to you confused me."

"Well, confusion is better than the disgusted looks I was getting last night." He grinned down at her, unrepentant. "Our housekeeper gets back tomorrow afternoon, Maggie. Would you have dinner with me tomorrow night? Just us, I promise. No boys or turtles or dogs."

Maggie gave him a long considering look. She should say no. Things were moving too fast with this man. He overwhelmed her, both physically and with his exuberant family. Besides, there was the project to con-

32

sider. They might find themselves on opposite sides of a very nasty debate before too long. Despite all that, Maggie found herself nodding.

"Yes," she got out, right before an errant soccer ball rocketed toward their heads and they both ducked, laughing.

CHAPTER 4

After the game Maggie spent the rest of Saturday and most of Sunday at her cubbyhole of an office. She might hold a Phi Beta Kappa key from MIT and have a good ten years' experience in environmental issues, but the complexity of Eglin's operations awed her. Like any professional, she wanted to learn as much as she could as quickly as possible.

34

Late Sunday afternoon she found the folder on the laboratory test under a stack of files. Although she felt comfortable with her initial assessment, she decided to go through the documentation again. Her growing personal interest in the man behind the test had nothing to do with it, she told herself. This was business.

The new chemical proposed as a propellant could make a major difference in the Department of Defense space program. Although highly volatile, it was inexpensive to formulate and readily available. Maggie had read a lot about it, had even been involved in another minor experiment involving it a few years ago. But this test represented a major milestone in its practical application. She spent a good hour rereading the report and doing her own analysis of the test parameters.

She sat back in her chair, brow furrowed and doubts still unresolved. The propellant was incredibly dangerous, more so than most of the exotic explosives and chemicals tested at Eglin. Maggie knew commercial concerns were just beginning to consider it as a possible source of power, but no one had figured out how to reduce its volatility to safe levels yet.

As she reviewed possible test impacts, Maggie began to appreciate just why Eglin Air Force Base covered an area larger than a small state. The test business involved a lot of unknowns—dropping bombs or firing missiles for the first time and recording their properties. The fliers and engineers required a large safety footprint for their tests. Unfortunately the footprint included habitats of several endangered species, highways that had to be closed during tests and encroaching civilian communities. All of them had to be considered in the environmental analysis for each major new test. Mac's staff hadn't adequately addressed all the environmental impacts if this propellant lived up to its dangerous potential.

She made a few hasty notes and stuffed the folder into her tote to take home with her for yet another look. She put the other folders back in her drawer and glanced at the wall clock. She wanted plenty of time to prepare for her dinner date this evening with her enigmatic colonel.

If Mac's soft whistle when she opened her door to

him later was any indication, her preparation time had been well spent. She felt the impact of his glinting approval from her hair, held up with combs on top of her head, down the length of the shimmery green silk pantsuit to her high-heeled sandals.

"I'm not exactly sure how anyone encased in cloth from neck to toe can manage to look mostly undressed, but you come close."

"I think I'll take that as a compliment," Maggie said, moving aside to let him in. "Wearing outrageous clothes is one of the few advantages a tall woman has in life over the dainty types."

Maggie smiled to herself as she turned to shut the door. She'd bought the outfit because of the way the silk clung sensuously to every curve. She didn't have that many of them, and if this little outfit helped Mac notice the few she had, it was worth every penny.

Mac would have disagreed with her assessment of her attractions had he known it. His eyes roamed appreciatively from her slender hips to her small high breasts. The jade-green tunic outlined them clearly, hinting at the nubs in their centers before falling in graceful folds. Surveying the way the fabric moved as Maggie did, Mac's feelings underwent a subtle change. From masculine appreciation, he began to experience a possessive desire to keep Maggie's curves to himself. He felt a surprisingly primitive urge to wrap her in a shapeless blanket so that only he knew what was beneath.

Unaware of his thoughts, Maggie turned to pick up her small gold purse. Mac barely stifled a groan when the silk outlined the delicious curves of her derriere as she leaned down. It was with a somewhat grim expression that he escorted Maggie to his car.

He managed to relax over dinner. The sight of Maggie demolishing a grilled red snapper, a generous portion of steamed rice and half a loaf of crusty French bread, along with a bottle of perfectly chilled chardonnay, restored his balance.

Maggie sighed as she leaned back in her chair. "That was heaven."

"It's nice to share a meal with someone who appreciates it," he responded, lifting his wineglass in her direction.

"Which is a very tactful way of saying I eat too much." Maggie laughed. "I guess being tall has another advantage, besides allowing me to wear outrageous clothes. It takes a lot more to fill me up. And I can enjoy every morsel." She grinned unrepentantly over the rim of her wineglass.

"Yes, and I can think of at least one more advantage." At her inquiring look, he stood and held out his hand. "I've been looking forward to dancing with someone whose nose won't tickle my belly-button. Come dance with me, Maggie m'girl."

Mac decided he liked the feel of the woman in his arms. Very much. She fitted him perfectly. Ignoring the glances other men in the room directed at Maggie, he enjoyed the feel of her warm flesh through the smooth material as he moved his hand slowly up and down her back. To distract himself from what he could feel at her front, he nuzzled a soft tendril of hair that had escaped from the topknot and resumed their lighthearted dinner conversation.

"So where did you work before coming here? You mentioned the Air Staff."

Held closely against Mac's hard body, Maggie had difficulty remembering her own name, let alone her career history. Only after she'd shifted away from the warm cradle of his arms could she collect her thoughts.

"Mmm, yes. I worked on the Air Staff in Washington for a year or so. It was exciting, but I didn't care much for the paperwork. I decided I liked fieldwork better.

"Houston was next," she murmured into Mac's obliging shoulder. Really, it was amazing she could talk at all. She found herself reveling in the sensation of dancing with someone whose shoulder was just the right height to rest her head on. Even with her high heels, the mountain retained his majestic proportions.

"How long at Houston?" he asked, his voice low, his breath teasing the wispy curls at her ears.

"Not quite two years."

"So why did you leave there to come here? That job must have paid twice what the government could pay you."

Maggie smiled into Mac's shoulder. "I think I had this conversation once before with Ed Stockton. The same answer still holds. There's more to life than money. I wanted to get back to hands-on environmental work, and Eglin has plenty of that."

38

Maggie leaned back in his arms to look up at him. Mac barely managed to suppress a groan as her breasts brushed against his chest. Damn that silk! He could feel the peaks of her breasts clearly through the material, distracting him so much he almost missed her soft words.

"My needs in life are pretty simple, Mac. Some nice clothes, a good car and a challenging job, in reverse order, about sums them up."

"Isn't there something missing from that list? Like a home and a family? Someone to cook for you?" he teased.

Much as she liked him, Maggie's habit of keeping her private life private was too ingrained to give Mac anything other than the barest details.

"I've come close once or twice," she admitted lightly. "But every time I thought I'd found Mr. Right, he turned out to be Mr. Wrong. Enough about me. What about you? What's on your list?"

"My priorities are pretty simple, too," Mac answered as he moved them in time to the slow dreamy tune. "The boys and the air force, not in reverse order. I'm lucky. Between those two devils and the demands of a military career, I've never been still long enough to be bored."

"And that's enough? What about someone to talk to in the night? About things besides soccer or Boy Scouts, I mean? Don't you want to marry again?"

"What makes you think husbands and wives talk in bed about anything other than Boy Scouts and grocery lists and who's going to take the kids to the dentist?"

At her mock scowl, he shrugged. "Like you, I've had a few close calls over the years. Being single and so physically big make me a real target it seems. But so far, it's just me and the boys. And Woof."

Maggie buried a small sigh of satisfaction in the fabric of Mac's shirt. She was glad Woof and the boys, and no one else, were taking up his time.

Mac led her around the dance floor a couple of more times, then leaned down to whisper in her ear, "Let's go, Maggie. I don't think I can take one more man sliding his eyes over you in that slinky getup."

Maggie gave silent thanks once more to Nieman Marcus for her outfit and smiled her readiness to leave.

She promised herself another shopping trip when Mac closed the front door of her apartment and growled, "Come here, woman. That thing you're wearing has been driving me nuts all evening."

Maggie allowed Mac's big hands to pull her close. He propped his shoulders back against the door, forcing her to put her palms on his chest and lean heavily against him. Her body was plastered against his from shoulder to knee.

"This is much better," he said, rubbing his hands up and down her back. He bent his head to taste a spot on her neck bared by the upswept curls.

Maggie kept her eyes closed. She kept her hands still where they pressed against his chest. But she couldn't keep her nipples from tightening as Mac rubbed her front against his, or a hot streak from shooting through her when his moist tongue left her neck and pushed gently into her ear.

Good grief, she thought, how did such a mountain manage to create such delicate shivers in every nook and cranny of her body? Then she forgot to think at all as his mouth took hers. He shifted her weight against his right arm. With his other hand he reached up to tug loose her curls. With a grunt of pure male satisfaction, he lifted his head to watch her hair spill down in a tumbling mass. That basic task done, he looked into her eyes.

"I want you so much it hurts, but I suspect you won't accept grits as a peace offering if I come on too strong again. So from here on out it's your call. You set the pace, Maggie. Tell me what you want."

She opened her eyes and gave him a clear direct look. "I want you, Mac. It'd be nice to get you and grits, too, but I'll settle for you."

"That's all I needed to know."

With an easy movement he bent and scooped her up in his arms, then headed down the hallway toward the bedroom.

CHAPTER 5

Maggie reveled in another totally new sensation as Mac carried her through the dim hall. Being carried was even more exciting than having a shoulder at just the right height to rest her head on while dancing. As best she could remember, no man had ever tried to hoist her off her feet before. *Talk* her off her feet and into bed maybe, but nothing quite this physical. She began to appreciate that there was a lot more to this seduction scene than she'd experienced before. She rather liked it, she decided, enlivening the short trip down the hall by exploring Mac's conveniently placed ear with her tongue.

Mac reacted to her explorations with satisfying directness. He dumped her on the bed with more haste than finesse and was beside her before she could catch her breath. This time his kiss was fierce and hot and demanding. Maggie kept her eyes closed once more, but now her hands roved as feverishly as his. She plucked distractedly at the buttons on his shirt, not content until she'd undone enough to slide her hands inside. Crisp hair curled over powerful chest muscles, teasing the

42

tips of fingers. She delighted in the touch and the scent of him, strong and hard and very male.

When Mac slipped his own fingers under her satin tunic and shaped one aching breast, Maggie gasped. He slanted his mouth across hers more firmly, demanding her response. With a slow sure movement he pulled her body under his and pressed her down into the thick comforter.

"Your body fits against mine as well horizontally as it does vertically," he murmured. "I like being able to kiss most of the important spots without getting permanent spinal damage."

Maggie's breath slammed out of her as Mac suited action to words. With a quick bend of his head, he closed his mouth over a breast. She felt him hot and wet through the silk. When his teeth took the nipple and teased it into taut stiffness, a shaft of pure sensation shot through her.

He found the side button of her pants and slid them and her lace panties down to her ankles. With a muttered curse, he sat up to fumble impatiently at the tiny straps of her sandals. He finally pushed shoes, slacks and panties off in one tangled mass. Maggie reached for him and he turned back to her, but he caught both her hands loosely in one of his and stretched them over her head.

"Let me look at you, Maggie. Let me drink in the sight of those long luscious legs and gorgeous gold curls."

Maggie blushed in the half-light. She felt indescribably wanton with her lower body naked and exposed to the cool night air, not to mention his decidedly hot stare and her satin tunic sliding sensuously over highly sensitized nipples. She twisted her hands free and undid the last of his shirt buttons.

"Your turn, Mac. Let me look at you."

She pushed his shirt off shoulders so broad they blocked out all the light from the hallway when he leaned over her. Her hands fumbled at his belt buckle. With an impatient movement, he got up to rid himself of the rest of his clothes. Maggie gave in to the pleasure of watching him, then quickly pulled off her last piece of satin.

She lay back and let her eyes rove with hungry appreciation over his massive body. He fumbled in his pants pocket for a small foil package and turned away for a moment. A warm glow lodged just under her heart at his unquestioned willingness to take responsibility for her protection. When he turned back, she eyed his rampant manhood in the dim light and bit back a grin. The man certainly ran true to size!

She wondered briefly if it was possible to have too much of a good thing, then gave up all attempt at rational thought as Mac lowered himself to her side. One of his legs nudged her apart, and he slid a callused palm down her belly. His fingers tugged playfully at her nest of curls, then buried themselves in her wet heat.

Maggie arched against him. Her breathing changed to shallow panting gasps as he moved his fingers in and out, slowly, deliberately, while his thumb explored the sensitive little nub at her core. His hands tantalized and roused her to fever pitch. When he lowered his head and took an aching nipple into his mouth once more, Maggie thought she would explode.

"Not yet, Maggie my sweet," he whispered. Removing his hand, he positioned himself atop her body. "First I want to feel you all around me."

Holding her head still with both hands, watching her eyes in the dim light, Mac pushed himself into her welcoming warmth.

Long hot moments later, after his hands and his mouth and driving manhood had taken her to incredible heights of sensation, Maggie gave a hoarse cry. Waves of pleasure swamped her, and the darkness behind her closed lids shattered into splinters of bright light. Mac echoed her panting cry as her tightness gripped him in rippling waves. He muffled his shout of satisfaction against her neck and thrust deeply, following her over the edge.

Hours later, or so it seemed to Maggie, she roused herself enough to run light fingers through the dark head resting on her breast. Mashing it to a pulp, really. Even with most of his weight on his forearms, Mac crushed her into the mattress. She wiggled and tried to shift to a more comfortable position, only to have him lift his head and grin down at her.

"So soon, Maggie m'girl? Without even a nourishing snack to sustain your energy? Well, we fly-boys aim to please. If you're ready, I'll do my best."

"You big lummox, stop grinning or I might force you

to make good on your boast." Maggie tried again to shift him. He let himself be moved off her body only enough to insert his hand between them and cup her breast.

"Boast? I never boast. But I need sustenance after a good workout even if you don't. I think a little midnight feeding will do it."

Before Maggie understood his meaning, he'd lowered his head and began a slow sweet suckling at her breast. His hand pushed the firm mound up so his mouth could draw at the nipple, then covered half her breast with hot wetness.

In total amazement, Maggie felt streaks of heat shoot through her again. And again, when he woke her up an hour later. Only after he'd pulled her on top of him and made her take her bedsprings to the limit of their endurance did he fall asleep himself.

She awoke again just as gray dawn was beginning to lighten the room. Without having to reach across the bed, she knew he wasn't there. She lay quietly, her eyes closed, while a series of incredibly erotic visions danced behind her eyelids. Lord, she hadn't really moaned like that, had she? Her raw throat and the tenderness between her thighs mocked her own denials.

She was about to bury her head in the covers at the thought of some of her more energetic activities when the unmistakable scent of fresh coffee reached her.

Heavens, he was domesticated, she thought. Untangling herself from the bedclothes, she slipped on the faithful short terry robe and padded down the hall to the living room. She pulled up short at the sight of Mac, slacks riding low on lean hips and shirt hanging open to display that massive chest. He was leaning casually against her desk with a steaming cup of coffee in one hand and an open folder in the other. Even from across the room, Maggie could see it was the propulsion-test folder.

The warm greeting bubbling on her lips died. Her eyes fastened on the folder in growing consternation. Was that what all this was about? Had he wined and dined and put on that admittedly spectacular bedroom performance to change her mind about that damned test? Doubts swamped her, even as Mac looked up and met her suspicious gaze.

His own slow smile of greeting died. There was no mistaking the direction of her thoughts as her eyes moved from the folder to his face. He watched her thoughtfully for a few moments, then greeted her in a neutral tone.

"Morning, Maggie."

If the woman had a problem, he wasn't going to help her with it. She could darn well spit it out.

"I see you make yourself at home, MacRae. Anything else you'd like access to? After my body and my private reports, that is?"

Whew! When she let loose, she did it with both barrels. Mac told himself to stay calm. There was nothing in this report he hadn't already seen. It was government property, for Pete's sake. Hell, he had a copy of it on his desk at work. Maggie's own people had sent it over, as she'd remember if she hadn't been so busy jumping to her angry conclusions.

Still, Mac knew he shouldn't have just picked it up and started reading while he waited for her to awake. He also knew he should apologize, but rational thought warred with stung male pride. The woman had just spent the night in his arms. How the hell could she think what she so obviously did?

Pride won. Setting his mug down with a thump that sloshed coffee over onto the damned report, he started across the room toward her. When she backed away from him nervously, he stopped short. His jaw tightened ominously.

48

"Dammit, Maggie, that report isn't private. I've seen it several times. It was lying open on your desk."

"The point is, it was on *my* desk, MacRae."

Even as the words tumbled from her mouth, Maggie knew she was making too much of the whole thing, but she couldn't help herself. She hadn't had that many lovers during her otherwise adventurous thirty-three years. But based on her limited experience, she thought what she and Mac had shared last night was special. It hurt to think it may not have been so special, after all, but something rather sordid. Angry and confused, she wrapped her arms around her waist.

Mac gave her a long hard look, then began buttoning his shirt.

"Fine, it's your desk. Nice to know you think I'm the kind of guy who has ulterior motives for sleeping with a woman, Maggie. You'll understand if I don't hang around for any more of your flattering comments. I have to get home before the boys wake up and put two and three together."

Miserable, Maggie stood stiff and silent as he gathered the rest of his clothes. When he let out an exasperated sigh and stopped in front of her, she set her jaw in mulish lines.

"Maggie, this is crazy. We need to talk this out."

"I don't want to talk right now," she said to the solid chest blocking her view. "Right now, all I want is for you to leave. It was fun, MacRae, but don't overstay your welcome."

Mac's breath hissed in at her flippant words. "Why the hell is it that every time we get together, it starts with magic and ends with an argument?"

When she refused to respond, he yanked the door open. "I'll talk to you later when we've both had time to cool off."

He was gone before Maggie had a chance to think of a suitably devastating response.

CHAPTER 6

Cool off indeed, Maggie fumed all through her quick breakfast and preparations for work. She didn't need to cool off, she needed space. Lots of it. She needed time away from a certain Colonel MacRae and his overwhelming presence. She needed… Maggie sighed and shoved the folder into her briefcase. What she needed was to put the whole incident into perspective.

It didn't help that she knew Mac was right, that she had overreacted. She felt slightly disgusted with herself as she wheeled her Jag through the crisp morning air. She knew darn well that much of her anger had stemmed from a combination of surprise and old-fashioned embarrassment. She'd never responded to any man the way she had to Mac. In the privacy of her car and her thoughts, the memory of their activities the night before still made her blush.

The early morning drive helped her relax. It took half an hour to reach the base from her rented condo in the little resort village of Destin. The most enjoyable stretch of her drive began when she crossed the high bridge spanning the channel connecting Choctawhatchee Bay to the Gulf of Mexico. Ahead of her was Santa Rosa Island, with its rolling dunes, feathery sea oats and blinding white sand. Emerald-green gulf water sparkled on the left, while the huge bay stretched to the horizon on the right.

The sunlight dancing on the water and the smooth rush of waves washing the shore restored Maggie's usual good humor. By the time she pulled the Jag into her parking slot behind the long low World War Two-era building that held her office, she had her ready smile back in place.

"Morning, team," she cheerfully greeted her small staff, who were assembled for their daily meeting. As she edged her way through the crowd in her tiny office, which had to double as a conference room, Maggie firmly suppressed a fleeting image of the spacious corner office in the Houston high-rise she'd left behind.

"Okay, we've got a lot to cover this morning. Let's start with the reds."

Within days of her arrival, Maggie and her staff had devised a color-coded system for dealing with the avalanche of issues facing them. Red signaled a potential hazard that required immediate attention to avoid danger to health or welfare; yellow, a hazard that could result in action against them by a regulatory agency but wasn't imminently threatening; blue, a task they felt needed attention but could wait; and green, a purely administrative requirement. The fact that Maggie firmly refused to waste her small overworked staff's talents on greens had won their immediate loyalty.

"We found a couple of more transformers leaking PCB last week, Maggie," said one. "I'm going out with the folks from the exterior electrical shop this morning to replace them. I'll try to get the shop to move a little faster on completing the survey."

Maggie nodded her approval. PCB, or polychlorinated biphenyl, was a highly toxic chemical compound used extensively in electrical transformers before its cancer-causing characteristics were fully understood. Eglin, like most cities across the nation, faced massive challenges in recording and replacing older transformers. The base was almost a year late in completing the survey of the hundreds of transformers used to channel power at all the test sites scattered across the half-million acres. Higher priorities had eaten away at the money and time needed for the survey, even with an extension. They only had a few more months to get it done before the extension ran out and they faced heavy fines.

"Do that, Jack. I know the shop is as strapped for manpower as we are, but we've got to get that survey done. Let me know how it goes."

An intense young woman opposite Maggie spoke up. "We found some seepage on Site 22 last week. I think it may be an abandoned underground storage area."

Maggie grimaced. Burying was the accepted method of disposing of toxic waste twenty years ago. The nation was just beginning to understand the effects as toxic waste escaped from rusted containers and seeped into

52

the ground. With all the tests conducted at Eglin over the years, they had dozens of known underground storage sites and probably as many that were never properly recorded.

"How bad is it?" she asked.

The woman looked at her notes. "There's a small pool of greenish liquid, with bubbling at one edge. I'm going out with the bio-environmental folks from the hospital this morning to take samples for analysis."

Telling her she'd join them, Maggie finished her short meeting. She was on her way back from the washroom, where she'd changed her linen skirt and high heels for the jeans and rubber wading boots she kept in her office, when her intercom rang.

"Dr. Wescott, it's May in Colonel Stockton's office. The boss just got a call from the lab. They'd like you to meet with them this morning to go over the propulsion test."

"I can't do it this morning, May. See if you can set it up for this afternoon and call me back. I'll be on my beeper."

Maggie replaced the phone with a twinge of guilt. She could've rearranged her schedule. After all, the test was a top priority. But the small act of defiance somehow made her feel better about last night. With a cheerful nod to her crew, she clumped out of the office and went off to explore the green slimy gook.

When she entered the armament lab's paneled conference room later that afternoon, she was once again in her skirt. The soft cream-colored linen was paired with a gold-patterned silk blouse and high-heeled sandals. A long strand of cultured pearls gave her added dignity, she thought. She suspected she'd need all the professionalism she could muster for this meeting.

The half dozen or so men present stood up as she entered. A couple of them, including an older distinguished-looking man who should have known better, stared outright. She wasn't quite the type of engineer they were used to dealing with, if Maggie read their assorted expressions right. Well, here we go again, she thought.

"Good afternoon, gentlemen, I'm Dr. Wescott." She moved to an empty chair on one side of the long polished table. Setting her briefcase down, she went around the room to meet each man individually. Pleasantries done, she sat down and looked inquiringly at the man who'd introduced himself as Dr. Ames, the lab's deputy director. It was their meeting, she thought. They could darn well take the lead.

The older man shook his head slightly and squared his tweed-covered shoulders. "Ah, Dr. Wescott, Colonel MacRae asked me to get the propulsion team together so we could discuss your objections to the test. I'm not sure we understand some of your concerns."

"My team's concerns were detailed in the draft report they sent over several weeks ago," Maggie responded coolly. Then, with a small sigh to herself, she relented. Ames probably hadn't even read the report. Besides, she preferred a cooperative mode of operation. "However, I appreciate the chance to discuss the project in detail with you. I understand it's an important test for Eglin, and I'm part of the team now."

"Good. We've set aside an hour for Major Hill to brief you and answer your questions."

Ames settled himself with a condescending smile into the chair at the head of the table and nodded to the young major standing by the podium. Maggie decided to ignore the pompous deputy, and turned to the man who should really know what this project was all about.

Three hours later, the once immaculate conference table was littered with coffee cups and scattered papers. Discarded suit coats lay over the backs of chairs and various charts filled a large corkboard. Major Hill had abandoned his canned briefing and was standing by a built-in blackboard, scribbling notes as the group worked their way through one particularly complex chart covered with annotations and formulas.

Mac entered the conference room through his office's connecting door. He stopped short at the sight of Maggie and his deputy bent over the table, trying to read one of the chart's more obscure formulas.

Waving the other men back into their chairs as they started to rise, he leaned against the wall and waited patiently for Maggie and Ames to finish. His eyes passed over the way the soft linen clung to her delectable tush, and he shook his head in despair. Her wardrobe was wreaking havoc with his self-control.

"Dr. Wescott."

Mac greeted her gravely when the pair finally finished examining the chart and straightened up. His firm handshake held Maggie's until she tugged it free.

"Colonel MacRae." She nodded curtly.

His small private smile gently mocked her. He held her gaze for a moment, then turned an inquiring look on his deputy.

"We're getting there, Mac," Ames responded heavily. "We've resolved most of the minor questions and are just getting into some of the major issues. Dr. Wescott has some valid concerns."

Mac bit back a smile at his deputy's reluctant admission. Ames had been a brilliant scientist in his time, but he'd peaked a few years ago. Now that he was close to retirement, he filled his time more and more with administrative duties and less with the research that was the lab's lifeblood. Mac bet Maggie had probably given him a real run for his money.

"Good. I won't interrupt you, then. Dr. Wescott, if you would, please stop by and see me before you leave."

Maggie tried to think of some important meeting she had pending, but Mac was gone before she could tell him he could go whistle Dixie—professionally speaking, of course.

It was several hours later when the group in the conference room finally gathered up their assorted papers. Maggie had a pounding headache and was in no mood to face Mac. She knocked irritably on his office door, then entered without waiting for an answer.

He was on the phone and waved her to one of the soft leather chairs in front of his desk. Maggie tossed her briefcase down but was too restless to sit. While Mac finished his conversation, she prowled around his roomy corner suite. It had most of the trappings of a military commander's office—the requisite set of flags, a large conference table, a computer on the credenza—but few of the plaques and memorabilia most military personnel liked to display. The only real personal touches were a small picture of Mac giving a thumbs-up in the cockpit of some sleek lethal-looking jet and a picture of him with the twins, their laughing faces surrounded by bright blue sky and a tangle of fishing tackle.

His call finished, Mac watched as she settled herself with a deliberate touch of defiance in the chair across from him. His small sigh wasn't lost on Maggie.

"I take it this isn't a good time to talk about what happened last night," he said.

He leaned back in his massive desk chair. It probably cost the government a fortune to build one big enough to keep from folding under his bulk, Maggie thought nastily.

"No, it's not," she snapped. "I just spent five difficult hours with the lab's best and brightest. And I'm tired."

She stopped abruptly as she remembered just why she was so tired. She hadn't gotten much sleep last night. A quick glance at Mac's glinting eyes told her he was remembering, too.

"Look, Mac. I'll do my best on this damn test. Just get off my back."

Maggie bit her lip in real chagrin. Her words conjured up another decidedly erotic memory, and hot blood crept up her cheeks. She ignored the wide grin spreading across Mac's face. She got to her feet and reached for her briefcase.

"Maggie, we need to talk."

She turned at his quiet words. "Not now, please. I'm still sorting out last night in my own mind. I know I overreacted to your reading the report this morning, and I apologize for that."

Mac felt a spear of relief in his gut. He'd worried that the damn report would stand between them like a wall. Maggie's candid apology eased his tense neck muscles, but her next words had them tightening into knots again.

"I think we've both moved too fast, Mac. We need to slow this—this relationship down a bit. Why don't you call me later in the week and we'll find a time to talk?"

Pure unaccustomed anger surged through him. He wasn't about to let her get away with this call-me-sometime crap. Not after last night. She'd given herself to him totally, and his every instinct told him she wasn't the kind of woman to do that lightly. He forgot his promise to let her set the pace. He forgot his own determination not to rush her, as he had that night in his truck. He wanted to pick her up, carry her to the couch in the corner of his office and show her just how slow she thought she could take it. Only the sight of her white face, with faint blue shadows of fatigue under her eyes, stopped him.

"All right, Dr. Wescott. You've got your reprieve.

But don't kid yourself that either you or I have much control over what's happening between us. Now go home and get some sleep."

He handed her her briefcase and very nobly resisted the urge to kiss her unconscious. She left with a definite flounce of cream-colored linen.

Mac watched from his office window as she crossed the street in front of the lab and climbed into her Jag. The sleek green sports car was the number-two priority in her life, he recalled. He was thinking seriously about rearranging her priorities, not to mention her clothes and her hair and her bedcovers, when his deputy, Dr. Ames, knocked on the door.

Turning, Mac greeted the older man. "Still here, Jim? Did you get everything resolved?"

"Not quite. We're going to have to modify the test significantly. That Wescott woman is stubborn as hell."

Mac made no comment. He wasn't about to argue about Maggie with anyone.

"Ed Stockton should have known better than to let her exercise veto power over this project."

"Why?" Mac asked coolly. "I've seen her credentials. She's certainly better qualified than some of the folks we've had reviewing our proposals."

"Oh, on paper, she looks good," Ames allowed.

Mac was thinking of a few other things she looked good on, as well, such as rumpled bedclothes, when Ames's next words caught his attention.

"Don't you think it's rather coincidental that she left a plush job with a corporation that's very much against alternate energy sources to come here? And one of the first things she does is put the kibosh on our test?"

Mac regarded his deputy steadily for a long minute. "What are you implying, Jim?"

"I'm not implying anything. I just find it interesting that this particular propellant has a lot of potential for commercial use. If our test succeeds, it could cut into the oil companies' profits. Be a threat to Dr. Wescott's former employers."

"We got the draft report challenging the test over a month ago, well before Dr. Wescott's arrival. Did the final signed report differ from the draft substantially?" Mac kept his voice level, fighting his rising anger.

Ames fidgeted with his tie. "I didn't read the draft myself. Major Hill briefed me on the key points. The final report included essentially the same issues, but in much more detail. Someone put a lot more work into that final product."

"Maybe if we'd put as much effort into our initial test design, we wouldn't have the problem we have today," Mac responded. "Stay with it, Jim. Let me know how you work out the remaining issues."

When his deputy left, Mac turned back to the window. The green Jag was gone. Ames's suspicions simmered at the edges of his mind, but he refused to accept them. Instinctively he knew the laughing, smiling woman that was Maggie wasn't involved in anything like what Ames hinted at. He also knew that his deputy was out of touch with current technology sharing. Transfer of the technology developed by the air force to com-

60

mercial use was a side benefit of their work. Mac knew his staff had already shared information on this particular propellant at a recent consortium of military and civilian scientists. There was enough material about it now in the public domain to preclude the big energy concerns from trying to sabotage their test.

Still, Ames had made Mac realize there was a lot he didn't know about Dr. Marguerite Wescott. Such as why she'd really left Houston. And why a woman with her credentials would be content with field-level work. They'd talked about a lot of things during dinner the previous evening, but most of it was lighthearted banter, the kind men and women engage in during the first part of any courtship dance.

After what they'd shared last night, Mac wanted to know more, a lot more. He wanted to know the woman beneath the easy smile and mop of curls. He didn't like the thought that there were still parts of Maggie he wasn't privy to. With a determined snap, Mac turned off his office lights and left.

CHAPTER 7

"Hey, Maggie!"

A loud bark almost drowned the enthusiastic yell. Maggie turned to see the twins waving energetically from the other side of the small cove. She waved back, then waited while Woof bounded toward her along the narrow strip of beach, with Davey—or was it Danny?—dragging behind on his leash. The other twin and a short stout woman followed in their sandy wake.

"Ugh, hello, Woof." Maggie tried to keep the massive paws off her chest and the wet slurping tongue off her face. She held him at arm's length while Davey/Danny struggled to reduce the dog's ecstatic greeting to a wagging tail, though even that furious action threatened to knock them both over.

"Whatcha doin' here? This is our favorite spot. Woof loves the water, but Dad says we can't let him loose where people go, so we always come here."

"I can understand why." Maggie smiled down at the boys while she held her shirtfront out with both hands to shake off the wet sand. Splotchy paw prints decorated the once-pristine white cotton.

"I'm here checking some erosion along the shore, and no, I didn't know it was your favorite spot."

"Mrs. Harris, this is Maggie Westlake. Remember, we told you? She likes grits." The boys knew their manners, even if they couldn't remember names.

"Maggie Wescott." She smiled at the older woman and held out her hand. As her fingers were encased in a hard grip, Maggie suddenly remembered Mac's saying his housekeeper was a former prison warden. Clearly this was she.

"Hello, Dr. Wescott. Colonel Mac mentioned he had dinner with you last week."

If the older woman knew that the dinner date had lasted until morning, her bland expression gave no sign. Nevertheless, Maggie felt a surge of self-consciousness as the woman's bright eyes assessed her from head to toe.

Luckily she was spared the necessity of answering when one of the twins tugged on her sleeve.

"You wanna come with us, Maggie? We've got a special place down the beach and nobody knows about it 'cept us and Mrs. Harris. We'll show you some real neat stuff."

Maggie glanced at her watch. After a long morning in her deserted office catching up on paperwork, she'd intended to spend a few hours checking for herself the erosion along Eglin's north shoreline. She'd become so absorbed in taking notes and clambering over uprooted tree stumps that she'd forgotten the time. It was too late now for the errands she'd planned to run this beautiful Saturday afternoon. Tossing aside her plans, she gave herself up to the boys' bubbly companionship.

"Sure, I'd love to see something special. If you guys and Mrs. Harris don't mind sharing it."

"Nah, she doesn't mind, do ya?"

The older woman's plump face lost its blandness when she smiled down with genuine affection at the twins. "No, I don't mind at all. Why don't you two and Woof lead the way?"

Maggie admired the woman's strategy as the boys and Woof charged down the beach, wildly splashing through the shallows. She fell in beside Mrs. Harris, and they followed at a more leisurely pace.

"We walk along this beach almost every afternoon," the older woman said. "I thought it would take some of the edge off their collective energy, but the air and the water only seem to revive them after a tough day at school. They especially love coming here on weekends when they don't have homework hanging over their heads. My name's Kate, by the way."

"Please, call me Maggie. The boys do."

"Yes, I noticed. They talked a lot about you after the soccer game last weekend." Kate cast her a shrewd look. "They like you. So does Colonel Mac, unless I miss my guess."

Maggie blinked at the woman's bluntness. She bit back the quick retort that evidently the colonel didn't like her all that much. He hadn't called in five and a half days—not that she was counting.

"I like the boys, too. They're lively and bright."

The woman beside her snorted. "Too lively on occasion. It's a good thing I've still got my nightstick. It's the one souvenir I took with me into retirement. I keep it hanging on a very prominent peg in the kitchen. So far, just the threat of it has worked."

Maggie chuckled, then asked, "How long have you been with them?"

"Well, I came down here a couple of years ago. I'd just retired from the Federal Bureau of Prisons and thought I'd just laze the rest of my days away in the sun. That lasted about a week. Luckily, Colonel Mac advertised for a housekeeper about the time I started counting damp spots on the walls for entertainment."

By the time they caught up with the twins, Kate had Maggie laughing delightedly with stories of her days "in the pen," as she termed it.

"C'mon, Maggie, look here!"

Two pairs of excited blue eyes and two very wide grins told her this was the special place. Maggie looked around the small cove with interest. A fallen tree edged the bank and scrub littered the narrow beach, but try as she might, Maggie couldn't see what held their interest.

"Here, right here."

Danny, yes, she was sure it was Danny, pointed. He was the one with the single dimple in one freckled cheek. He grabbed hold of her hand and together they waded toward the north end of the cove, where the water of the bay lapped right up against the rugged shore. It wasn't until they were almost upon it that Maggie noticed the indentation halfway down the bank.

"It's a cave. Dad says Indians used to camp here in the old days. This was one of their hiding places. See, it goes way back behind the bushes and has all kinds of neat stuff in it."

Danny pulled her closer to the hole and bent his body half into the shadowed darkness. Maggie resisted the urge to pull him out. So far she hadn't seen any snakes or wild creatures in the area, but she didn't much care for dark holes, inhabited or otherwise.

"There're bunches of arrowheads in there and some old pot bits," Davey explained while his brother continued to root around in the cave. Danny emerged, grimy but triumphant, gripping some small stones. He took Maggie's hand and poured them into her palm. Sure enough, they were arrowheads.

Maggie didn't know much about archaeology, but she did know that northwest Florida has been home to several prehistoric tribes. They'd hunted the vast forests and fished the rich waters of Choctawhatchee Bay. In fact, the bay was named for one of the early tribes. There were several major historical sites and hundreds of minor finds scattered across the Eglin complex.

Her staff had briefed her about the consultant from Florida State University who was on call for archaeological matters. He was supposed to help catalog finds and do the necessary paperwork whenever there was any test activity that might affect a historical site.

66

"Dad says we can't take them 'cause they have to be registered or something. But we can play with them if we're careful."

Maggie knew there was a whole storeroom of as yet uncataloged artifacts somewhere on base. But archaeological-consultant fees ranked low on the list of the base's priorities.

"Go ahead, look inside and see how many there are."

"Ah, no, thanks, Davey. I'll take your word for it." No way was she going to stick her head or any other part of her anatomy into that hole.

"Chicken!" Dave taunted over Maggie's laughing protests. His twin took up the refrain, with enthusiastic accompaniment from Woof. Mrs. Harris added her voice to the general cacophony, telling the boys to lay off. Then a deep voice interrupted them all.

"You have to learn to take a lady at her word when she says no, boys."

"Dad! You're home."

The boys scooted up the bank, Woof at their heels, and threw themselves at their father. Mac wrapped a big arm around each of them, only to let go to ward off Woof's happy greeting. The boys shouted with laughter when Woof managed to sneak in a wet swipe at their father's face on one of his bouncing tries.

Maggie watched the four of them. Whatever else the exasperating man might be, he was a good parent. Their unabashed joy in each other shone through like a beacon.

She and Mrs. Harris climbed the slight bank as Mac finally calmed dog and boys.

"Hello, Kate. I expected to find you and the boys here, but I didn't expect to find you had company."

Maggie sucked in her breath as the corners of Mac's mouth pulled up in a slow easy smile. Damn, one smile and he could make her forget five-and-a-half days without a call—almost.

She started to return his greeting, only to lose his attention to a demanding nine-year-old.

"Did you fly the F-15 back, Dad? Did you? How'd it handle?"

"Yes, Dave, I flew it back. And it was worth waiting a week for. It cuts through the air like the Eagle it's named for. Come on back to the house and I'll tell you all about it." He ruffled the boy's hair, then turned to Maggie.

"Why don't you come back with us? I smelled something delicious when I passed through the kitchen on my way out here." His twinkling eyes told her he knew very well she could resist *him,* but probably not the offer of food.

"Yeah, please come, Maggie," said Davey. "Mrs. Harris made lasagna. You'll like it better'n grits, even."

"How can I pass up an offer like that? But I left my car parked back up the beach. I better go get it."

"We'll go with you, so we can show you the way."

The boys slithered eagerly back down the bank. Mac managed to grab Woof's collar just in time to keep him from joining them. He could just see Maggie driving down the road with a big hairy hound sticking out of the sunroof of her Jag.

"See you at the house." He smiled and turned to join a very interested Mrs. Harris.

By the time Maggie made it back to her car, answered the boys' excited questions about just how fast the Jag could go and followed their somewhat disjointed directions to their bay-front home, she'd managed to get a few questions of her own answered. So Mac had left unexpectedly for California to participate in some special test at Edwards Air Force Base. So he just got back this afternoon. So maybe that was why he hadn't called....

CHAPTER 8

Three hours, two helpings of lasagna and a long laugh-filled game of Monopoly later, Mrs. Harris sent the protesting twins to bed. She went upstairs herself soon after, with only one or two significant glances and a slightly smug grin.

Mac poured brandy into large snifters and led Maggie out of the cluttered den to the deck that ran the entire length of the back of the big house. The last rays of the sun streaked through dark clouds drifting above the bay. With a contented sigh, Maggie slouched down in a redwood lounge piled with weather-beaten cushions and stretched her long jean-covered legs out to rest on the deck rail. Woof immediately plunked his massive head down on her knees. Two soulful eyes gazed up at her in the dim light until she got the message and began to scratch behind his ears.

"I'm sorry I didn't get a chance to call before I left for California. I didn't like leaving things unsettled between us. I thought the conference would never end."

Maggie turned her head to study the man next to her.

He was as relaxed as she in a huge battered chair. His face was hard to see in the fading light, but she could feel his eyes watching her.

"It was a long week for me, too, Mac." Her admission surprised her. "I half expected you to call to make sure Ames and I hadn't killed each other trying to resolve the rest of the test questions." She could see his white teeth as he smiled in the gathering darkness.

"Well, *you're* still alive. Is he?"

"Barely. The man is more stubborn than I am. We still haven't closed on one or two issues," Maggie warned softly. "If we don't resolve them this week, you may have to scrub the test."

"To tell you the truth, I'm sick and tired of that damn test," Mac grumbled. "I'm still carrying the scars from your raking me over when you found me reading your report. I was hurt by your thinking I'd had an ulterior motive for sleeping with you."

"I'm sorry, Mac," Maggie murmured as she swirled the brandy around in the heavy crystal goblet and scratched Woof's shaggy head absently. "I knew there wasn't a thing in that folder you hadn't already seen, but I was too upset to admit it. I'm not normally a suspicious person. I don't know what it is about you, about us, that makes me overreact so."

Mac grinned at her. "I've noticed that your emotions do run a bit high. Seems like every time we've been together, I've had to beat a hasty retreat. That's not a very satisfactory state of affairs for a military man."

"Well, why don't we declare a truce?" she asked lightly.

"Nope. No truce. A truce implies both parties shake hands, retire from the field of honor and go their separate ways."

"A cease-fire, then? An end to hostilities."

"Not good enough. Nothing so imprecise for us."

"Well, for heaven's sake, what *do* you want?" Maggie asked, exasperated.

"I won't settle for anything less than unconditional surrender."

Maggie bristled. She'd been her own woman too long and was too comfortable in her independence to accept his casual ultimatum.

"Whose surrender? Yours or mine?"

"What difference does it make?" Mac asked with a low chuckle. "If it matters, I give!"

He rose, then reached down to pull Maggie to her feet. Taking the glass from her suddenly nerveless fingers, he sat back on the rail and pulled her between his legs. Maggie gave a devout prayer that the railing was up to holding his weight before he tugged her head down to meet his.

A loud slurping sound brought them both back to consciousness long moments later.

"Woof, for Pete's sake, get away from that brandy!"

Mac eased her out of his arms to move toward the dog. Pulling a crystal goblet off the end of a long hairy nose, he shooed the grinning hound into the house.

Maggie waited silently in the dark while he tended

to the dog, using the brief respite to try to settle her spinning senses.

"Come on, I'll take you home." His shape materialized beside her in the dark.

"You don't need to. My car's here."

Mac took her chin in his fingers and turned her face up to his. "We'll come back for it in the morning."

If there was a question in his words, Maggie didn't hear it. She heard only quiet conviction.

"You've filled my mind all week, Maggie. When I saw you with the boys this afternoon there on the beach, I felt like I'd truly come home. I've been aching to hold you in my arms all evening. Let me take you home."

With a sense that she was committing herself to something she wasn't quite ready for, something deeper and stronger than she'd ever felt before, Maggie nodded slowly.

With that nod, she knew she'd crossed a line, one she'd had in front of her throughout her varied personal and professional life. She'd always kept things light and kept herself on the move. Even the upwardly mobile and short-lived fiancé hadn't drawn the unspoken commitment from her that Mac had. In fact, one of the main reasons she'd left Houston was to distance herself from the man who'd started pressuring her to put down roots, to take her position in the corporate world more seriously. Yet here she was, less than two weeks after meeting Mac, driving through the dark to a night of loving in his arms. Throughout the long trip back to her condo, she wondered just who had surrendered to whom back there on the deck.

As they rolled silently through the glowing Florida moonlight, Mac, too, examined his feelings, trying to understand the fierce satisfaction he felt to have this tousled, exasperating, wholly fascinating creature beside him. When he'd seen her there on the beach, laughing with the boys, a sense of absolute certainty had jolted through him. He wanted this woman—in his bed and in his life. Tonight he'd try to make her want him, too.

He smiled when he closed her condo door behind them. She stood uncertainly in the middle of her living room, looking at him with a slight frown.

"Don't worry so, Maggie. I won't ask anything of you you're not prepared to give."

"Damn that smile," Maggie said with a resigned sigh as she walked into his open arms. "It constitutes a lethal weapon."

Mac let her set the pace as she explored his lips. He contented himself with running his hands over the rear so obligingly at arm's reach and available to him in the tight jeans.

His smug confidence that he could control the pace shattered when she ran her hands down his chest, then lower still. When they moved slowly, deliberately, over his manhood, Mac sucked in a quick breath and pulled her hands away. Maggie tugged them free and went back to her erotic massage. The bulge in his jeans turned rock hard under her hands. Mac stood it as long as he dared, then groaned and pulled her hands away once

74

more, this time twisting her arms behind her back and holding them there with a gentle grip.

"Maggie," he said on a shuddering breath.

"Don't worry, Mac," she looked up at him with a teasing glint in her green eyes. "I won't ask for anything you're not prepared to give."

That did it. With a low growl, Mac had her flat on her back on the soft carpet. Her arms were still twisted behind her back, causing her breasts to arch up invitingly toward him. Mac gave her a mocking smile that promised retribution, then bent his head and took one nipple into his mouth, his teeth worrying it until it grew hard. Maggie gasped as he continued to nip and suck at her aching breast through the soft cotton shirt. She tried to free her hands.

"Oh, no, Maggie m'girl. Not yet. I owe you for that little bit of teasing."

Mac pushed one heavy leg between hers and used it to pry her thighs apart. His free hand roamed down her front, to the deep jean-covered V between her legs. Maggie held her breath as he cupped her mound and ran his fingers along the seam of her jeans. She felt the heat of his hand even through the thick material. And it felt wonderful.

Mac, too, could feel her heat. For a few moments more he struggled to hold on to his own control as his hand shaped and stroked her femininity. He bent down to still her thrashing head and capture her soft moans in his mouth. All vestiges of playfulness disappeared. He gave in to the deep primal need of the male to cover his mate.

Maggie lay helpless as he released her arms and methodically removed both her clothes and his own. He made undressing a new erotic experience as his mouth touched everywhere his hands uncovered. By the time he had taken the few seconds to protect her and had repositioned himself at the juncture of her thighs, she barely had the strength to lift her legs around his waist as he directed. Mac tried to cushion her on his arms as he moved into her in long sure thrusts. Her back was spared, but her hips ground against the carpet with every move.

Mac took a handful of soft curly hair in both fists and held her head steady so he could look down into her face. He could tell by her soft moans and the gathering spasms of her satiny sheath that she was near her peak. For some reason, it was vitally important to see her face when he brought her to pleasure. Only after she'd arched under him and he'd seen, as well as felt, her shattering climax, did he allow himself to close his eyes and follow her over the edge.

76

CHAPTER 9

"Well, I see the mountain has come to Muhammad," Ed Stockton tossed at her with a grin several weeks later. They'd just finished a meeting on a new education center to be built on base. Unfortunately the chosen site was right in the middle of a nesting area for red-cockaded woodpeckers, one of Eglin's endangered species. The meeting had been lively, to say the least, and Ed was glad it was over so he could turn to more interesting matters.

Maggie didn't pretend to misunderstand his sly comment. She stopped gathering up her papers to grin back at him. "Let's just say we met on the road to Mecca."

Ed had teased her once or twice about her pet name for Mac—The Mountain—since the rumors began that she was seeing the lab commander for reasons other than business. This was the first time she'd acknowledged their relationship publicly.

"The word is you and MacRae are making all the local hot spots together, kiddo."

"What there are of them," Maggie laughed back. In

addition to the various official functions on base Mac had taken her to, they had explored the rich fare in their corner of northwest Florida. Under the twins' enthusiastic tutelage, Maggie had been given a crash course in the local haute cuisine.

Quick visions of restaurants with paper place mats and plastic baskets piled high with shrimp and mouthwatering fried amberjack filled Maggie's mind. Mac had taken them all out to various local eateries, seeming to derive as much enjoyment from watching Maggie and the boys together as from the food itself. Mrs. Harris enjoyed the treats, too. She ate the local fare heartily, but insisted they all go "home" for dessert. Somewhere in her long career she had picked up a fatal weakness for gooey, saccharine-sweet confections, and always had something freshly baked in the pantry. Maggie and Mac discreetly scraped off layers of frothy icing and passed the goo to an appreciative Woof rather than dampen Kate's pride in her culinary achievements.

But the desserts were nothing compared to the sweetness that followed when Mac drove Maggie home. When it wasn't too late, when one or the other of them didn't have an early conference or a flight, or the boys weren't expecting him back, Mac would stay the night and they would make long lingering love. Other times, when he couldn't stay, they shared more kisses and heavy breathing than anything else.

"Jim Ames was over here yesterday. He mentioned that their big test is set for next week." Ed Stockton's

78

voice interrupted Maggie's private thoughts. She frowned.

"Yes, I know. It was a struggle getting them to agree to all our conditions. The last issue was the height of the dike around the ignition site. Mac approved the change—and the associated costs—over Ames's objections."

"Ames was also asking a lot of rather strange questions," Ed continued after a pause. "Like why you left a big oil conglomerate to come to this little corner of God's country. Particularly when we're about to test a new energy source that might make your former employers very, uh, nervous."

Maggie stiffened and turned slowly to face her boss. She let the implications of what he was saying sink in fully before she answered.

"And what did you tell him?"

Ed blinked at the ice in her voice. "Hey, hold on there. Don't shoot the messenger. I told Ames he was nothing but a fussy old woman— Oops, sorry!"

Ed had a tendency to forget that some of the old euphemisms were taboo in the current, more sensitive work environment. Maggie usually didn't hesitate to correct any of her crusty old boss's lapses, but this one she let slide.

"I just thought you'd want to know what you're dealing with."

Maggie gave him a hard clear look, then nodded. She walked back through the bustling yard to her office, for once not noticing the activity teeming around her.

Industrial espionage—that's what the old fart was implying. She thought indignantly of all the hours she'd humored the man, maintaining a polite respectful demeanor even when he asked the same question for the third or fourth time. Despite herself, she couldn't help wondering whether Mac knew of Ames's suspicions. Surely, he himself didn't think that about her, not after all they'd shared.

Mac came by early that evening to pick her up for a formal function at the base. He could tell something was wrong as soon as she opened the door. She'd caught her hair up with glittering rhinestone combs, and was wearing a long slinky red thing that almost covered her tall frame, except for the slit up one side that appeared to go all the way to her armpit. It was an outfit only someone with Maggie's long lithe beauty could carry off, and one that made Mac's mouth go dry. The look that should have gone with that getup was sultry and smiling. Instead, there was a slight furrow on Maggie's brow, quickly erased as she took in his full glory.

"Lord, Mac. I didn't think they made uniforms with padded shoulders like that," she teased.

"It's the shoulder boards. And this damn cummerbund. They make a man look like he's all trussed up."

Not hardly, Maggie thought, as she feasted on the sight of Mac in his dress uniform. The short tailored jacket of midnight blue sported a glittering array of medals, topped by shiny wings. It fastened with a single button at his trim waist, showing a deeper blue cummerbund, pleated white dress shirt and a jaunty satin bow tie.

"Is this the same man whose standard dress is worn jeans and old sweatshirts?" she asked with an awe that was only half-pretended.

"One and the same, Maggie m'girl. I'll prove it."

And he did, with a kiss that left them both breathless. Maggie was still trying to steady her racing pulses when he put a finger under her chin and tilted up her head.

"Your dress is spectacular—what there is of it—and I love your hair up. The only thing missing is the smile in your eyes. What's the matter?"

Maggie wasn't ready to talk to him about Ed Stockton's disclosures, nor the doubts they raised in her. Not now, with a big function ahead of them. Later, she thought. Later they'd talk.

"Nothing, Mac. I'm a little nervous about tonight's do, I guess. I haven't been to one of these before."

The Maggie he knew wasn't nervous about anything. Mac decided not to press the issue until they had time to thrash out whatever was bothering her. Later, he thought.

"Don't get your hopes up, honey," he warned as he escorted her outside. In honor of the occasion he'd brought his little sports car instead of the Jeep. "The Air Force isn't very old. We're the baby military service, don't forget. We're still feeling our way between ironclad British-mess traditions and fighter-pilot free-for-alls. What you'll see tonight will probably be a mixture of the best and the worst of both."

His words proved prophetic. Maggie couldn't remember ever attending any function where dignitaries were marched to a noxious-looking grog bowl for real or imagined slights. Everyone forgot the rules of the mess in the general hilarity and camaraderie that filled the ballroom. She laughed at the silly rituals and was moved to tears by the guest speaker. The former POW spoke quietly about his experiences in Vietnam. Looking around the room during his stark moving speech, Maggie noted fierce feelings of pride on the faces of the men and women in uniform as they listened to their comrade-in-arms. With a rush of indefinable emotion, she took in Mac's clenched jaw and intense eyes. The speaker finished with a simple prayer for the warriors left behind.

Mac held her close against him as they danced after the official part of the evening ended. Even when the music sped up and the younger couples around them gyrated across the floor, he held her close and moved to his own beat. They were among the last to leave.

If Maggie thought the long dinner, the numerous toasts and the intimate dancing had made Mac forget her earlier pensiveness, she soon learned her mistake. When the door of her condo closed behind them, he led her over to an armchair and sat down, pulling her onto his lap.

She was going to have to invest in some sturdier furniture, Maggie thought as the chair creaked ominously under them.

"Okay, now tell me why your eyes have had a shadow in them all night."

She looked up at him, surprised. She hadn't even thought of Ames's ugly insinuations for whole hours at a stretch tonight. How in the world had Mac seen through her laughter and tears to the worry beneath? She took a deep breath. Better to get it out than let it fester. Besides, it wasn't her nature to dissemble or hide her feelings for long.

"Ed Stockton told me Dr. Ames seems to think I have some ulterior motive in my objections to the propulsion test. Something to do with loyalty to my former employer."

Mac cursed his bumbling deputy roundly. "Ames is a fool, Maggie. You probably talked circles around him, and he reached for something to justify his own inadequacies. The test is a go for next week, isn't it?"

She nodded, a troubled frown creasing her brow.

"My people resolved every one of your objections, didn't they?"

She nodded again. "I had my deputy review the proposed changes, as well—he's the one who wrote the original draft report. He's satisfied with the new parameters."

"So that proves you're not trying to sabotage the effort." Mac ran his thumb lightly along her furrowed brow. "Don't let Ames's dithering bother you."

Maggie let her breath out on a ragged sigh. "I'll be

glad when the darn thing's done. It seems as if this test has been hanging over us forever." Swallowing, she looked up at him. "It's still awfully dangerous, Mac."

"That's the nature of the test business," he reminded her quietly. "You know that as well as I do. We're pushing the edge of the envelope, stretching into the unknown with every new plane we take up, every new chemical or explosive we test. All we can do is ensure all possible safety factors are considered."

Maggie huddled against Mac's solid chest. She wanted desperately to believe his steady measured words. Normally she wouldn't have let a man like Ames bother her in the least. She had supreme confidence in herself and her professionalism. But she felt vulnerable lately, as if by giving in to Mac, she was laying open a part of herself that had been hers alone up till now. Her confidence had developed a soft spot where he or anything to do with him was concerned.

"Look at me, Maggie," Mac's quiet voice commanded. "I refuse to let you be bothered by Ames. Forget it. Forget him!"

Maggie couldn't hold back a smile at his crisp order. "Yes, sir!" She tried to sit at attention in his lap and give him a smart salute.

Mac groaned as her fanny wiggled against him and held her still. They both forgot Ames and the lab and the test and their own names for a good long time.

In fact, Maggie managed to push the propulsion test to the back of her mind. She'd done everything required by law or common sense to protect the environment and the people involved, and had other equally demanding projects to occupy her energies. Added to her pressure at work, Mac had given her some more things to fill her mind, not to mention her body and her heart. He'd begun to get downright grumpy about the evenings he couldn't stay with her and had to leave for his own home. And in a man as big and normally even-tempered as Mac, grumpy was definitely a state to be reckoned with.

"Something's got to give, woman. I don't like crawling out of your bed and sneaking back into my home like an adolescent."

Mac nudged Maggie out of her sleepy lethargy and settled her boneless body in the crook of his arm. She snuggled into his warmth contentedly, wishing he'd let her just drift off to sleep. They'd had this discussion several times already.

"I love you, Maggie."

That got her attention. Her heavy lashes fluttered open to find him staring down at her, a determined expression in his eyes.

"I hate leaving you at night. I want us together, in our own bed, every night. I think we should get married."

As proposals go, Maggie had had better, but none that tempted her as much. None that called out to her heart to grab hold of something permanent, something wonderful. She wanted desperately to say yes.

"I…I think we should think about it." She forced herself to meet Mac's eyes. "I think I love you, too, Mac.

But I've thought I was in love before, and it didn't work out. We owe it to the boys to take this slowly."

Mac's eyes narrowed. "Don't use the boys as an excuse. This is between us. And what's between us deserves better than this sneaking around. I want to marry you."

Some of Maggie's independence reasserted herself. After all, it was her bed and her bedroom and her life.

"You need to work on your technique, Colonel. Men usually ask women to marry them, not order them." She tried to slip out of bed to put some distance between them.

"Oh, no, you don't." Mac pulled her back easily. "I want an answer, however the question was or wasn't phrased."

"I told you, I need to think about it!" she snapped. At his hurt look, Maggie relented. "Mac, you don't understand. I…I'm nervous about marriage. I came really close once, and when I did, a trapped feeling overwhelmed me and I bolted at the last minute. I left a good job in Houston because I just wasn't ready and my fiancé was."

Well, at least now he knew why she'd come to Eglin, Mac thought. For a long moment, he studied her. He knew her too well to think she was being coy. It hurt him more than he was prepared to admit that she had doubts when he had none at all. He'd known she was the one he wanted in his home and his heart from the moment he'd seen her up to her knees in water, poking in that dark hole with the boys.

"Okay," he said finally, levering himself off the rumpled bed. "Think about it. But think hard, Maggie m'girl. I may be big, but I'm not particularly slow or patient."

He reached down, took a handful of her hair in one fist and held her steady for his kiss. When he left, closing the door carefully behind him, he was breathing as fast and as painfully as she was.

CHAPTER 10

Maggie was learning. She followed Mac's orders and thought hard over the next few days. She remembered her feelings of panic when her former fiancé had pressured her, although not quite as forcefully as the mountain had. She remembered how she'd run from him and her Houston job to escape her feelings of being trapped. And she compared those feelings to the intense urge she felt to accept Mac's hand and heart.

She didn't feel trapped with Mac, she felt…confused. Ten years or more of lighthearted wandering wherever her will and her talents took her were at stake. Suddenly they seemed trivial compared to what she suspected she might find with Mac and his two, correction, three, holy terrors.

Maggie had just tossed another page of doodles into her overflowing wastebasket when the crash phone rang. With Eglin's active flying mission, there were usually one or two in-flight emergencies a day, most of which ended routinely. Maggie or one of her staff monitored every call on the crash line. If the incident being reported turned out to be serious, they needed to respond. She picked up the receiver quickly.

"This is the Eglin command post. We have a report of an explosion on the range. The base commander has directed the disaster-response team to assemble immediately at Base Operations. Acknowledge."

Maggie's heart turned over in her chest. Telling herself not to panic, she waited until the command post rapped out her office code, then responded with the approved call sign.

Don't let it be the propulsion test! Dear Lord, please don't let it be the test! Her mind screamed the silent prayer as she grabbed her boots and jeans, slammed her office door shut and tore off her skirt and slip. Her fingers trembled, fumbling on the snaps. She grabbed her hard hat and was just pulling the thick disaster-response team checklist out of the bookcase when her intercom rang. She started to ignore it, but a quick glance told her it was Ed Stockton's direct line.

"Maggie, we just got a call. There's been an explosion."

She sucked in her breath. "Yes, I know. I just took the notification from the command post. I'm on my way out the door."

"Did they tell you the location or nature of the accident?"

"No." Maggie's last hope died at Ed's flat hard tone.

"It was Site 32. The propulsion test. Something went wrong."

"I was afraid it was," she rasped out. "Ed, Mac's out there!"

And Jack, her deputy, along with a lot of other people, she thought. She swallowed her gut-wrenching fear. Gripping the phone so hard her hand hurt, she forced herself to ask. "Any report of casualties?"

"Not yet. The fire department's on the scene right now. The chief himself went out for this one. He'll do whatever's necessary until the disaster-response team gets there."

Ed's words recalled Maggie with a jerk. "I've got to go. The team's assembling at Base Ops now. I've got our van with the radio in it. Please, please, let me know if you hear anything."

90   She knew the fire chief would be in direct contact with Ed, probably before he even called the command post to update them.

"Will do, Maggie. Be careful, okay? You know better than anyone how dangerous this may be."

She didn't need that reminder, Maggie thought as she forced herself to drive the speed limit the short distance to Base Ops. She knew it would take longer for the rest of the team to arrive, some coming from the hospital all the way on the west side of the base.

Please let Mac be okay, she prayed over and over in an unconscious litany. *Let me see him again.* They hadn't been together since Mac had delivered his marriage proposition three nights ago. Maggie refused to call it a proposal—it had really been more of a command—but it had filled her mind almost to the exclusion of everything else. She rubbed her eyes with a fist to hold back the threat of tears.

Forcing her personal fears from her mind, she made herself focus on her professional responsibilities. Mentally she reviewed everything she knew about the test. She'd gone over it with Jack again just this morning. Since he'd done the original analysis and wanted to cover the actual test, she'd agreed. Maggie refused to give in to the sick guilt that threatened to swamp her. She should have gone out to the test site, instead of Jack. He knew the test, knew all the properties of the chemicals they were using, knew the dangers. But it was her responsibility. And Mac may be hurt.

By the time she reached Base Ops and unloaded her gear, she had forced herself to an icy calm. She'd practiced with the disaster-response team a couple of times since coming to Eglin. The team took their responsibilities with deadly seriousness. Their practices were frighteningly realistic. They had to be. Eglin had an active flying mission and the population of a medium-size city. Any type of accident could happen, from gas-main explosions to fires to airplane crashes. The exercise-team chief enlisted schoolchildren, wives and on-base civilians as participants in simulated bus crashes, hostage situations and major explosions of all types. Hospital personnel painted gory injuries on the players. The more realistic the better.

Their practice stood them in good stead now. As the

various team members assembled, they ran through their checklists with brisk efficiency. The on-scene commander briefed them on what he knew, which wasn't much more than what had been relayed by the command post. Each team member then described what he or she knew of the test and the site. Maggie forced herself to detail calmly the environmental hazards to the other team members. Everything inside her wanted to scream at them to get on with it, to move faster. Her rational mind knew the danger of plunging blindly into an accident site. But emotionally, she wished she could jump in her van and take off without waiting.

After what seemed like hours, but was only minutes, the on-scene commander directed the team to an entry control/safe point coordinated by radio with the fire chief. Maggie ran to her van, accompanied by the chaplain and two bio-environmental techs. Her four-wheeler could handle the rough range roads easily. She wheeled the van into the convoy of vehicles that drove off the main base, led by a police car with its siren screaming.

She kept the radio tuned to the fire-station crash line all during the long ride to the site. The firefighters were real pros, and the chief especially so. He kept chatter over the open radio to a minimum. Their lines were unscrambled and often monitored by civilians off base. There was no need to panic the general populace until they knew the scope of the disaster.

"It's Jack. Thank God!"

Maggie all but shouted as her van pulled up to the

circle of police cars and fire trucks gathered at the entry-control point. Even from a distance she recognized her tall bearded deputy. Before the van had completely stopped rolling, Maggie slammed it into park and leaped out. As she ran toward Jack, she could hear the roar of flames and smell the sharp acrid scent of smoke in the air. Tall pines blocked the accident scene from sight.

"Jack, are you okay?" She grabbed his arm.

"I'm fine, boss. I wasn't on-site when it happened. I'd just come back to my car for some notes I needed."

"What happened? How bad is it?"

"It wasn't the propellant, Maggie. The stuff hadn't even been unloaded from the containers."

Maggie clutched his arm hard in relief. All during the long drive to the site, she'd dreaded hearing reports of toxic clouds spreading over the area.

"It was some kind of a freak accident. The crane lifting the firing tube into place snapped a cable, which in turn whipped into the mechanized loading vehicle. From what I can gather, sparks ignited the vehicle's fuel and caused the explosion. I wasn't there, though. The fire chief has the real poop."

Maggie glanced over to where the chief was briefing the on-scene commander. She turned back and asked the question eating at her soul.

"Jack, did you see Colonel MacRae before or after the accident?"

Jack shook his head slowly. He, like most of the engineering squadron, knew Maggie was dating the lab commander. Maggie caught back a ragged sob, then made herself take several deep breaths.

"The chief might know something," Jack volunteered. "He just came out of the accident area a few minutes ago."

Maggie knew she couldn't interrupt the fire chief as he huddled with the on-scene commander, but she watched them closely. When the commander turned away to take a radio call, she approached the sweating helmeted fireman.

"Chief, Colonel MacRae was supposed to be on-site for the test. Have you had contact with him?"

The stocky grizzled man turned to face Maggie. He admired and respected this vibrant young woman. She'd ridden with his fire crews during a couple of exercises and had spent a full day with his hazardous-materials team. If Maggie's own credentials hadn't already won his professional respect, her willingness to listen and learn from his people would have done it.

"Sorry, Dr. Wescott. I haven't seen him. There's still a lot of confusion in there." He nodded toward the flames they could see leaping above the treeline. "We should hear something soon."

He turned away to answer a call from the on-scene commander. They talked for a moment, then the commander called his team together. Maggie knew the man in charge both personally and professionally. She and Mac had been seated beside him and his wife at more than one social function. Maggie gave grateful thanks that he'd been in the job for more than two years and knew his stuff.

"Okay, this is what we have so far," the commander said. "A vehicle fire and explosion occurred just north of the control center at Site 32. Burning fuel sprayed several workers in the area. The fire crews have stabilized at least two people with severe burns, but there may be more."

He nodded to the senior medical rep. "Doc, make sure your folks call back for more burn-trauma kits, just in case. Additionally, the fuel ignited both structural and brushfires that are still burning. The lab folks moved the propellant and main rocket fixtures off-site immediately and they're out of range. Thank God we don't have that to worry about. But there may be other chemicals stored or brought out for the test. Fire crews are surveying the area now."

He took a deep breath, then finished with, "There were several lab and range control crews on-site. We're trying to get a firm head count. I'm going in with the chief now. Doc, you better come with me. The rest of you wait until I call you in."

Maggie bit her lip in an agony of frustration. Now that her worst fears of a major chemical disaster were allayed, every nerve and fiber in her body screamed for word of Mac. She forced herself to review again her disaster-response checklist, going over the sections on chemical and natural fires. Together, she and Jack added to the grease-pencil annotations on the checklist. She'd have to either call or fax a detailed report to both state and federal environmental agencies as soon as the imminent danger passed.

"Dr. Wescott, over here, please. Major, you, too."

Maggie looked up to see the on-scene commander returning. She and the senior bio-environmental medical engineer hurried over.

"Look, there are some barrels burning close to the control center. We couldn't find any lab folks who knew what they contained. The senior test engineer is one of those seriously injured. The chief has what markings his people could get off the barrels. I need you to get with him immediately and see if you can figure out if we have a danger of a secondary explosion on our hands."

Maggie and the young major hurried over to the worried fire chief. "What do we have?"

"I think they're chemical-waste containers, waiting to be transported to main base for disposal. I've called the numbers into the National Emergency Materials Center, but I need you to take a look and see what you think."

Maggie knew the twenty-four-hour hotline should respond within minutes. But even those few minutes could be too late for the people facing the danger of a secondary explosion. She pulled out her own copy of the materials directory and frantically scanned the listed agents that contained the numbers the chief cited. All were flammable, but should burn steadily, not explode. The men around her sagged with relief at the news. The

96

call from the center confirmed her numbers a few minutes later.

"Thank God," the chief muttered. He picked up his hand radio and barked a series of short orders.

"The fire crews have contained most of the fires," the on-scene commander told his assembled team less than fifteen minutes later. "I'm moving the command post forward. Get your stuff. Public Affairs, you need to leave someone here to handle reporters. I don't want them on-scene until we ID the injured. Call me if anyone gets too persistent about wanting to film the scene. I want to clear it before you bring anyone forward. The rest of you gather your gear and move up."

Maggie, with Jack crammed between her and the chaplain, maneuvered her van over the bumpy road leading to the test-control facility. Several ambulances passed in the opposite direction, moving back toward the main road with lights flashing and sirens wailing. As soon as Maggie's van reached the site, the chaplain jumped out to hurry to the small triage area set up.

Maggie and Jack stood back to observe the devastated control facility and its surrounding area. Flames had scorched the earth all around and peeled the paint from the main metal building and its adjacent utility sheds. Electrical lines hung loose and snapping on one side of the building. Maggie directed Jack to get on the radio to the architectural section back at the main base. They needed a general idea of the floor plans of the main facility so they could check for underground drains that might carry burning fuel. While Jack was on the radio, Maggie desperately scanned the crowd of hurrying people.

She identified firefighters, security police, disaster-response team members in their distinctively marked hard hats, medics and a couple of frantic-looking civilians huddled to one side of the site. But, try as she might, she couldn't see any figure that came near Mac's dimensions.

She shivered with gut-wrenching fear when the chief approached her, his face grave.

"The doc just confirmed that Colonel MacRae was one of the injured. His burns aren't too bad, but he inhaled a lot of smoke pulling one of the crew out from under some burning debris. They've already transported him to the hospital."

He reached out a hand to steady her as she rocked back on her heels. "I'm sorry—I wish I could tell you more about how he is. But maybe Doc—"

Maggie was racing toward the clump of medics before he could finish.

The doctor assured her that Mac's condition, although critical, was stable. He was unconscious, and they feared lung damage. The doc couldn't, or wouldn't, say more, but he did add that the hospital commander, a noted surgeon, was already with the emergency-room crew awaiting the ambulances. Mac would be in good hands.

Maggie worked frantically with Jack to cover her

checklist items. She guessed it would be at least three or four hours until the initial assessment was complete, and then there'd be days and weeks of investigative reports. But Jack could handle it from here.

The on-scene commander took her report, agreed Jack could handle the cleanup, then arranged a ride for her back to the main base in one of the police cars. With a grim shake of his head, he returned to the business at hand.

CHAPTER 11

"Maggie!"

The thin wavering cry greeted her as she got off the elevator and hurried down the pale hospital corridor toward the intensive-care unit. She recognized Davey's voice even before two figures came hurtling toward her from a small waiting room to one side. She knelt down to hug one small body in each arm.

"Don't cry, Danny," she whispered to a dark head buried in her shoulder. "I talked to the doctors downstairs. They're sure your dad will be okay."

Actually, the hospital commander, whom she'd met at a couple of parties, said he was sure Mac would pull through. Something about his being a tough son of a—

"Maggie, they say Colonel Mac has burned his lungs. That he's on a respirator." Mrs. Harris joined the group in the middle of the hallway. Maggie held out her hand and Kate gripped it hard.

Maggie loosened her hold on the twins. "Come on, troops. Let's get out of the hallway before the hospital orderlies sweep us up and out."

When the small group were seated in the waiting area, Kate wadded her handkerchief into a tight ball. "Did you say you talked to the doctors, Maggie?"

"Yes. The hospital commander stopped me on my way up here. He'd just checked on Mac and said he was doing as well as could be expected. I guess that's medical jargon for hanging in there. He's well enough for them to allow me a quick visit, anyway. Have you seen him?" she asked the boys.

"No, they wouldn't let us in," Davey answered waveringly. "The nurses have been real nice, though," he added after a quick swallow. "They come out every so often to let us know how he's doing."

"Well, I got the okay from the big man himself, so I'll go check. I'll see if they'll let you in."

Maggie wiped her finger gently across Danny's cheek to catch a lingering tear. She ached to kiss them both, but wasn't sure just how nine-year-old boys felt about kisses. She contented herself with one last ferocious squeeze.

The nurse in charge led her to one of the six beds that formed an open circle in front of the monitoring desk. Maggie wasn't prepared for the sight of Mac lying so still and helpless. He had a respirator tube taped to his mouth and various intravenous lines running into one arm. Gauzy tentlike structures covered both arms almost to his shoulders. A light gauze pad ran down one side of his face, from forehead to chin.

"Oh, Mac," she whispered. She wanted desperately to hold his hand, touch some part of him, but was afraid to disturb any of the bandages or cause him pain. She looked helplessly at the nurse standing on the other side of the bed.

"Don't worry," the woman said with a sympathetic smile. "He's doing fine. They've already decided not to send him with the others to the burn center in San Antonio. All these tubes make him look a lot worse off than he is."

Maggie smiled her thanks as the older woman turned to leave. She spent the next few minutes in a chair pulled up close to Mac's side, whispering softly to him. She could never recall afterward just what she tried to tell him in those first worry-filled moments.

The boys and Kate waited for her anxiously, along with a gathering crowd of Mac's co-workers and friends. Several officers who knew Mac were there already, some with their wives. The Eglin commander, a major-general almost as big as Mac, arrived within a half hour. He spoke to each of the boys and to Maggie and Kate after he'd taken a quick look in on Mac. The boys were allowed one short visit, which they took surprisingly well, before agreeing to go home with their friend Joey's dad.

Time passed in a blur for Maggie after that. It seemed as if there was a constant stream of folks coming to inquire about Mac. A surprising number knew her and knew of her relationship with him. Finally, late that evening, the traffic died down and it was just Kate and Maggie. They were allowed brief visits on the hour. Throughout the long night, the two women took turns making trips into the intensive-care unit, and their shared worry brought them closer.

Maggie spent her short spells at Mac's bedside perched on the edge of a hard chair, whispering soft nonsense to the accompanying hum of the hospital machinery. She finally worked up the nerve to touch him gently on his sheet-covered thigh. With every light stroke she thought about their last conversation, when he had told her he wanted them to marry. And with every stroke, she knew that was what she wanted, too, more than anything else in the world.

The same pattern repeated itself the next day. Kate convinced Maggie to bring some things to the house and stay with her and the boys, rather than make the long lonely drive around the bay to her Destin condo. She moved into a spare bedroom and managed to keep Woof out long enough for a brief nap in the afternoon before heading back to the hospital.

Mac's father arrived that evening. Maggie would've felt awkward if he hadn't greeted her with a warm twinkle in his blue eyes, which looked so like his son's her breath caught in her throat.

"So this is the little girl Mac's told me about." He grinned. The older man carried his years well on his big frame. "I understand you're soon to become part of the family," he added, taking her hand in both of his.

Maggie nodded slowly, but without hesitation. Another line crossed, she thought. "If he still wants me. I'm afraid I've given your son a rough time."

"Good," his loving dad replied with deep satisfaction. "Nothing worthwhile is ever easy in life."

He spent several hours at the hospital before Maggie convinced him to go home with Kate for the night.

Much later, when the hospital had settled into that peculiar somnolent state during which patients rested and the staff worked quietly, Maggie went in for her hourly visit and found Mac awake. He tried to grin at her around the tube taped to his mouth and failed miserably. It was the most gorgeous grimace Maggie had ever seen.

"Hello, Mac." She smiled down at him. "'Bout time you decided to rejoin the living." She sat down and began what by now was an unconscious light stroking of his thigh. "Kate and the boys and your dad were here earlier. They're all okay," she told him. She knew the boys would be his first concern.

"How...how long?" he managed to get out around the tube.

"Two days now. I'm not sure how much you remember. There was an accident, a cable broke and hit a vehicle."

Mac nodded. He remembered everything. Including the screams of the man trapped under the burning vehicle.

"Three men were hurt. They're still not sure if the one you pulled out will make it. They were all taken to the burn center in San Antonio."

He lifted one singed brow in query and nodded at his 104 arms, still under their light gauzy tents.

"You've got second-degree burns on both arms and on one side of your face. The doctors were afraid you'd seriously damaged your lungs, but it's not as bad as they first thought. They'll give you the details now that you're awake."

She turned to alert the nurse of Mac's consciousness. A swarm of medical specialists soon surrounded him, and Maggie retreated to the waiting room. Alone in the dim light, she huddled in one corner of the couch. She drew up her legs, rested her folded arms on her knees and gave way to the tears she'd held back all those terrifying hours.

When she finally went back in to see Mac, he was asleep again. She looked at the tube taped to his mouth and wished with all her heart it was gone, so that she could hear her mountain rumbling in her ear again.

CHAPTER 12

A week later, Maggie almost wished the tube was back in Mac's mouth. He'd turned out to be a terrible patient, one of those men who were never sick and didn't believe anyone who tried to tell him his body needed time to heal. He responded gruffly to the nurses' orders and was extremely vocal in his opinion of the food they served. He told the doctors not to order any drugs or painkillers after just two days. If his burns pained him, he wouldn't admit it. As Maggie came up for her afternoon visit, she could hear his deep gravelly voice halfway down the hall.

"I don't care what the doctor says—I want up! I refuse to use that blasted bedpan again."

"Colonel, you can't, ah, do anything for yourself with those bandaged hands. This is better for you until—"

"I'll manage, dammit!"

Maggie shook her head at his clenched jaw and angry blue eyes as she strode into the room. Two young nurses turned to her with palpable relief. The ward staff had learned quickly she was the only one who could control their patient. The two nurses gave her a thankful glance and left.

"For heaven's sake, Mac, act your age. You've got to stop terrorizing those lieutenants. They're just trying to do their jobs."

Mac watched her toss down a pile of magazines and stand at the foot of his bed, hands on her hips. The sight of her pile of curls tied up with a blue silk scarf and matching soft silk shirt made his frustration level rise dangerously.

"They can damn well go ply their trade on someone else," he grumbled. "And take their bedpan with them."

"You know you can't do anything for yourself with those bandaged hands," Maggie tried patiently.

"Oh, yeah?" His grumpy look was replaced by a decided leer. "Wanna bet? These bandages are the only things that stand between you and being kissed senseless. I think I can manage at least a demure peck or two, even with them on. Come here."

"No way! The last time I got close, you ended up showing your buns to the general's wife when you tried to wrestle me onto the bed just as she came in. Nice conduct for a senior officer!"

"Maggie, come here."

She eyed him for a long moment, then gave in to the soft command. Better the bed than his trying to chase her around the room.

He sighed as she settled gingerly next to him in the wide hospital bed. "I've been waiting for you all afternoon," he said, nuzzling the golden head beside his on the pillow.

Maggie sighed. She relaxed contentedly and let the scent and feel and warmth that was Mac surround her.

"By the way," he added with seeming casualness, "Dad was here again this morning. He wants to know what we want for a wedding present. Does he know something I don't?"

Maggie looked up into his face in dismay. It was her own fault, she told herself. She should have said something sooner.

She'd been trying to bring up the subject of their future ever since Mac had regained consciousness. She wanted desperately to tell him that all her wanderlust was gone, burned up in the flames that almost took him, as well. To her dismay, she'd discovered that taking a man up on a marriage offer he hadn't renewed was a little tricky. She and Mac had had precious few moments alone since he'd been moved out of intensive care to a private room. It seemed the man knew half the people on the darn base. Someone was always there, even late in the evenings.

Well, it looked like her future father-in-law had made the first move for her. As long as they had a few moments alone now, she might as well follow up.

"Your father seemed to know about your rash offer, or rather, order, of marriage. If the order still stands, Colonel, I want very much to marry you," Maggie told him softly.

"Dammit, woman, you picked a fine time for this!" he roared.

"What?"

Maggie bounced off the bed. She'd have whacked the jerk with his own bedpan for startling her so if she wasn't so confused by his response.

"Hell, woman, I've been aching for you ever since I regained consciousness and found you stroking my thigh. Do you have any idea what that does to a man who's numb everywhere but one particular unburned spot? The nurses are going to have to build another little tent pretty soon to cover the evidence of my frustration."

Dumfounded, Maggie gaped at him.

108 "And then you have the nerve to bring up marriage when I can't even take you in my arms and kiss you and...do all the other things a man should do when the woman he loves says she'll marry him."

"You idiot," Maggie shouted. "First you order me to marry you, now you won't even take yes for an answer when I give it. Well, I've got news for you, Alastair Duggan MacRae—yes, your father filled me in on the Duggan—we're going to be married and that's that. The boys are already planning the ceremony."

Maggie took devilish satisfaction in Mac's surprised look. "They're part of this, too," she went on. "They've got a great idea for a guitarist for the reception. Someone with a safety pin in his ear, I think." She ignored his low groan.

"And Kate is already designing the cake. She's got

visions of a pile of sweet gooey frosting five layers high."

This time she grinned at Mac's long moan. She was beginning to enjoy herself.

"Your dad is making reservations for the honeymoon. It's a toss-up between Disney World and fishing in Michigan. The boys are torn, but I think the vote is going to be for Disney World. Kate's never been there, you see."

Maggie's green eyes sparkled in pure mischief. She imagined there wouldn't be many times she'd have her mountain lying helpless. She enjoyed the rare sensation of having the upper hand.

Mac gave her a long-suffering look.

"And if you don't behave yourself and follow the doctor's orders we may line up Woof to stand in for the groom. He's about the same size, but has a much better disposition."

The corners of Mac's mouth turned up in his slow, lazy, incredibly sexy smile. Maggie thought she might drown in the flow of emotion that washed over her. Lord, she loved that smile. Not to mention the hunk of male that went with it.

"Well, you may think you have all the details covered. But I've got news for you, too. *I'm* going to pick out the wedding dress."

And he did. It was a loose, baggy creation with yards of netting that somehow managed to hang on Maggie's every curve.

THE END

Behind the Scenes
from Eglin Air Force Base:
A Day in the Life of Merline Lovelace

Serving as the wing commander at Eglin Air Force Base was the highlight of my military career. It was comparable to being the mayor of a city. The more than 3,000 men and women I commanded provided essential medical, law enforcement, communications, engineering, transportation, supply, housing and morale/welfare/ recreational support to everyone who lived or worked on base.

Every day brought new adventures—some fun, some not so much. During my tenure, a C-141 crashed in the swamp, killing all aboard, a tornado caused more than $10M worth of damage and we mobilized for the first Iraqi war. Each of those events reinforced my tremendous respect for the highly trained, incredibly dedicated civilian and military personnel who serve their country.

I thought you might enjoy a glimpse at my typical schedule during those busy, wonderful years at Eglin. I've also included a dictionary of useful acronyms and favorite expressions. I've cleaned those up considerably for public consumption. Hope you find both Sierra Hotel!

A Day in the Life of a Base Commander

0245	Call from command post, Hurricane Bertha forming in Caribbean
0433	Call from command post confirming Bertha's projected trajectory
0530	Reveille
0630	Breakfast at airman's dining hall with first sergeants
0720	General's morning stand-up with senior commanders
0800	Ground-breaking ceremony for new communications center
0930	Briefing by Hospital/CC re: Medical Accreditation Inspection
1000	Visit mobility center, review schedule of troop deployments
1130	Guest speaker, NW Florida Mayors' Conference
1330	Review hurricane preparation/response plan with key staff
1430	Update by OSI on counterterrorist activities
1500	Present diplomas at kindergarten graduation
1630	Throw out first ball at base softball tournament
1800	Dinner with Junior Officers' Council reps
1900	Accompany security police on marijuana bust
2200	Quiet time in office to plow through paperwork
2330	Return to quarters, snuggle in with hubby
2357	Call from command post—Bertha heading up Gulf
	Order recall of key staff and activation of hurricane plan

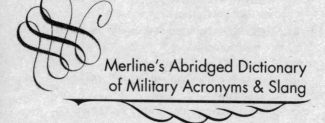

Merline's Abridged Dictionary of Military Acronyms & Slang

The military have their own unique language—they even have an alphabet used exclusively by them. Read on to discover more.

Auger In—Not a favorite expression with pilots, it means to dig a hole with an aircraft while still at the controls.

Black Hat—An army drill instructor or other creature of a similar nasty nature.

Bravo Zulu—Letters from the international civil aviation alphabet (see below) meaning a job well-done.

BDU—Battle Dress Uniform, either desert tan or forest-green/black/brown. Although why anyone would designate these baggy pants and loose shirts as a "dress" uniform remains a mystery to all.

Butter Bar—Second lieutenant (ensign in the navy), one of nature's most pathetic life forms.

Ground Pounders—An aviator's term for everyone without wings.

Hangar Queen—Either an aircraft that's always down for maintenance or one of President Clinton's Don't Ask/Don't Tell recruits.

Lost On Post—Where you say you'll be when you have to run errands.

MRE—Meals Ready To Eat: a packaged meal that includes snacks, main course, sweets, drink, heating element and a sanitary pack with utensils, napkins and dental floss. No excuse for gum disease in today's military!

NCO—Noncommissioned Officers, generally known as sergeants. Top-ranking NCOs are usually called Chief or Top.

PCS—Permanent Change of Station, where you pack up kids, pets and grandmother's quilt for a move to another base.

Ranger Pudding—Made from sugar, a packet of powdered coffee creamer and cocoa mix in the MRE. Mix with a little water from your canteen and heat. Yummy!

Roger That—Air force-ese for yes. Why use one word when two will do?

Sierra Hotel—An expression of approval, also from the international alphabet. The cleaned-up translation is Super Hot.

SNAFU—A holdover from WWII. The polite version is Situation Normal, All Fouled Up.

TDY—Temporary Duty at a location other than your home base.

The Old Man—The commander of a squadron, base or wing, unless he happens to be a she, in which case the correct appellation is simply The Boss or CO, for commanding officer. Similar to the Skipper in U.S. Navy talk.

Trash Hauler—Any cargo aircraft or the crew thereof.

And just in case you've always wondered, here's the International Alphabet used by U.S. military personnel and just about everyone you talk to when making hotel or airline reservations these days....

A—Alpha	J—Juliet	S—Sierra
B—Bravo	K—Kilo	T—Tango
C—Charlie	L—Lima	U—Uniform
D—Delta	M—Mike	V—Victor
E—Echo	N—November	W—Whiskey
F—Foxtrot	O—Oscar	X—X-ray
G—Golf	P—Papa	Y—Yankee
H—Hotel	Q—Quebec	Z—Zulu
I—India	R—Rome	

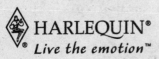

SAGA

The five McCoy brothers are about to meet the newest member of the family…their sister!

National bestselling author

Tori Carrington

A brand-new, longer-length story from the miniseries The Magnificent McCoy Men.

A REAL McCOY

In the next twenty-four hours, defense attorney Kat Buckingham will discover she's adopted, that her biological father is very much alive and that she has five very protective older brothers—all working in law enforcement. Oh, yeah, and she'll be wrongfully arrested…for the murder of her fiancé!

Available April 2005.

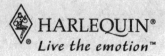

HARLEQUIN®
Live the emotion™

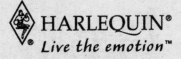

LOGAN'S LEGACY

Because birthright has its privileges and family ties run deep.

**Follow her quest for love and
his determination to avoid it...
until fate intervenes.**

RIGHT BY HER SIDE

**A new Logan's Legacy story
by *USA TODAY* bestselling author**

CHRISTIE RIDGWAY

The news that he was
going to be a dad shocked
the heck out of sexy
executive Trent Crosby!
But despite his doubts
about Rebecca Holley—
the accidental recipient
of his sperm donation—
Trent soon found himself
yearning for marriage
and family.

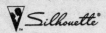